Love, LOSS, AND HONOR

VOLUME III: BETRAYAL

By

HERBERT WIENS

H.P. Waterhouse Publishing

ISBN: 9798985408386 (Paperback)
ISBN: 9798985408393 (eBook)

TABLE OF CONTENTS

CHAPTER ONE
BETRAYED

After almost twenty years as a law enforcement officer in some of the worst areas of Los Angeles County, Paul Taft's hands rarely shook. Today, while he packed the pictures from his living room wall into a moving box, he couldn't calm them. Bubble wrapping the last framed picture of his wife and two children, the tape dispenser fell to the floor, his fingers too weak to hold it. His knees giving out, he sat on the coffee table—the only piece of furniture the secondhand store workers hadn't carried out yet.

They were gone. Without them, the house became a mere echo chamber of memories. Holding the picture to his chest for a few minutes, fighting to control his emotions, he resolutely bent over and picked up the tape. Paul carried the last box out to his vehicle and drove to his tiny apartment. It was time to begin his new life alone.

As months passed, each day was a clone of the day before for Paul in this God forsaken place where human decency no longer existed. Everyone he reacted with had intentions of harming someone else—either physically or financially. At least that's what it appeared like from his perspective. It was why his wife was no longer with him and his children not underfoot when he got home after his shift.

Every now and then, he'd swing by his mini-storage and drag another box home to sort through and dispose of meaningless crap. Today's box of old case files was no different. Pulling out file after file and glancing at them, he'd throw irrelevant ones in a trash bag.

The bottom file in the box caught his interest. Not because it was still active but because it involved his cousin's wife. The Pressure Washer Killings had stopped years before. The original suspect had died in front of multiple witnesses. An alternate suspect surfaced in the Maldives but had disappeared again. It was assumed the second suspect had also met his own untimely demise.

Even though he had never been part of the investigation, Paul sat the file on the kitchen counter. It was the only piece of his favorite cousin's memory he had left. It was coming up on the anniversary of Peter's death from an IED explosion in Afghanistan.

Paul put on his ballistic vest, grabbed his weapon out of the lockbox, picked up the garbage sack for disposal, and left for his twelve-hour shift.

Twelve hundred miles away, Carrie Bennett climbed out of Bill Schmidt's old beater pickup in the high school parking lot. Since his family had moved to the small town after his dad was killed in combat, the two of them had been best friends. Bill's stepfather had saved Carrie's life twice and rode a horse through a wildfire to save the Bennett ranch.

Upon getting his driver's license, it had become a habit for Bill to drive out of his way to pick her up for school. It just wasn't acceptable for seniors to ride the bus. Willa Roberts, the new girl, flew in next to them with her expensive foreign convertible.

Willa's father was one of the bigwigs in a corporation buying up most of the smaller local farms. Wanting an escape retreat from large city frenzy and liking the area, he'd recently built a huge house on the highest hill in the area. Willa felt entitled, more sophisticated than the local rubes, and was a huge flirt. Tall with dark hair and perfect makeup, *all* boys were expected to fawn in her presence. Other girls were just side attractions.

"Hi, guys." Willa hopped out of the car and blew past Carrie to be next to Bill. The two old friends were seemingly immune to Willa's manipulations. Therefore, she made it her mission to flirt with Bill, date him if she could. "I'm having a party this weekend. You're both invited."

"We can't," Carrie replied for the both of them. "This weekend we're vaccinating and dehorning the calves."

"Ugh! That's disgusting." Ignoring Carrie, she took Bill's arm. "You sure you can't come?"

"Yeah, I'm sure." He gently pulled his arm free, but not quick enough for Carrie. "We don't get done until late and are pretty hosed by then."

"Next time, then." Willa merrily strutted on her way.

Carrie slugged Bill's arm. "Quit encouraging her."

"What?" He didn't get it. Carrie was jealous. Barely five foot two inches with dishwater blonde hair and minimal makeup, Carrie felt inferior compared to Willa.

Even though they had been best friends since he moved to town, Bill and Carrie only officially started dating the previous summer. He cared a great deal for her but thought she considered him just her lovable lackey.

After the calving and branding seasons were over, life at the ranch relaxed a little until the start of the haying season. The weekend before graduation, Carrie and her mother, Beth, went to Spokane for a girls' weekend shopping trip. She hadn't told her mother she was looking for a dress to become a woman in.

She deeply loved Bill and wanted to spend the rest of her life with him. Her problem was how to make the transformation from friends to lovers. With only a month until graduation, Carrie made her plans. She'd get all dolled up and get him out on a date for only the two of them. She was going to give him her virginity.

Solely to appease her mother, Carrie had sent an entrance application to Beth's alma mater in New York state. Carrie's free-willed grandmother, Kate, still lived on Long Island where Beth grew up. After Beth's sophomore year at college, and a summer in France, she transferred to the university where she met Carrie's father.

Carrie had been accepted but, wanting to stay close to home near family and Bill, didn't take it too seriously. Both teens had been accepted into Washington State University in Pullman.

Bored, Bill pulled his truck into the parking lot of the town's tiny drive-in restaurant for a burger. Willa's convertible dove in next to him.

"What are you doing?"

"I just thought I'd have a burger." Bill shrugged.

"Where's your sidekick?"

"Oh, Carrie and her mom went to Spokane for the weekend."

"You poor baby. You've been abandoned." Willa instantly shifted into full flirt mode. "I have an idea. Why don't we go to the county seat for a real meal and a movie? We can take my car. You drive."

"Me drive?" It was the most expensive car Bill had ever been around. The temptation of driving it overrode his common sense. "Sure. Let's go. I just have to call my mom first so she doesn't get worried."

"Why don't we leave your truck at my place since it's on the way." Willa smiled. "That way I won't have to double back when we're done."

While he drove, Willa kept patting his arm and laughing, no matter what he said. Bill had a hard time keeping his eyes on the road when she bent forward to adjust the sound system, intentionally letting him look down her tank top. She made sure he noticed the way her tiny mini skirt rode up when she twisted toward him.

In the theater, Willa wouldn't let up. Constantly finding reasons to lean against Bill, she whispered in his ear, "to not disturb others" while commenting on the movie. Finally, the temptation became too great, and he let her kiss him. The movie transformed into a necking session. On the drive home, Willa constantly stroked his arm.

In her driveway, she insisted he kiss her goodnight. "It's still early, why don't you come in for a while?"

"I don't know," the inexperienced Bill stammered. "I should go."

"Oh, don't be a wuss." Her arms around his neck, she pressed against him. "My parents are gone for the weekend and the house is so lonely. Just a little while."

"I guess. Just for a little while."

Willa knew she had him. Giving Bill a quick tour of the house, they ended on the second floor. When he became antsy, she asked, "Something wrong?"

"I need to use the restroom."

"The guest bathroom is right there." She pointed down the hall.

When he came out, she was nowhere to be seen. "Hello?"

"In here," she called back. "In my bedroom."

"Where are you?" he walked into the plush room.

"In my bathroom. Look at the view out of my window. It's spectacular." Willa put her arms around him from behind. When he turned, she was naked. "My bed's right here. Want to try it out?"

Open mouthed kissing with her fingers twirling his hair and nude body rubbing against him, he desperately wanted to try it out. When they were done, Bill stared at the ceiling. He'd never kissed a girl in a passionate way before, much less had sex. It dawned on him what he'd just done.

"Oh my god!" he whispered to himself. "Carrie."

"What's that, babe?" Willa scooted next to him.

"Nothing, nothing. I've got to go." Bill jumped out of bed and hurriedly dressed. "You can't tell anyone about this, okay?"

"Of course not," she cooed. "I don't want it getting around that

I'm not a virtuous girl. Come back anytime. I want to show you my new horse."

Willa watched Bill run out of the house. Having no intention of telling anyone—except Carrie—she smiled and fluffed her pillow. It had been a good night.

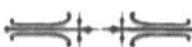

Wednesday afternoon was graduation. Carrie wore her new dress when Bill picked her up for the after party. Tonight was the night. Tonight, she was going to become more than just his kissing buddy. The following morning, Bill had to take his younger siblings to their grandparents' house for a traditional two-week summer visit.

Without asking, she scooted next to him in his old truck. At the party, she glued herself to his side, but he seemed nervous. When Willa walked in, Carrie thought Bill was about to faint.

"Well, don't you two make the cutest couple." Willa smiled sweetly. "You're a lucky girl."

Suspicious, Carrie didn't know quite what to make of the usually snarky girl's comment. "Thank you. I think we are." Carrie leaned against Bill, smiling up at him.

"Yeah. I mean, he's the *best* kisser." Willa winked at Bill. "And, well, that *other* stuff."

Carrie gasped and looked up at Bill. His mouth was moving, but nothing came out. By the look on his face, no one needed to explain what "that other stuff" meant. "Take me home, *now*." She stomped off, climbed into his truck, and slammed the door.

"Let me explain," Bill pleaded as he drove.

"Don't talk to me." Carrie held up her hand and pressed against the passenger side door, silently staring out the window.

"We'll talk when I get back," Bill pleaded as she got out.

Carrie walked off without answering. When he reached the end of the driveway, out of earshot, she replied to his vehicle's rear bumper, "You bastard." Carrie sat on the back steps, fuming.

Finally, she pulled out her phone and dialed. "Hello, Gramma? Yeah, I know it's after midnight there. Can we talk?"

Mandy, Bill's older stepsister by a year called him. "Dude, you need to talk to Carrie. She didn't tell me what was wrong in her texts, only that it had to do with you. She's *pissed*."

"I've been trying, but I think she blocked my number." He was beside himself with worry. "She's even unfriended me everywhere. I don't know what to do other than go over there when we get back."

"Well, whatever you did, you need to apologize." Mandy was adamant. "I mean *really* apologize."

"Tell her that I'm sorry and I'll be there as soon as I can."

"Sorry, bro. This is all on you. She's made it clear that I can't ever mention you. If I do, I'll lose her friendship."

Bill bounced off the walls during his obligatory two weeks at his grandparents'. Once home, the other kids scarcely had time to jump out of the vehicle before he spun a donut in the driveway and sped toward the Bennett ranch. He knocked on the back door instead of just walking in as usual.

Beth opened the door and greeted the very contrite young man. Her devastated daughter didn't tell her what had happened, only that it concerned Bill. From the look on his face, it must have been bad.

"May I talk to Carrie, please?"

"I'm sorry, hon, she's not here."

"When will she be back?"

Barely able to hear him as he mumbled toward his feet, she reached out and put her hand on his arm. "Carrie's not coming back—at least for a while. She's gone to her grandmother's house on Long Island for the summer."

Beth didn't have the heart to tell him that Carrie had already pre-registered at her old alma mater in New York state and may not return in the fall. She watched the slump shouldered young boy shuffle back to his truck. After leaning his forehead on the steering wheel for quite a while, he started the engine and drove slowly down the driveway. Little did she know this spat between friends would turn into a years' long saga of pain.

CHAPTER TWO

FIRST SUMMER APART

Beth and Karen sat at their traditional weekly luncheon comparing notes on their kids. Beth shook her head. "I don't know what happened, but it must have been major. Carrie was adamant about visiting my mother this summer."

"For the last five years, those two kids have been inseparable." Karen shook her head. "Now, he's almost incapacitated with grief. None of the other kids near their age in church know what happened—only that it was the night of the graduation party."

Beth replied, "Carrie's adamant that his name not be mentioned in our conversations."

"I tried pumping Mandy for information as soon as she came home from college," Karen said. "But as one of Carrie's best friends, she was tight lipped, not wanting to get in the middle."

Beth pulled little Peter, Karen's toddler, onto her lap. "I hope they work it out soon. Those two going at it puts everyone else on eggshells. I just don't know how they're going to do that if they're not communicating."

Grandma Kate gave Carrie a part time summer job at her gallery. Even though she grew up herding cows and riding horses, Carrie had spent enough time at Beth's art shows to be comfortable around the aficionados. But still, a small coastal village on Long Island wasn't anything like the Palouse.

To keep the wounded girl distracted, Kate took her along to visit friends. All of the stops magically seemed to have either children or grandchildren close to her granddaughter's age. One friend even owned a stable with horses needing exercise. With new two- and four-legged friends, Carrie's anger and hurt over Bill became resentment. Her self-confidence and indomitable personality started shining again.

"You need to find a social life. Quit sitting around moping." Kate leaned over her granddaughter to see what she was working on and put a hand on Carrie's shoulder, the nearest thing to caring intimacy she possessed. Hugs were out. "You need to find a boy to distract you. Go on some dates."

"I don't know how to do that." Carrie couldn't fathom her mother, a complete moral opposite, being raised by this woman. "The closest thing to an actual date with a boy I've ever been on was to a movie in a group."

"Oh, you poor dear! Well, we're going to change that. It's no wonder you're roaming around here all depressed over one silly boy. You need to expand your horizons. Explore life! How do you know which car you want to buy until you've test driven a few?"

"Gramma!" Carrie blushed. "You make it sound so easy!"

"But it *is*, dear. I guess a better analogy for you would be horses. You don't stable the first horse you've ever ridden. You ride a bunch first to see which one feels the best under you. And remember, just like a horse, don't let boys control you. You're the boss."

"Oh, my *god!*" Carrie fled the room. This wasn't the Palouse. Gramma Kate and her mom were *definitely* different women.

With her grandmother's constant pushing, Carrie started dating. She'd always wanted to lose her virginity to Bill, but he'd cheated on her. Yes, she'd kissed him and wanted to go further.

With their history as best friends, going further proved to be more complicated than she expected. The big blow up ended that dream.

Full of anger, resentment, and hurt, Carrie spitefully set about losing her virginity like another needed task back on the ranch. She reincorporated her motto: "Buck up, cowgirl, there's a job to be done."

None of the boys felt right. Mid-June, Carrie was currying a horse she'd just ridden when a guy she'd seen around the stables walked up. "Boy, it's sure a muggy one today, isn't it?"

"Yeah." Carrie smiled at him. "I'm all gross from sweat. I can't wait to get home and shower."

"You're Kate's granddaughter, aren't you?" He picked up a brush to help her. "Name's John—John Spencer. My uncle owns the place."

"It's a nice facility. A lot fancier than what I'm used to." She started to wonder where this was all going. "Do you work here?"

"Yeah, my uncle gives me a job during the summer to appease my mom. My shift is over though." He opened the stall gate. "It *is* muggy today. I was going to the beach for a swim. Wanna come?"

"I don't have my suit with me. I need to take Gramma's car home and change. Maybe some other time." All excuses, she couldn't swim well. The Palouse near her ranch had no public pools and few swimming holes.

John grinned at her. "Hey, I *know* where Kate lives. I'm not giving up that easily. I can pick you up. Maybe we can have dinner too."

That was their first date. Three years older than Carrie, he would be entering his junior year at Stanford. Glad to see her granddaughter coming out of her funk, Kate was tickled to let her have all the time off from her made-up job that she wanted. After a few weeks of constantly knocking around together, they became almost attached at the hip. John (and Kate) subtly pushed to further their relationship past kissing.

He made a not so veiled proposition. "The people using our

beach house have left for the season. Why don't you come up for the weekend?"

"Won't your parents mind?"

"They won't know. My parents live in Southern California and don't use it very often. I'm getting tired of the guest room at my uncle's place, so I think I'll put the cottage to use."

"I don't know." Carrie feigned mulling it over. Really liking John, she'd already made up her mind not to return from the weekend a virgin. "I'll think about it."

Grinning, he said, "I promise there's no ax murderers anywhere near the place."

Free spirited Kate not only approved but encouraged the trip—anything to get that wretched boy in the Palouse out of her granddaughter's heart. Carrie was eighteen and needed to spread her wings, so Kate pushed the little bird out of the nest. "Go, go. Just bring me back some chowder from that place just up the shoreline from there."

John took Carrie's bags into the beach house's guest room. "This is your room. Change into your bathing suit, and I'll see you in the courtyard."

When she walked onto the ocean view patio, John was already stretched out sunbathing. "It didn't take long for you to get started," Carrie commented.

He smiled. "Hey, I can't wait forever. It takes you women so long to get ready for anything. Here, lay down. I'll rub some lotion on to keep you from burning."

His hands on her like that felt so good, she wanted them to go everywhere. When John untied both the neck and back strings on her bikini for "easier lotion distribution," she knew where he was headed. Wanting to take that journey with him, Carrie smiled and rolled onto her back without her top. John became her first lover instead of that idiot Bill.

Monday morning before driving back to Kate's place, John cooked breakfast while Carrie sat at the patio table thoughtfully watching the ocean. He put one hand on her shoulder as he placed the plate on the table. She lifted her hand and caressed his. Smiling up, she said, "I could easily get used to this."

He kissed the top of her head. "I want to get out from under my uncle's thumb, so I'm moving my stuff to the cottage. Why don't you stay here too?"

Spending most of their free time together at the cottage for the rest of the summer, the start of the school year was bittersweet. Even though they became extremely close, possibly bordering love, John and Carrie knew that with their schools thousands of miles apart, the end of summer was the end of their relationship.

"I don't want to leave without you." John pulled her close while they strolled on the beach.

"Me either." She leaned her head against his arm. Coming to Long Island to mend a broken heart had resulted with another. She and John had become too close, even though they both knew better. "Please stay in touch. I want to see you during semester breaks."

"I'll try. But my family tends to create obligations for me without asking."

They kissed, then John left for California.

CHAPTER THREE
MR. ROBERTS

Bill worked on the Bennett ranch during the first hay cutting but wouldn't make eye contact with either Beth or her husband, Randy. Then, he roamed around the county doing odd jobs on other spreads to make college money. One day, in the mercantile, Willa's father approached him.

"I hear you're a good worker. I need someone for the company's various operations."

"Doing what?"

Bill didn't want to go anywhere near the man's daughter, the cause of so much pain. Even though what she did was to intentionally break him and Carrie up, Bill couldn't blame her for everything. He knew he'd been impulsive, immature, and just plain stupidly horny.

"You'll be going around to our various properties checking irrigation pipes, maintaining equipment and the like. Interested?"

Bill was, as long as he didn't have to go near the man's house or his daughter. The money was good and the work familiar. Toward the end of July, Mr. Roberts stopped by the irrigation pump Bill was working on.

"I need you to come by my place tomorrow. The carpenters who built the stables left a few small things unfinished. It isn't worth my time to call them back out. Know anything about horses?"

Bill winced and thought about quitting on the spot. "I know a little . . . . Is Willa around?"

Oh good, Mr. Roberts thought, *one more hornball boy following my daughter around.* Then, he replied, "No. She's running around Europe with a bunch of her friends. My wife's idea."

Bill was relieved. "I'll be there. What time?"

"How about six, before it gets hot."

Everything went fine until mid-August when Willa descended back in town with a group of her rich friends. Bill tried to blend in to the background, but he needn't have bothered. She breezed by, showing the others her horse in the stables. He might as well have been a pitchfork leaned up in the shadows, something disdainful only to be touched by the help.

After work, spurred by the rich girl's return, he swung by the Bennett ranch to see when Carrie was returning. Filled with hope, he found Beth in her art studio. "School's starting in a couple of weeks. When's Carrie coming back?"

"I'm sorry, sweetie." Beth had held out as long as she could. It was time to break his heart. "Carrie's not coming home. She enrolled in my old alma mater and will be staying in New York."

Gut punched by her words, Bill staggered back. Both hands shaking on the end of limply dangling arms, he turned. Slump shouldered, on his way to the door, he said, "Oh. Well, give her my best."

Beth watched the devastated young man shuffle out of her studio, feeling conflicting emotions. She felt sorry for heartbroken Bill. Yet, she was angry with him for doing whatever he did to her daughter. Beth had been deprived of Carrie's presence for almost three months. Now, it looked like the next opportunity would be during the holiday break.

It was a madhouse when Bill got home. His stepfather, Charlie, was playing with toddler Peter. Bill's younger sister, Nettie, was arguing with Heather, her stepsister of about the same age. Heather's little brother, Ricky, was blathering on to Bill's mom, Karen, about a wounded coyote he saw running across one of the upper fields. The only one who seemed semi sane at the moment was Mandy, sorting clothes to pack for her sophomore year at college.

"I need to talk to you." Bill nodded out the laundry room window. "In private."

"Sure. Let's go for a walk." Mandy walked beside her second best friend past the outbuildings into the recently harvested grainfield. She knew what Bill wanted but, not wanting to betray Carrie's confidence, had kept silent all summer until he found out from someone else. "What is it?"

"Carrie's not coming back. She's going to school in New York."

"I know."

"I need to talk to her," he said, desperation in his voice. "I need to make things right between us."

"Sit." Mandy motioned to the stubble covered ground. She leaned against him. "You need to let her go. Move on."

"I can't. I need her back."

"You have to," Mandy teared up in sympathy for Bill, "because *she's* moved on."

"No. Carrie wouldn't do that. We belong together."

"There's no easy way to say this, but she's been dating other guys all summer." Mandy grimaced, then tore the bandage the rest of the way off. "She's been seeing the same guy for almost two months. From what she tells me, it's pretty hot and heavy."

Bill gasped and stared at his older stepsister for a few moments, then collapsed into a fetal position, sobbing. Mandy leaned over him from behind, resting her head consolingly on his shoulder. He pushed her away.

"Leave me alone."

When Mandy walked into the house by herself, Karen gave her a questioning look. Mandy looked sadly at her. "He probably won't be in for supper. I'll stop by the clinic at lunch tomorrow and fill you in."

Willa's friends only stayed for a few days. Since no one else seemed to care, Bill was mucking out her horse's stall when she came strutting into the stable.

"We haven't had a chance to talk since I came home. I'm bored. Let's visit."

"Get away from me." He pushed the wheelbarrow toward the compost pile.

"That's no way to be," she whined. "I'm *bored*."

"Why not work with your horse? That's why you have one, isn't it?"

"But I want to hang with you," she pouted.

"I don't want to talk to *you*!" he snapped. "You ruined my life. Now you want to be all nicey-nice? Get away from me!"

She saw her father passing the stable door. "Oh, Daddy! Can I see you for a moment?" When he walked up to her horse's stall, Willa pulled the helpless daughter routine. "Daddy, my horse doesn't mind me very well. She seems to be just fine around the hired hand. Could you have him escort us on a ride to show me some tricks?"

Bill's mouth fell open. That girl didn't need to be shown any tricks. She already had most of the dirty ones well in hand.

"That's a good idea, Willa. Bill, saddle up my horse and go with her. He could use some exercise." Furious, Bill saddled the horses. Mr. Roberts stood beside his daughter, watching. "I'm leaving for a business trip to Seattle. I'll be gone all weekend. Will you be alright by yourself, dear?"

"Of course, Daddy. If something goes wrong or breaks, I'll just call your hired hand and he can handle it."

"Good idea, Willa." He looked at Bill. "Hear that? My daughter's got you on call until I get back. Understand?"

Thinking Willa had the whole male manipulation thing down pat, Bill just nodded. He finished saddling and led the horses out of the stable as her dad disappeared down the driveway. "Let's go."

Obviously trained by someone else, someone who knew what they were doing, the horse behaved just fine. Riding toward the backside of her family's property in silence, Willa just couldn't let it be.

"So, why are you so mad at me?"

"I told you. Because you couldn't keep your mouth shut, Carrie broke up with me. You ruined my life."

"Aren't you being a little dramatic? Didn't you guys just talk it over and make up?"

"Talk and make up? She hasn't said a word to me since that night. She's moved to New York and is going to college there." He started to shake with anger. "She has a *boyfriend*. No, we aren't going to talk and make up. Satisfied?"

"Oh, sorry," Willa offered what sounded like a sincere apology. "I didn't realize you two were so into each other."

Riding along in silence for a while, Bill calmed down a little. He told himself it wasn't totally her fault. After all, he *was* a more than willing participant in what happened. That was what bothered him the most. In the end, he had no one to blame but himself.

"So, why are you alone this weekend? Where's your mom? I don't think I've ever seen her."

"Right now, I think she's in LA with her new boyfriend. My parents split up two years ago." She had a lost tone in her voice Bill hadn't heard before. "Because of that, Daddy won't let me attend the college I wanted back East. In fact, he won't even let me go to the University of Washington. He wants me close by to keep an eye on me. I have to go to Washington State in Pullman. Just where I wanted to go—a cow college."

"Huh."

"Isn't that where you're going?"

"That was the plan. My stepsister's already going there."

"We can hang out." Willa glanced toward Bill.

He sighed. "You're really pushing it."

Back in the stables, she actually helped put the horses away and feed them for once. When Bill was loading up his gear in the truck, she followed expectantly. As he reached for the driver's side door handle, she finally said what had been on her mind.

"Would you stay for supper? It isn't much. Just a couple of TV dinners. I don't want to be alone. Please?"

Helping her warm the dinners, then during their meal, Bill saw another side of Willa. Buried underneath the brazen, manipulative flirt was an insecure girl lacking parental attention. He still hadn't forgiven her. He wasn't even close to forgiving himself. But he at least could talk to her. After supper, sitting on the sofa, she put her hand on his arm.

"Would you stay with me tonight?"

"*What?*" He couldn't believe she would still ask such a thing. "Why would I do that? After everything that's happened?"

"I know. We're too different. I don't expect forever—just right now."

Lost, emotionally hollow, with the only person able to fill that void forever gone, he called home and told his mother he had a sick critter needing constant monitoring. He didn't know when he'd be home.

Though wounded by different weapons, Bill and Willa became each other's bandage. Now a couple of convenience, they dated each other because there just wasn't anyone else who understood their needs.

CHAPTER FOUR
DEALING WITH CHANGE

It didn't take long for Carrie to make friends at college. The girls in her dorm were fun to be around for the most part. Now that the Bill-caused wounds were buried under a layer of heartbreak over John, she made an effort to stay away from boys.

Her new friends had other ideas, pushing her to date as many young men as possible just to see what was out there. Often, Carrie discovered that, what she thought would be a girls' night out was a blind date set up. It was on one of those occasions she remembered a discussion she'd had with Grandma Kate before leaving.

"Remember the horses. I want you to ride at least ten before I see you again."

"*Ten?* I don't want to be a slut!"

"I didn't mean it *that* way. Just have no qualms at all about saying yes to a date. If the boy's interesting enough, you can decide about the other thing." Kate hugged her granddaughter for the first time ever. Oh, and I want names to make sure you're not fudging."

"I promise."

Having been raised differently, Carrie had no intention of honoring that promise. But slowly, with her new friends' urging, she dipped her toe into the dating pool.

She'd been a loyal friend to the boy who shall not be named. What had being chaste and pure, waiting for them to be together, gotten her? Still bitter and attempting a recovery from John, Carrie went overboard and became a bit of a tease. However, since flirting was the limit of her involvement, none of her dates hung around for long.

It was going to take another special young man like John for her to become intimate again. Staying in touch, Carrie sent feelers to her summer love, hoping in vain to see him during the holidays.

John messaged back, "Unfortunately, my parents are taking us to a Swiss skiing chalet. They've also pushed me into accepting an internship in asia next summer. With my family's desire to expand their business into the far east, I'll probably have to do my senior year at a university there. I really miss you."

Feeling emotionally hollow and wanting to go home during Christmas break, Carrie called her mother to check out the situation. Enough time had passed that maybe she could stand to see Bill's face again. Possibly, she might let him explain. Deep down inside, she still loved him.

"Hello?" a strange male voice answered the phone.

"This is Carrie. Who are you, and why are you answering my parents' phone?"

"Carrie? Oh, hi! Haven't seen you since last spring. It's Steve. Remember me? You were a year ahead of me in school."

"Yeah, yeah. Hi, how're you doin?" Well, at least the house wasn't being robbed—maybe. "What are you doing in my house?"

"Oh, oh yeah. I came in to wash my hands. Your mom heard the phone ring from outside and told me to answer. Want me to get her?"

"No, that's all right." Carrie thought this might work out better. From what she remembered, Steve was clueless about much of anything past video games. He'd be perfect to pump for information. "So, you're working there now? Is there enough work that Charlie and Bill can't keep up?"

"Bill?" Steve sounded confused. "He hasn't worked here since last June. I took his place."

"Really? Where'd he go?"

"Oh, he got a job working for that corporate farm and spent most of the summer caretaking the Roberts' spread." Steve paused, then continued with an envious tone, "He's one lucky dude. I think he and that hot Willa chick hung around together. I heard they're both at WSU now."

Carrie squeaked out, "Oh."

"You want me to run out and get your mom?"

"No . . . no, that's all right." Carrie could barely breathe. "Just tell her that I won't be able to come home for the holidays . . . something important has come up."

She sat on her dorm room bed staring at the floor. Bill and Willa hooking up wasn't just a one-time thing. Was that what Bill had been trying to explain to her the night of the graduation dance? Was he intending to break up with her to be with that other girl but too big of a coward to be up front about it? Carrie wondered how long they'd been seeing each other behind her clueless back.

One thing was for certain. She was done thinking about that scumbag back home. It was time to date as many boys as she could just to see if there was a decent one in the bunch. Carrie's social life went into hyper-drive, and her grades started to slip.

Even Kate became concerned. "Yes, I encouraged you to see what's out there, but you might be going overboard. All of the continents can't be adequately explored in one year."

Trying to throttle back after spring break, Carrie started going out with Ethan, a sophomore at her college. A product of a broken marriage, his parents gave him everything he needed, except parental supervision. Even though he could be a little self-centered at times, Ethan made up for it in other ways. Nowhere near in love, Carrie kept seeing him just to not be alone.

"I've got a plan." Ethan kissed Carrie. "I've never been to Spain. You speak Spanish. How about you and me going there this summer?"

"I was planning on heading home and spending some quality

time on horseback." Then, it hit Carrie. Returning to the ranch meant a high probability of running into Bill again. "Tell me more about your idea."

"A few guys I hang out with are from there. One of their parents has a villa on the Mediterranean coast and said we could use the guest cottage." He pulled her into a spoon position. "I asked, and there's a stable nearby where you can ride horses. We can go anywhere in Europe and use their place as a home base."

Carrie really wanted to see her parents and the ranch again—except for Bill. But it *was* a free trip to Europe. "Okay, I'm in."

Beth was hurt when her daughter didn't come home for Thanksgiving, enraged at Christmas. After Steve relayed Carrie's message, she stormed past her husband, working on the dually in the shop. "I trusted him! I made him part of our family!"

"What are you talking about?" Randy leaned back from the truck's engine compartment. Confused, he asked, "*Who* are you talking about?"

"Bill!" she shouted. "Carrie isn't coming home for Christmas! I don't know what he did to her, but she can't even stand to be on the same side of the continent as him anymore."

"Maybe it wasn't all him . . ." Randy's attempts to reason with his wife weren't heard. She'd already slammed the door to her studio.

Beth's artwork started to suffer. Usually, her paintings were uplifting scenes of wildlife, nature, or quirky people. With Carrie's absence stretching on, the mother's work became dark, without hope. When Carrie announced she'd be heading to Spain for the summer, Beth bottomed emotionally.

"Aren't you at least going to come home for a visit before you go?"

"I would, Mom, but the scheduling just doesn't match up," Carrie lied. She thought she'd outgrown such a primitive lifestyle and wanted nothing to do with the Palouse. Her parents and horse, yes, everything else, no. "I'll keep in touch. I promise."

"I'm disappointed. I'd fly out there to visit but I've already committed to some shows." Having spent a summer in France herself, Beth understood her daughter's desire to expand her horizons. But her once close daughter stretching their emotional bond past the point of elasticity broke Beth's heart.

"Have a good time, dear. Call often."

It was that boy's fault. He had broken her family. Beth and his mother, Karen, had been good friends. They'd even covered up each other's crimes. There literally was a buried body in her upper feedlot and the ashes of another sent to its owner's relatives to cement their bond. Bill was tearing the two families apart.

CHAPTER FIVE
OFF TO EUROPE

A week after finals, Ethan and Carrie arrived in Spain. His tendency to be self-centered immediately began testing her patience. Then, her boyfriend and his Spanish buddies decided to go to Greece and party their way around the Mediterranean coastline.

Carrie texted Mandy, "I feel like I'm just arm candy used as bait to attract other girls. I'm seriously considering ending our relationship, but Ethan is my ride. I can't break up until we're back in the States."

Her friend messaged back, "Keep me posted. Meanwhile, try to get the most out of your trip. Maybe go sightseeing on your own."

Later, when Carrie and Ethan were finally alone, she grumbled, "I'm getting tired of this. It's not what I signed up for. I want to go back to Spain."

Ethan acted like he got the hint. His buddies left on their own adventure while the couple spent one more night in a coastal tourist town before leaving.

"Let's go to the club district tonight. I heard of a perfect one for just us."

"I suppose." Carrie sighed. What she really wanted was to be sitting quietly along a Long Island beach.

Full of high rollers, the club was obviously out of their league.

An intimidating man in his mid-thirties, surrounded by lackeys and fawning women, closely watched them from a private balcony. Ethan came back from the restroom, elated.

"Come on. We've been invited to the VIP level. It'll be fun."

Reluctantly, she went to the area reserved for the man who'd been watching them. Large, muscular, with a commanding presence, Nicolas was obviously the one in charge. Sitting next to him in the dark club, she thought he was strikingly good looking. With his short sleeved shirt half unbuttoned, his very hairy chest and arms reminded her more of a bear than a wealthy man. As her boyfriend blathered, the man kept nodding as if he was listening, but his eyes stayed on Carrie.

When an alcohol filled bladder forced Ethan to excuse himself from the table, Nicolas turned to Carrie. "I haven't had a chance to get to know you. Tell me about yourself."

She shrugged. "There's not much to tell. I start my college sophomore year this fall."

"Oh? What are your courses?"

"Right now, I'm mostly taking business courses but minoring in art history."

"Interesting," Nicolas said, leaning toward her like he actually cared.

Tired of Ethan's inattentiveness, she'd had enough when she saw him making eyes at another girl on his way back from the restroom. Scooting closer beside Nicolas to elicit jealousy backfired. Not even the rich man's hand on her thigh seemed to phase her boyfriend. Amping up her flirting, she cavalierly looked at Ethan when Nicolas put his arm around her shoulder. Uncomfortable with how far she'd gone when the rich man kissed her neck, she feigned illness.

"I'm sorry, but I'm not feeling well." She looked up apologetically at Nicolas. "I'm going to have to call it an evening and return to the hotel."

He smiled sympathetically. "But of course. You should rest and recover. It was nice to meet you."

Initially not happy he had to leave the bar with his girlfriend, Ethan recovered when the high roller held him back for a momentary chat. Walking to the hotel, he was ecstatic.

"The big guy really liked my ideas. He needs to visit a few places to conduct business tomorrow and we've been invited to tag along so he can pick my brain. Then, we'll go to his private island for a few days."

"I don't want to go," Carrie grumbled, thinking this was just one more nail in their relationship coffin. "I thought we were returning to Spain."

"Oh, come on." He kissed her cheek, but she pulled away. "It'll be fun. He's sending a limo in the morning."

"When we get back, we're going to have a serious talk."

Suspicious from the start, an angry Carrie wondered why a couple kids from the States slumming around Europe rated a trip to a private island. The next day, when the limousine dropped them off at a cafe for breakfast, Nicolas and his security detail were already there.

Ignoring Ethan, Nicolas asked Carrie, "Are you feeling better this morning?"

"Yes, thank you," Carrie tentatively answered. "It must have been the food I ate earlier."

He laughed. "That happens to a lot to tourists. They eat in places with the fanciest exteriors and the worst kitchens."

Ethan interrupted, "She'll recover. Carrie has the strongest stomach of anyone I know. We should get down to business. Where do you need my advice?"

"I'm interested in purchasing an olive grove and processing plant." Carrie could hear restrained irritation when Nicolas replied, "I was thinking you two would like to accompany me to look at it."

Touring the plant, Carrie was struck by the contrast of her immature boyfriend next to their host. She'd always known Ethan hadn't grown up yet, but his constant yammering about things he knew nothing about drove the point home.

Mid-morning, at the wharf, there was a collection of party type men and women she'd seen in the club, businessmen, and what appeared to be bodyguards boarding the small ferry. One of the business types intercepted Ethan and took him aside for a talk. When it was Carrie's turn to board, her boyfriend ran up, ecstatic.

"Boy, have we lucked out. They've invited me to examine a couple more business opportunities on the way out."

"Okay . . ." Carrie knew there was a "but" coming.

"Yeah, the big guy's flying out this afternoon in his helicopter. He has to check on some of his charity projects. He remembered you saying that you studied art, so he wants you to stay behind to view some historical places and fly out later with him."

"No." Being offered up as a carrot to further Ethan's aspirations irritated her. "I want to stay with you."

"It'll be a boring ride with all the business talk. Besides, you don't have to worry, look at all the security around his limo."

With the guard holding her arm, she watched Ethan on the ferry deck surrounded by women from the club. Her boyfriend making separate arrangements without asking ticked off Carrie. He was more interested in his own ambitions than spending time with her. When the driver opened the car door and Nicolas was waiting in the back seat, she stood tentatively, unsure if she wanted to get in.

He laughed. "Come on. It's not that nefarious. I'm done with my business earlier than expected. Last night, you seemed to be a lot less offensive to be around than anyone else. I can show you the local historical ruins and still beat the ferry to my island."

Spending most of the day with him as her tour guide, Carrie was glad she got in the car. She gave him a questioning look when he led her past the closed sign at one of the sites usually not available to normal tourists. He winked. "They know better than to tell me no."

She asked, "What's the history of this site?"

Having left his security detail outside, Nicolas described the ruins in down-to-earth, pleasant conversation. The consummate gentleman, he opened doors and held her hand in uneven terrain—sometimes uncomfortably long. By the time they went to a small cafe only frequented by locals, she automatically reached for his hand at the smallest obstacle.

When they climbed into an empty aircraft cabin, she asked her host as the engine revved for takeoff, "We're it? Where's everybody else?"

He laughed. "I told you, those other people get on my nerves. I'm pleased that I took a chance with you being an acceptable companion to keep me company."

Now more relaxed around her host, Carrie started asking more personal questions. "How come you speak English with hardly any accent?"

Nicolas smiled. "I spent time at a boarding school in Florida, even went to college in California. My father pushed for New York, but I didn't want to endure the weather there."

Looking down at his approaching island, she thought it would have been a very defensible Middle Ages fort. Surrounded by high cliffs, it only had one well-guarded dock in a small cove.

Upon landing, she found her boyfriend and their luggage in a separate guest accommodation building from the main house. She wasn't that worldly, but it looked like most of the other females present were "on the clock." Friendly with all of the men, none looked to be attached to any individual.

"I don't know why we're here. We've nothing in common with these people." She left out that she enjoyed Nicolas's company as a tour guide and the opportunity to be away from her grating boyfriend for a while.

"Relax, babe, the big man really likes me." Ethan's self-centered opinion of his importance to the world had never been higher. "I'm doing some good networking here that'll benefit the both of us in the future."

"Well, I don't trust any of this. Be careful." Carrie was just talking into thin air. Her boyfriend had tuned her out on his way toward the inner circle.

The over-the-top partying beside the pool didn't impress her much after the privately guided tour of historical sites. When Ethan became involved in a card game, Carrie shook her head. She'd played with him a lot back at college and always won. A terrible player, he took too many chances and had huge tells. Yet somehow late that afternoon, possibly because Nicolas was paying more attention to her than the game, Ethan seemed to be constantly winning.

Taking Carrie aside after the game, her boyfriend pushed her to be friendlier. "You're kind of a stick in the mud. We came here to have fun." Looking past her, he winked. "You need to be a better guest."

"Better guest?" Turning, she saw one of the "professional women" smiling at him.

Carrie snapped at him, "When we get back to the mainland, I'm going home."

After Ethan shrugged and walked off, Nicolas came up and asked, "Problems?"

"No, it's all right," she said, glowering in the direction of her soon to-be-ex-boyfriend. "He just gets on my nerves."

"I see. If I can be of any assistance, let me know."

"I need some time away from him." Carrie paused, then asked hopefully, "I don't suppose you have another room? Maybe I can stay with one of the other girls for a night?"

Nicolas laughed. "Oh, you *don't* want that! I'm sorry but the guest quarters are at capacity." Thoughtfully eyeing her, he said, "Although, I have a room in the main house reserved for special visitors. If you want, I can have your luggage moved there."

"That's too much." She couldn't believe his generosity. "I don't want to be a bother."

"Nonsense. Consider it done." He pointed to a maid. "When you're ready, she'll show you to your new room."

Later, tired of being ignored by her boyfriend, Carrie found the maid and was led to her room. Before entering the main house, she saw Ethan chatting it up with the woman who'd smiled at him.

Taking her to the second floor, the maid opened the last door before a staircase to the third floor. "Don't go up there. It's Nicolas's private quarters."

As promised, Carrie's luggage was waiting, and the bed was turned down. Not caring why she rated such a nice room and private bath, she fell asleep on the luxurious bed. Coming out of the shower the next morning, she found a note on the bed. Her presence was requested on the back patio for breakfast.

Nicolas, the only person at the small table, stood and held her chair. "Did you have a good night's rest?"

"Yes," she replied. When a plate was set in front of her, Carrie asked, "Where is everyone?"

"Most are still asleep. They partied late last night." He sipped his coffee. "Visitors usually have breakfast in their rooms. I dine alone unless . . ." he smiled at her, "they are special guests."

Not knowing what to say to that last comment, she changed the subject. "What's there to do here during the day? Surely it's not all partying."

"I mostly work. Guests just fend for themselves."

"What? You're on an island and you don't even fish or water-ski?"

"You fish?" He didn't wait for an answer, pushing the button on his intercom. "Ready the fishing boat. One guest and I are going out." Not giving Carrie a chance to decline, a half hour later, they were aboard a fully crewed vessel pulling away from the dock.

"I'm not used to this larger tackle." She picked up one of the poles. "I've only shore-fished in Palouse streams and our ranch's stock pond for catfish."

"Palouse? What's that?"

"It's where I'm from." Carrie struggled with the pole. "It's an area in Eastern Washington state and Northern Idaho."

"I should go there someday. Here, let me help you with that."

A patient teacher, Nicolas spent the day with his arms around her, helping with the rod. She suspected he was more interested in holding her than the pole but didn't care anymore. Not getting any attention from a boyfriend of uncertain standing and flattered that a handsome man wanted to be near her, she continually asked for more assistance.

Mid-afternoon as they were coming up the hill from the dock, she thanked her host. "It was a fun day. I think I'll take a shower to wash off the fish goo. I probably smell gross."

"You're fine. Just take a dip in the pool while I check on the other guests. I'll have the cook prepare our catch for supper tonight."

Carrie laughed. "There's barely enough for two people."

He smiled. "That's all we need. Everyone else will probably drink their dinner."

Seeing Ethan and the girl lounging next to each other by the pool elicited a flash of jealousy. Trying to calm down, Carrie told herself that she'd just spent the day with another man and nothing nefarious had happened. Although, the possibility was starting to intrigue her.

"You're back." Ethan jumped up. "How'd your day go? Boy, you're doing a good job schmoozing. At this rate, we'll have all kinds of great contacts when we go home."

"You keep using the word we," she snapped. "I'm pretty sure the *we* part of us is on thin ice."

"Shhh." He pulled her out of hearing range. "Don't ruin it for us, babe. We'll talk about it back on the mainland. But for now, these guys have to believe we're still a couple. We are, aren't we?"

Glancing toward the girl in the lounge chair, she growled, "Yeah, if you say so."

"Although," he looked in Nicolas's direction, "if an opportunity came up to influence our host by being *overly* friendly, you have my permission. It'd be good for both of us in the long run."

Speechless that Ethan blatantly suggested she sleep with Nicolas for his own professional gain, Carrie turned and dove into the water.

Ignored, bored, and daydreaming while watching the sunset, Nicolas's voice brought Carrie out of her trance. "Dinner is served. Would you care to join me?"

"Sure. I'd *love* to. I'll stop by my room and change out of this swimsuit if that's okay."

Walking toward the house, she saw Ethan sitting next to that girl again. Carrie put on a sundress just in case he'd see her and, more importantly, she wanted to look nice for Nicolas.

This time, she wasn't so surprised that only she and Nicolas were at the table. "Wine?" he asked.

She apologized. "I don't drink. I've never developed a taste for it."

"Oh, this stuff is so weak, it's almost like drinking fruit juice." He poured her a glass. "Try it. Besides, the water is terrible."

Carrie understood her host's need to be away after spending what little time she had around those people. Gaining a good rapport during her guided tour and the fishing trip, their conversation over dinner was much more intelligent than the nonsense back at the pool. Seemingly enjoying her lifelong outspokenness, Nicolas's intense eyes never strayed from her face—as if she were the only other person in existence. Mesmerized and drawn to him, she was still surprised when he said, "I have an extensive art collection. Would you like to see it?"

"Sure. I'd love that." Carrie took his arm without asking.

Maintaining body contact, he escorted her around the house explaining each wall hanging and statue. Comfortable with his touch after spending the day with him teaching her how to hold a rod, she pushed closer when he held her waist or shoulders while looking at the art.

"I keep my most stimulating artwork where unapproved eyes cannot view it." Arm around her shoulder, he led her up the stairs to a second-floor security door directly across the hall from her room. Smiling devilishly, he placed his palm on the keypad. "Ready to join me in my lair?"

The wine being stronger than advertised, Carrie giggled. Now overtly wanting him to desire her, she flirtatiously followed her suave host into the room. "You weren't fibbing. These are really valuable." Gasping when he led her to a room full of erotic art, she blushed. "Oh my!"

"This is where I take special ladies to impress them." She tingled when he put his arms around her waist from behind and kissed her neck. "Are you impressed?"

"Very." Completely under the spell of her worldly host, Carrie turned her head and kissed him on the mouth. Then, she pulled away. "I . . . I can't. I have a boyfriend."

"You mean this idiot?" He led her across the hall and pointed out her bedroom window. "Him?" Nicolas's pager buzzed. "I'll be right back."

She stared down at her boyfriend and the girl sitting on his lap without her swimsuit top. Looking at an unseen person, the girl nodded then led Ethan toward the guest quarters. High from the wine, Carrie didn't care anymore. They were definitely done.

Nicolas returned and closed the window. Carrie was so angry when he tried to hug her again, she couldn't stand to be touched. "I'm sorry. Would you mind terribly If I just called it a night?"

"But of course. It's been a long day for you. I'll see you for breakfast."

Sleep took its time overcoming Carrie's active mind. Curled up facing the window, her hurt and anger directed at Ethan collided explosively with what she considered her irrational jealousy. After all, she now fully intended to break up with him after securing her stateside return ticket.

Punching her pillow, Carrie rolled over, facing her room's interior wall. The same wall just across the hallway from Nicolas's art gallery. The room where she kissed him. She told herself he was twice her age and not really interested in her. Yet, Carrie drifted off dreaming about what it would feel like with his bearlike arms holding her against his hairy chest.

CHAPTER SIX
BUYING TRIP

The next morning, there were four settings on the patio table. Nicolas and one of his advisors were already there. Halfway through the meal, bleary eyed Ethan finally showed up. She rolled her eyes that he could be so inconsiderate.

"Well, it's good to see you survived the night." Nicolas's sarcasm was lost on Ethan but not Carrie. "I have a dual pronged business proposal I'd like you to consider."

Egotistically thinking his host was serious, Ethan replied, "Sure, I'd be happy to lend you my expertise. Just as long as I get a piece of the pie."

"Excellent." Nicolas smiled and nodded toward the fourth person at the table. "I'd like you to consult with my associate over the next few days. It requires a bit of travel."

"No problem. Carrie isn't going to get in the way, is she?"

"Absolutely not." Their host turned and smiled at her. "In fact, that's the second part of my proposal. While you're off making my business more profitable, I'm going on a short art buying trip. I thought she could accompany me and help choose the items."

"That sounds great!" Ethan was bubbling with excitement. "We'll both do a good job for you, right babe?"

Carrie couldn't believe how clueless he was. The sparks which had been flying between her and Nicolas should have been obvious to a blind man. Was her boyfriend that tied up in himself not to be jealous? Or was Ethan *really* serious when he virtually told her to sleep with their host? Either way, she left to pack for the trip while the men continued their discussion.

"Ethan," Nicolas said, "why don't we have a private chat about you securing investment opportunities while Carrie gets her luggage?"

"That's an excellent idea," her boyfriend gushed. "I was about to ask about that!"

As she headed for the helicopter an hour later, Carrie saw Ethan watching with a strange look on his face.

She was torn between her promise to her grandmother about test riding horses and the unfortunate technicality that, since they hadn't had the chance to talk privately, she and Ethan were still a couple. Starting with Bill's betrayal, it was always her that walked away from a relationship.

The only exception was John where they both knew the beginning of the school year would be the end of their romance. John was three years her senior, the largest age difference of anyone she'd been with. The man beside her in the limousine was twice her age. That disparity only added to her curiosity.

Driving between art galleries in a two car caravan, one for her and Nicolas and one for his security detail, her physical attraction toward him continued to build. There was just something about his quiet but powerful demeanor. She'd lost the will to resist his gravitational pull. Smiling, Carrie turned her head away and bit her lip, knowing she would sleep with Nicolas if he tried again.

Wearing the only other dress she'd packed for the trip to dinner at a fancy restaurant, she blushed feeling his constant gaze.

"You are positively radiant tonight." He poured her another glass of wine. "Do you dance?"

Her face flushed and she replied, "I will with you."

Carrie stood and took his hand. As the evening progressed, his every action indicated that he wanted her. From gently brushing her hair from her face at the table during conversation to the way he held her on the dance floor, it all pointed to her spending the night in his bed. She did everything possible to encourage him short of coming right out and saying what she wanted. Later, when they said goodnight outside her hotel room, he pecked her on the cheek and left.

Unsure if she misread his signals, she leaned back against the inside of her closed door with shaking legs to catch her breath. Disappointed, Carrie kicked off her shoes, removed her earrings, and undressed. She heard a soft knock on the door between their adjoining rooms. When she opened it wearing only a hotel housecoat, Nicolas stood shirtless, lust on his face. Gazing up into his intense eyes, she slid the robe from her shoulders, letting it fall to the floor.

Nicolas woke her the next morning with a cup of coffee. "Good morning."

She sat up in bed and kissed him. "It's a *great* morning. My European vacation became a whole lot better last night."

"As did my buying trip." He smiled. "Since we seem to be getting along so well, how would you feel about extending it by a few more days?"

"I'm game. Where to?" After spending the last few days with Nicolas, then a night in his bed, Carrie knew she'd never go back to her boyfriend. Her grandmother had proven correct. There were definitely better horses in the stable. "What about Ethan?"

"Don't worry about him. My business associates are keeping him busy. As for you, how much adventure are you up for?"

"What do you have in mind?"

He kissed her forehead. "Get showered, we're going to Vienna." He stopped on the way out of the room. "But first, we need to expand your wardrobe."

"I don't need any more clothes. That's what hotel laundromats are for."

"I like you in dresses during the day. The rest of the time, I plan on keeping you naked." He walked back and kissed her. "I assume we'll only need one room from now on."

She blushed and giggled. "Okay."

The short buying trip extended into one, then two weeks. After a couple days in Austria, his jet flew them to Prague, Budapest, and Sofia. Carrie was having the time of her life. During the whole trip, she couldn't get the smile off her face. She had never been fawned over so much, even by the ranch dog back home. She discovered on their very first night that the women she saw competing for his attention in the night club weren't just after his money.

On one layover where the gallery was closed for a holiday, they spent the day at an associate's private estate. With the friend occupied elsewhere, Carrie and Nicolas sunbathed by the pool. As he fastidiously applied lotion to every part of her pale skin, including between her toes, she wondered if this attention to detail was how he built his empire.

"I sure will be sad when it's time to end my summer fling," she snuggled next to him during the limo ride back to the Sofia airport, "but we have to return to our normal lives sometime."

"Yeah, sometime," he replied, sounding distant.

Instead of returning to the island, they went to a compound in north central Greece. After a couple of days, her "boyfriend" and a few of Nicolas's "financial advisors" drove up. Ethan greeted her like they had only been apart for a day.

Carrie wondered how he could be so naive not to have figured out that she and Nicolas had been sleeping together. Then, thinking back to their conversation beside the pool, it dawned on her—he did know, and somehow it served his purpose. Either way, since there was never a really good time to end a relationship, she decided to get it over with.

"We need to talk."

His tone indicating he already knew, he asked, "Yeah? About what?"

"We haven't been getting along for a while." Carrie put her hand on his forearm. "I think we should part ways."

Ethan shocked her with his almost nonchalant reply. It was as if he expected or wanted the breakup. "You're probably right. We should go back to the States and get on with our lives. We can leave tomorrow."

"You go. I'm staying a while longer. Nicolas has a list of archeological sites to show me. I want to experience as much local culture as I can before returning to school."

"No," Ethan insisted, "I *really* think we should leave together."

Nicolas walked up. "Is there a problem?"

Carrie gave him a forced smile. "Not really. We're just having a small difference of opinion about our travel plans."

"Oh." Nicolas eyed them both. "May I have a word with Ethan? I have a business proposition he should be *very* interested in."

She watched her ex-boyfriend and current paramour walk off, having an apparent serious discussion. Ethan returned tense and on edge.

"Nicolas made an offer I simply can't refuse. I'm going to take him up on it."

When he quickly walked off, she was curious what new scheme Ethan had up his sleeve. Whatever it was, he made it sound ominous. *Nothing new there*, she thought. He always leaned toward the overly dramatic. At least she had done the right thing and broken up with him. Now, she had a clear conscience.

Nicolas returned. "I'm hosting a nice dinner for the guests. I took the liberty of having a dress delivered for you to wear. I hope you like it. Take a nap and I'll see you in a couple of hours."

After dark, Carrie walked into the formal dining area set up in the courtyard wearing the most expensive dress she'd ever donned. The waiter seated her next to Nicolas at the head of the long table. Ethan sat at the far end with lower tier guards.

During dinner, Carrie tried to ignore Ethan but intermittently glanced in his direction. *Now he's paying attention to me*, she thought as he constantly stared at her, acting like he had something important he wanted to say. No longer caring about her traveling companion's opinion, she nervously talked with the powerful men near her when addressed and hung on to every syllable her generous, and very virile, host uttered.

After dinner, Ethan discreetly pulled her aside. "You're doing a good job entertaining Nicolas. Keep it up. *Both* our futures depend on it."

"What do you mean, both? There is no both anymore."

Rolling her eyes, Carrie walked off, only seeing him once more that evening. After she called it a night and was heading for the house, he stood off to the side watching her with the same expression he'd had at dinner. Then, he got in a car with some "advisors" and left.

Nicolas met her in the main foyer. "You look exquisite in that dress."

"Thank you." She blushed. "You have good taste."

"May I escort you upstairs?"

"I'd like that." In their room, she reached up and kissed his cheek. "I don't want to risk damaging this new dress. Could you unzip me?"

Just as she'd been desiring all evening, his hands didn't stop with the zipper. Having never been around a man who made her feel so special, intimacy with Nicolas wasn't even a question anymore. No longer inhibited by guilt over having a boyfriend, she wantonly gave herself to her Greek lover.

CHAPTER SEVEN

ENTRAPMENT

After another few weeks of being treated like a queen, escorted everywhere by a security detail when not in Nicolas's company, Carrie had visited every historical site within a day's drive of the compound. Knowing it wasn't love, she had a strong infatuation with him.

Although he tried to keep her away from his business dealings, she began to pay attention to some of Nicolas's associates. The executive types appeared and acted as she expected. The lower-level errand boys, for lack of a better word for them, looked like they belonged in a cage fighting arena instead of an office. Somehow, the suits they wore just didn't match.

The first week of August, Carrie started to get antsy, knowing she should start toward home. "I've loved being with you, Nicolas, but I should leave soon. I need to get ready for fall semester."

"I suppose you're right," he answered. "My business here is concluded anyway. We need to return to the island."

"I can head for home from here if you need to go."

He smiled kindly. "I can't have you leave without a proper send-off. Come to the island for a few days. You know how much you liked it there, and I need your advice on displaying the art we purchased together. This way we can say goodbye without any regrets."

"Okay. I guess I can stay another week."

With her luggage loaded in the helicopter's baggage compartment, they left for the island. It was exactly what he promised—fun filled days and romantic evenings. She never questioned why they didn't use his third-floor quarters. They always slept in her original second floor room where he claimed it was more intimate. He went all out to make her last night special.

In the morning, Carrie rolled toward Nicolas. "I've enjoyed my stay with you, but it's time I start working my way back to the States."

He kissed the top of her head. "No, I want you to stay. I'll give you a good life."

"I don't doubt that, but I need to leave." She kissed him. "You can come visit me sometime at my college in New York. I could even take you to see the Palouse."

His face darkened. "You're not going anywhere. You're mine now."

"I'm sorry," she said, patting his chest. "I really need to go."

"You didn't hear me." As if someone had flipped a switch, Nicolas's voice became firmer. "You're mine now."

"What? No, I'm leaving." It was starting to sink in that the situation had spun out of her control.

"I told you. You're not going *anywhere.*" A now complete stranger kissed her forehead. "I'll be back tonight to pick up where we left off. Clean yourself up. Your meals will be delivered."

After he walked out, Carrie ran to the door. It was locked from the outside. Her luggage was missing. She opened the window to jump out but it was barred, as was the small bathroom window. She was trapped. Confused, she lay sobbing on the bed for two hours.

With nothing else to do during the day, Carrie lay on the bed thinking. Was her present situation the result of a meticulous plan? It was obvious that Ethan had been played. Using his naivete and exaggerated sense of self-worth, he was distracted by paid women and the promise of wealth. What about her? She entered in to her relationship with Nicolas with eyes wide open. Or had she been masterfully seduced? But why?

The only clothing available was her previous night's dress and a robe hanging in the bathroom. Sighing, Carrie took a shower to wash off the dirtiness she felt from her mistake. When she opened the curtain, Nicolas was standing there, holding out a towel. Grabbing it to cover herself, she shouted, "Get out! Leave me alone!"

"No. I told you this morning I'd be back to finish what we started." He yanked the towel away.

Trying to push her way past him, she snarled, "No. I'll fight you!"

"Don't be a tease." Grabbing her by the back of the neck, he shoved her up against the barred window. "Look around. What do you see? See anyone out there who's going to stop me?" Opening his robe, he pressed against her back. "Everyone is gone. The only people out there are my men. You will get on the bed and please me or I'll give you to them—*all* of them."

Shoving her on the bed, a completely different Nicolas used one hand to hold Carrie's arms above her head. Using his weight to control her, his free hand explored her body. As much as she fought to resist, he was just too strong.

She begged ineffectively, "No, please don't."

Physically unable to stop him, she lay perfectly still. Zoning out what was about to happen, she stared at the ceiling. After a seeming eternity of being pawed, waiting to be brutalized, nothing happened. The hairy body on top of her went limp, its weight pressing down upon hers. She could barely breathe with what felt like a flesh quilt filled with lead compressing her into the mattress.

Finally, he sighed, stood, and put on his robe. "This isn't working for me. We'll talk more tomorrow about your stay here. You have free reign of the house. Make yourself comfortable."

Confused, she sobbed until her emotionally betrayed body dissolved into a black, slumbering abyss. Late the next morning, after hearing her door being unlocked, she nervously came out of her room and crept toward the kitchen. As if she was merely part of the woodwork, no one looked at her. In the kitchen, the maid smiled kindly and sat a bowl of meatball soup in front of her.

Carrie finished the soup and, hungrier than she thought she was, had a second helping. Used to carrying her own load, she was washing the bowl when a middle tier lackey entered the kitchen.

"Nicolas will see you now."

Taking what he said to be more of an unrefusable command than a simple statement, she placed the bowl in the drying rack and followed. Positive her captor had recovered from his momentary bout of impotence, and she was about to be raped, Carrie mounted the stairs with quivering legs. Desperately, she scanned every crevice for a possible weapon to defend herself even though it would do her no good. There was no escape from the island.

The man knocked on the only door of the villa's third floor. Entering after invitation, he led Carrie through the expansive master bedroom suite with two bathrooms—one on either side of, curiously, a standard king sized bed. Opposite the foot of the bed were ten wall mounted video monitors behind open bi-folding cabinet doors.

Wearing a bathrobe and slippers, Nicolas sat at a balcony table scattered with papers, working on a computer. Holding a conversation into a one-eared headset, he paid little attention to his guests. The man pushed her into a chair at the table then left.

Continuing to work for another five minutes, Nicolas finally closed the laptop and looked at the scared girl. "Are you ready to discuss our future together?"

"I don't know what you're talking about." Carrie's ranch girl bluster just came out. "All I know is you've changed, held me prisoner, and tried to rape me."

A quick succession of expressions flashed across his face—surprise, anger, and hurt. "Well, aren't you the mouthy one." Nicolas smiled and leaned forward in his chair. "We'll have to work on that. As for me raping you, that just isn't possible. I can't rape something

I own. I merely utilize my possessions in the manner they were intended."

"You don't own me!"

"Oh, yes I do. It seems your male companion wasn't a very honorable man. In my line of work, honor is the most valuable trait there is. First, in order to get capitalization for some investments, he leased your services to me during our art buying trip."

"*What?* He had no right!"

"Maybe not, but be that as it may, you didn't seem to mind fulfilling my needs. Unfortunately, his investment choices were bad, and he lost that money and more. When you and I returned, he couldn't repay." Nicolas leaned back. His robe fell open, revealing his naked body. "Then, when *you* ended your relationship with him, I sent him away. He didn't fight for you or even protest. In fact, he transferred ownership of you to me permanently to settle his debt . . . . No, he wasn't a very honorable man."

"Did you *kill* him?"

"I'm done talking about someone no longer in the equation. Let's discuss us." Nicolas spread his legs. "First, let me make this clear: Your sole purpose on this island is to be my willing companion. You will provide that service as long as you are here."

"*What?* No, I don't want to."

"What you want is of no concern to me." He looked back down at his paperwork.

"How old are you?"

"Nineteen."

"Huh, that's a good age. You'll bring a high price if that's the option you choose."

"You said options." Carrie knew full well there could only be a couple. "What are they?"

"Option one is as I suggested. I sell you to the highest bidder to soothe my bruised ego. The other option is you return to being my lover."

"Doing exactly what?"

"The same as we've been doing all summer. Tonight, you will become my sex partner again. There's no negotiation. It's up to you how that goes. You can either comply or I *will* sell you."

"What about option three?" she asked. "I could just jump off a cliff and bring this all to an end."

"Huh, I hadn't thought about that. It's never come up before." Then, he smiled. "Well, willingly at least."

"If I choose option two, what are the terms?" Carrie didn't really feel the bravado inside. It was all bluff. "You said you're an honorable man. How am I to know that you'll honor the agreement?"

"You will conduct yourself around the villa and in front of guests with decorum. You will not embarrass yourself or my company." Nicolas looked down at his manhood. "Most importantly, you will satisfy my needs immediately, without complaint, whenever it is my whim. I need a fully involved sex partner. You've already shown you're capable of that. As for the honorable part, you'll just have to watch and observe. If you don't think I'll be honorable, you can always revert back to option one. And again, if the quality of your companionship lags at *any* time during our agreement, I *will* sell you. Do you agree?"

"For how long?"

"Six months."

"*Six months?*" His terms took her breath away. "I'll miss the whole fall semester at college. My friends and family will go berserk wondering where I am!" She started to tear up.

"Those are the terms. They're a lot more generous than I've made to others in your position." He closed his robe and leaned forward. "Because I am not an uncaring man, if you do satisfactory work, I will allow a single email or text to *one* person later this fall. Your dishonorable male companion told me that no one was expecting you back until at least September.

"In fact," he placed her phone on the table. "While the helicopter was refueling on the mainland, my associate took the liberty of sending a message to everyone on your contact list. See? It says you're excited to have been offered an internship recovering arti-facts. The project is in a remote area, and you'll be out of contact for at least six months. I've also been monitoring all of your con-tact with the States. You have never once mentioned me by name. I assume you wanted to keep secret your involvement with an older man. That was a mistake for you.

"If you're mulling trying to flee the island, my staff has gone through your possessions and placed your money and passport in my safe. It's your decision. You *will* be here in my room tonight at eleven. Your performance decides your fate. Until then, you have free run of the island."

The intercom buzzed. Nicolas pushed the headset's button. "Yeah . . . okay, did you get all of the information out of him? Yeah . . . you know what to do . . . yeah, in the usual way." Nicolas pushed the headset's off button and looked at Carrie. "Why are you still here? I dismissed you."

She stumbled into the bedroom at the base of the third-floor stairs. Her luggage had been returned. After dressing, she crept out one of the villa's back doors. No one tried to stop her. No one seemed to notice or even care. Hearing the helicopter power-ing up, she ran around the house hoping to persuade the pilot to carry her to safety.

Before she got close, two armed men led a beaten, bloody man from an equipment shed toward the chopper. Deciding it was a ride she probably didn't want to be on, Carrie stepped behind a bush to observe. Roughly shoving the man into the helicopter, they lifted off.

Walking around the island, the only place where she was de-nied access was the path down to the docks. She kept scanning the horizon. No other land was visible in any direction. Making crude guesses of direction by the sun's movement did her no good. She hadn't paid much attention during the rides from the mainland. If she tried to swim or steal a boat, would she head toward safety or into the middle of the Mediterranean?

Staring over the edge of a high cliff, Carrie tried to gather the nerve to jump. She told herself it was what any self-respecting woman would do to keep her body out of the hands of these men. The will to live so overpowering, her feet wouldn't budge. Instead, she sat sadly gazing into the desolate distance.

Returning to her room, a transparent robe lay on the bed. Having to make a decision, Carrie stared at herself in the mirror. Say no to the brute in charge and either be killed or sold into sex slavery, leap off the cliffs, or be his indentured concubine with a chance of freedom in six months. Her inability to jump now reduced the options to two. Initially drawn to Nicolas, she admitted he was the best lover she'd been with, thoroughly enjoying her seduction and their first weeks together. Now, she feared him. But at least he was a known quantity. If he treated her even close to what he had in the beginning, her time here might be bearable.

"Buck up, cowgirl. There's a job to be done."

That night, scared, wearing the silken robe, Carrie walked into Nicolas's bedroom and faced him. Moving behind her, he gently opened the negligee, and his hands explored her naked, shaking body.

"Please don't hurt me."

"I won't as long as you obey the rules. My first rule is that you will be an active participant. You *must* enjoy what you're doing. If not, I might just as well sell you off. Are you ready to be my partner?"

"Yes, sir."

Nicolas removed his robe and sprawled face up on the bed. "Prove to me you want to remain here."

Swallowing her fear, Carrie smiled weakly and mounted the hairy man with her eyes closed.

"Open your eyes," he demanded. "Keep them open and look into mine."

Convinced refusal meant she'd be on the first boat heading toward a middle eastern whorehouse, she complied. Gazing down into Nicolas's eyes while she rocked on top of him, Carrie began her life as a billionaire's sex slave.

CHAPTER EIGHT
LIFE ON THE ISLAND

Carrie quickly figured out that, like all men, her custodian had a weakness. His was his ego. The strong trait which allowed him to make other men bend to his will was his Achilles heel in bed. It didn't matter which Nicolas he was at the moment, he *needed* to believe he was the best around when it came to the bedroom.

The morning after her first session as his "intimate employee," she hid in her room, curled up in shame, sobbing. He walked in without knocking. "Why are you here when breakfast is waiting for you?" His demeanor was somewhat gruff. "What's that on your face? Have you been crying?"

"No . . . well, yes." Unable to hide her tear stains, Carrie thought fast. She answered truthfully but used kinder phrasing, "I was just overcome with emotion after our lovemaking last night. You're the most experienced lover I've ever been with."

His face lit up. She could see in his eyes that, if she enjoyed what he was doing, it pleased him. There it was. His ego demanded he take care of her needs first.

"Good answer. You're a smart girl. But your eyes say differently." Smiling kindly, he reverted to the good Nicolas who seduced her. "You feel dirty, don't you? I don't want that. Come with me." Putting out his hand, he led her back up the stairs to his suite. While she ate breakfast on the balcony, he filled his huge bathtub. "Get in."

Using her hands to modestly cover herself, she meekly did as told. When Nicolas dropped his robe and slid in behind her, she asked, "What are you doing?"

"Bathing you." With soap and a washcloth, he tenderly washed every inch of her. After shampooing and rinsing her hair, he pulled Carrie back against his chest. Gently moving her wet hair aside, he started kissing her neck. "You did good last night. I want your stay here to be as pleasant as possible. As long as you obey my rules, I will do my best to help you enjoy it."

Lips slightly parted, she leaned back against Nicolas while his hands worked. With his experience, if she tried to fake, he'd know and punish her. Not a good actor, she immersed herself in what he was doing. It was mandatory for her survival.

After a week of hiding in her room during the day then reluctantly attending to Good Nicolas's manly needs at night, Carrie began to relax physically around him again. Demanding she be an active participant, he insisted kissing was part of the deal. Confused at first, she realized it was the only time he allowed himself to be close to anyone.

He *needed* intimacy, another chink in his armor. He showed his appreciation for her, and she quickly learned how to react to his subtle signals. Not knowing which Nicolas she'd be dealing with at any given moment, she was still scared stiff. During the day, she felt like a trapped animal. But at night, because of his ego, he took his time with her.

It wasn't the same outside of the main house. Assuming she'd be just like any other soon-to-be-discarded boss's toy, the men hovered nearby with anticipation. While exploring the island, Carrie overheard Sergei's underlings (Nicolas's apparent top lieutenant) talk about her.

"The things I'm going to do to that entitled little whore when it's my turn." One man laughed and said, "She's not going to be able to walk straight for a month."

"Don't worry," another agreed, "she'll bore him soon and we'll all have our turn."

Carrie ran back to the main house. Intermittently frightened by Nicolas, she was constantly terrified of the men.

Confusing his need for intimacy in the bedroom for leniency elsewhere, Carrie became a little too comfortable around the villa. Not recognizing Nicolas was in one of his bad alter ego phases, she made the mistake of publicly backtalking. He detonated and banished Carrie to her room. A few days later, a yacht docked at the island wharf with a central African supplier on board.

After supper that night, Nicolas summoned her to his balcony and pointed to a chair at the table. "I need to keep Mosi away from the island for a few days. It seems my friend has never fished from a boat. It's obvious you don't value how well you're being treated here so I've decided you need to view the other side of the coin. You will go on his yacht, teach him to fish, and keep him distracted."

"That's not part of our deal." Knowing what he meant by "distracted," she started shaking. "I was just supposed to be with you. You're turning me into a whore."

He yanked her out of the chair by her hair. Lifting her by the throat, he pinned Carrie against the wall on her toes. "You are *my* property. I will do with you as I please. You disrespected me, and this is your penance. Maybe next time you'll think." He started to walk away but turned back thoughtfully. "Your stuff is being moved into the guest quarters."

Assured that she knew enough about fishing to get the job done, Mosi's yacht left the wharf with just him, a terrified Carrie, and the crew. She thought about jumping overboard, but the only visible land was Nicolas's island. Barely having left the harbor, they passed another boat coming toward the island.

When he led her to his state room, she looked at him questioningly. "Shouldn't we be getting the tackle ready? We should start fishing before we get into deep water."

"Fishing can wait," he replied in broken English. "Now, we have business."

"What do you mean?" She knew but was trying to stall.

He started undressing. "This first."

As much as she wanted to during the excursion, Carrie was never alone and couldn't cry. She didn't dare to show negative emotions Nicolas might hear about. Mosi only fished about one hour then became bored. He entertained himself by making her sunbathe naked in front of him and using her body in the stateroom. It was little consolation to the devastated young woman, but at least he wasn't brutal.

Three days later, Nicolas met them five miles out from the island with his fishing boat. While he settled business with Mosi, Carrie's gear was transferred onto the smaller vessel. Sensing he was still in one of his bad phases, she cowered below deck during the return trip. Once back on the island, she fled to her room in the now crowded guest quarters.

Nicolas had brought in women to keep the men from the second yacht entertained during negotiations. Both businessmen and "hostesses" stayed in the guest complex. Every night, a different themed party was scheduled in the villa's courtyard.

Nicolas walked into Carrie's room. "Well, it seems you made a very favorable impression on Mosi. He's offered quite a substantial amount for you. So much, in fact, I'd make a tidy profit." He studied her for a moment. "Let's see if our Turkish guests will beat his price."

She couldn't say anything. She dared not say anything. Somewhere in the void between desperation and resignation, Carrie silently stood quivering.

"Cute, little blonde girls like you are a novelty where they're from. I'm in the middle of delicate negotiations with my competitors and need to keep them distracted—and a little off balance." Frightened, she shivered as he stroked her hair. "You're the perfect distraction." He handed her a silken wrap dress, closer to a toga. "You will wear this tonight."

Omar, the visiting group's leader asked, "Where have you been hiding *this* one?"

"She's my personal assistant." With his arm around Carrie's shoulders, wanting to keep attention away from Mosi's visit, Nicolas smiled and deflected. "She's been occupied elsewhere and has just returned."

"Your *personal* assistant, eh? She must do excellent work." Omar pulled Carrie onto his lap and ran a hand inside her dress.

Nicolas flinched. Mosi was one thing. The Greek billionaire liked and trusted him. He knew his African supplier to be honorable and not very violent. These Turkish syndicate rivals were a totally different matter. If they weren't in the middle of some very delicate territory overlap negotiations, Nicolas would have had his men shoot Omar on the spot for daring to touch her. Outmaneuvered, he bit his tongue and bided his time.

She shook with humiliation while being publicly groped for the remainder of the evening. As a show of dominance, Omar made it clear that he would take his host's prized toy to his room for the night. The villa's guards and Sergei's men hovered, leering expectantly. Surely this meant their boss had lost interest and was soon to give her to them to do with as they pleased.

Her original intent was to pretend to enjoy whatever Omar felt like doing, but he had different ideas. Slapping Carrie as soon as the door closed behind them, he pushed her onto the bed and mounted her. When she cried out in pain from the rough treatment, he grabbed a fistful of hair and bent her head forward.

"It hurts," she gagged out, chin against her chest with her body bent doubled over.

He gleefully laughed. "Of course it hurts. That's how all you stupid whores like it."

Slapping, twisting her into unnatural positions, and pulling hair—anything which would elicit a cry of pain from Carrie, he did. The louder she whimpered, the more he enjoyed himself. Believing Nicolas was probably watching his monitors, she stared at where she thought the camera would be. The next morning, she hid in her room sobbing.

That night, even though Nicolas had brought in a fresh batch of professional women as an attempted distraction, Omar forced her to sit on his lap during the after-dinner socializing by the pool. Making sure everyone saw, the sadistic man kept his hands under her dress, torturing her while maintaining eye contact with Nicolas. Carrie couldn't quite make out the expression on her owner's face. Was he enjoying watching what was being done to her, or was it some sort of poker face to knock his opponent off balance? Were they playing some kind of negotiation chicken to see who cracked first? Either way, hysterically fearful inside, she pretended to like it.

"I think you need to throw this one in to sweeten the deal."

"It's a thought. She's been pretty disrespectful lately." Nicolas turned to Carrie and uttered the words she feared the most, "And she's getting boring."

"Oh, I think I could keep her in line." Omar's exploring fingers pinched her. She flinched and gasped. "You'll obey me just fine, won't you?" He pinched her again, harder.

That night, when she dutifully reported to Omar's room, he wasn't alone. All of his men were there wearing bathrobes. Carrie looked around panicked.

"No . . . no." She started to back out the door, but he caught her.

He laughed, nearer to a turkey gobble. "You're not going any-where. My men want a group activity. They're close like that." Grabbing her hair, he snarled, "You're mine now. Tonight's just a little taste of what it'll be like after I take you with me. If you say a word to anyone, it'll be your last." He snickered as he walked out, "Break her in right, boys."

Dropping their robes, the men surrounded the terrified girl. It was a long, humiliating night with sweaty, grunting savages. Unable to cope with what was happening to her, Carrie's mind snapped. Seeing only blurry images, she catatonically endured whatever their twisted minds decided to impose on her. Every bar-baric sound became roaring white noise in an out of focus hell.

The next day, bruised and mentally broken, she lay in her room positive she was mere merchandise in an already completed transaction. Now used goods, her value as a sex toy to her captor had plummeted. Hearing the guests preparing to leave, she had to do something. Desperately glancing around the room, the only thing remotely resembling a weapon was a long fingernail file with a plastic handle. Her door burst open, and one of the men from the previous night, only recognizable from the others by a deformed right ear, walked in.

"Let's go. The yacht is waiting."

Stalling, she replied, "I have to pack my clothes and put on shoes."

He let out a guffaw, "Hah! You won't be needing either. You're going to be spending all of your time on your back with your feet in the air."

Unable to bear the thought of being Omar's possession, Carrie stabbed Cauliflower Ear's hand with the file and bolted from the room. Ducking past Omar's other luggage carrying men, she ran out of the building and toward the cliff. Death was a much better option.

No matter how scared she was, Nicolas's guards were faster than a limping, barefoot girl. Tackled, laying facedown in the dirt with a man's knee in the middle of her back, Carrie sobbed, "Let me go. Let me die. Kill me."

The guard's two-way radio crackled, "Lock her in her room. Remove all sharp objects."

Carrie cowered in the corner of her room, listening to garbled shouting outside her guest quarter's window. When the shouting stopped, her room became deathly silent. There were no footsteps in the hall, or even the usual sound of sea breeze blown branches brushing against the building's exterior wall. In a complete sensory vacuum until the next morning, the maid finally opened her door and brought in a breakfast tray. Smiling kindly, she placed the tray on the bed.

"They're gone. You're staying here." She then left, locking the door behind her.

Relieved to still be on the island after Omar's departure, Carrie was convinced she was about to be sold off or imprisoned in a whorehouse. After she calmed from her dash toward death, her door was unlocked. But she remained confined in the guest quarters.

Nicolas made an obvious point to look the other way when she was around. Still borderline suicidal, Carrie slinked around the villa like a scared mouse looking for safe shelter. To keep her resale value up, the helicopter landed, carrying a doctor who administered a round of prophylactic shots and patched her Omar-induced wounds. Watching expectantly, the guards waited for the latest devalued woman to be given to them to do with as they pleased. Summoned back to the balcony after a week in exile, she applied concealer makeup over her bruises and meekly complied.

"Do you know how close you came to leaving on Omar's yacht?" he asked without looking up from his work. "Have you learned your lesson?"

Emotionally shattered, she replied, "Yes, sir. I'll never disrespect you again. *Please* don't send me away. I'm here to fulfill your every desire."

Still pretending to concentrate on his work, he opened his robe without looking up. "Very well, you may resume your duties."

"Anything to please you, sir." Obediently, Carrie knelt and crawled under the table.

After a few minutes, Nicolas gently lifted her head by the hair and studied her face. Nodding toward the bedroom, he said, "Go prepare yourself on the bed. I'll be in when I'm finished here."

"Yes, sir."

Expecting to be brutalized again, she was relieved when he was more tender with her than he'd ever been before.

CHAPTER NINE
THIS ISN'T FOR ME

In Pullman, Bill and Willa went on a few dates, but it didn't take her long to find a more socially acceptable crowd to hang out with. He tagged along with Mandy if she wasn't on a date of her own. Mostly, he moped around campus alone.

When his stepsister went home for Thanksgiving, Bill, not wanting to cause any more friction between the two close families than he already had, stayed on campus. Mandy managed to drag him home for Christmas, but he shied away from all public events where he would run into anyone having Bennett as a last name.

During the spring semester, an exasperated Mandy confronted him, "It's all I can do to hold you together. Bill, you drink too much at parties and have lost all ability to talk to girls. Your GPA has plummeted. It's as if you just don't care anymore."

If it wasn't for Karen's insistence, Bill wouldn't have gone home during the summer break. He would have looked for part-time employment in Spokane or across the border in Idaho. Definitely not wanting to work on the Bennett ranch, he hired back on with Mr. Roberts.

With Willa roaming around the world, Bill became a hermit, hiding in the back reaches of the corporate farm's properties.

The only thing which seemed to hold his interest for long was helping his stepfather, Charlie, in the metal shop learning about blacksmithing. Since Carrie's dad, Randy, had given him quite a few lessons over the past few years, Bill was a pretty good welder.

Mandy decided to transfer to Eastern Washington University near Spokane to finish her psychology degree. Spokane was much larger than Pullman, had more employment opportunities to help pay for her education, and most importantly, her boyfriend lived there.

On the heels of his older stepsister's decision, Bill announced, "I'm not going back to college in the fall. Nothing interests me there." Karen calmed somewhat when he said, "I'm going to welding school in Spokane to get certified. Good welders can find work almost anywhere. If all else fails, I can work with Charlie and have our own metal shop."

He became Mandy's roommate at the beginning of the school year.

Hung over, Paul reluctantly climbed out of bed. He hated his job but, since he hadn't seen his wife and kids in over two years, it was all he had to keep him from putting a bullet in his head.

Stumbling into the pigsty of a kitchen, he dumped too many grounds into the coffee maker basket and spilled water on the counter while filling the reservoir. The same thing he did every morning. He knew the reason for water dribbling on the counter was because he always overfilled the carafe, but kept repeating the error. It was the only way the counter got washed, at least in the area near the coffee maker.

While waiting for the coffee, Paul made breakfast. One bulk, prepackaged cheese, bean, and beef Chimichanga topped with a handful of shredded cheese and Louisiana Hot Sauce, nuked for one minute thirty seconds. The same every morning.

After eating, he filled his thermos, including the overflow grounds in the pot. He refused to drink the overpriced crap from pretentious baristas who invariably gave his uniform disapproving scowls.

Halfway through their shift, Paul waited outside their usual lunch stop—somewhere they knew the cook didn't hawk loogies in their food—while his partner hit the head. He heard a child's scream, squelched in the middle like a hand had been placed over her mouth. Instinctively, he ran toward the sound, an alley two buildings away. A hundred feet down the alley, he saw a man dragging an adolescent girl toward a car.

Putting a hand on his weapon, Paul yelled, "Stop! Release her!"

It took a split second when the man spun around for the two to recognize each other. Paul thought, *What's that gangbanger doing out? I arrested him two years ago for child trafficking. He should be locked up for at least twenty more years.*

When the thug loosened his hold on the girl to reach for a weapon, she bit his other hand and ran for the safety of the policeman. Thousands of thoughts raced through Paul's mind as he shouted at the lowlife to drop the weapon while shielding the girl behind him.

Why didn't I just kill him the last time? My finger so wanted to pull the trigger. No one would have even questioned the shooting considering the circumstances.

"She's mine, and you've got no backup!" the thug snarled. "Give her back. It ain't worth your life!"

The one thing the banger didn't count on was that, with Paul's wife and kids gone, he just didn't care anymore. Someone else's bullet ending his life was just as good as his own. That scared, pretty, little girl quivering behind him—her safety was all that mattered.

"Not on my watch! Not this time!"

Paul's partner had just come out of the diner and started toward their cruiser when the sound of gunfire erupted in the other direction.

CHAPTER TEN
ISLAND ENDURANCE

Moved back into her original room, Carrie despondently wandered the island in the daytime, collecting wildflowers, interesting rocks, and weird sticks. Without asking, she started doing artwork in her room. Combining natural elements into pleasing shapes seemed to be the only expression of beauty left in her.

Staring at a broken twig, she felt trapped, technically a well-kept indentured servant, but still a prisoner. Carrie stopped herself. She was a sex slave, nothing more than an object to a master who insisted all of his possessions be cared for. As property, she could be disposed of, just like the twig, merely upon the whim of her owner.

She could tell by their leering expressions that his disappointed male lackeys still wanted a go at her. If they didn't fear their boss so much, they'd force themselves upon her.

Still, Carrie was ignored enough, she overheard conversations she probably shouldn't have. With so many different languages among his employees, they tended to lean on English as the most universal. In one conversation, the men grumbled about all the wasted effort they expended during the weeklong visit by Omar. Apparently, his yacht mysteriously exploded a day after it left the island.

One of the men laughed. "Maybe the boss didn't like what he saw on the hidden cameras in the guest quarters."

"Possibly," another one replied. "His competitors mistakenly stayed away from their yacht the whole time they were here."

The first one laughed. "What a coincidence. Too bad the little whore wasn't on the boat with them."

Those conversations made her even more fearful. A few men thought she was a distraction to their boss in need of elimination. Most just wanted to demote her to be their group plaything.

"Hey, what are you walking so fast for?" A handful of lower echelon thugs were taking a smoke break out of sight from the main house. One of them blocked her path. "You should get to know us better. It's not going to be long before the boss tires of you."

"Yeah." Another one stood behind Carrie and sniffed her hair. "Then we all get to enjoy you—maybe at the same time."

She pushed her way past the first thug and ran toward the house. He called after her, "Maybe we won't wait that long. We'll just do it while he's gone on business."

Good Nicolas had been her owner's predominant persona since Omar's departure. Him getting bored or angry again, reverting into Bad Nicolas and either being given to the men or sold, was her ongoing worst nightmare. Fixated on not letting that happen, she focused on satisfying his desires. Because of the cycle of reward for pleasing him and punishment for not, she tried extra hard in bed when terrified. Over time, she developed an involuntary tic. The higher her fear level, the more abandoned she performed. Pleasing him led to her own experience becoming involuntarily more intense.

Being completely isolated from anything normal as time went on, Carrie's reality twisted. Her nighttime duties became her favorite part of the day. She looked forward to her skin pressed against his extremely hairy body. Her fear/pleasure tic didn't happen often, but Nicolas seemed to enjoy her loss of control when it did.

After months on the island, Carrie immersed herself in her daytime artwork as a distraction. Hearing a noise behind her, she turned and caught Nicolas watching her work, smiling. The next day, her wreaths and other artwork adorned prominent areas around the villa.

He moved her clothing into his suite, and she stayed the whole night in his bed. When her birth control supply ran low, it was magically replenished. She assumed the maid had been assigned to keep an eye on her.

Carrie was consumed with paranoia. Even though she believed he personally wouldn't lay a hand on her, Nicolas frightened her. With a flick of his finger, she could be disposed of—or worse. Being separated from him scared her more. The only place on the island she felt completely safe was sharing his bed. No one would dare harm her there. Captor became protector, savior. Her fear transposed irrationally into lust. She felt safest looking into his approving eyes while satisfying him.

Driven by Nicolas's comment to Omar about her getting boring, she constantly searched for new ways to please him beyond just in the bedroom. Needing reassurance in her safety, Carrie slavishly catered to his every whim. Taking on the role of his personal groomer, she gave him manicures, pedicures, and his daily shaves. Anything gaining that look of approval in his eyes, she did enthusiastically.

Dressing seductively, she actively searched him out to give herself to him. She wanted, *needed*, their intimacy as often as possible. Passive submission became wanton, noisy passion.

Two months of complete commitment after the Omar visit, Carrie went searching for new natural art supplies. On top of the island's highest cliff, she laid her little tool bag near the base of an interesting wind-distorted shrub. Pulling out her small pruning shears, saw, and opened folding knife, she laid them on the ground. While deciding where and how to prune the bush for best artistic usage, she heard someone walk up behind her. Turning her head, she saw Sergei standing above her.

"Oh, hello. Am I needed back at the villa?"

Grinning maliciously, he said, "No. You're too much of a distraction for the boss."

Nervously, she started to scoot away and asked, "What do you mean?"

"I *mean*, the boss thinks you're this innocent, pure little goddess he needs to fawn over." Sergei removed his shirt and started to undo his trousers. "You won't be going back there. I'm going to take away your purity then throw you over the cliff."

"You're not going to get away with that." She desperately looked for an escape route but couldn't find one.

"Yes, I will. It's my word against yours." Grinning, naked, he shoved her onto her back. "Oh, wait. You'll be dead so you can't refute my story. You tried to seduce me. When I pushed you away, you fell off the cliff."

Her life depending on it, Carrie fought with everything she had. With him only able to hold one of her arms while he ripped her clothes off, she grabbed the largest rock she could reach and hit Sergei above an ear. As he shook his head to clear the fog, she hit him again. When he collapsed on the ground, she hit him one more time to make sure he was unconscious.

Kneeling over her latest attempted rapist, Carrie realized Sergei was right. Most of Nicolas's employees thought of her as merely his personal whore. She *would* be blamed. He'd have no other choice but to kill her to maintain loyalty within the ranks.

She was enraged. She'd put in all of that work for the last few months to save her life. Now, those sacrifices and degradations were for nothing. No, she wouldn't give in that easily. She was going to die but, refusing to go alone, Carrie stabbed the unconscious man's chest with her utility knife.

Insane with anger and fear, she kept stabbing. The maid and one of the cooks, out for a midday stroll between their busy times, walked up. The maid shrieked but quickly recovered when she saw the look of despair on the young woman's face and the blood covering her body. The cook ran for the villa.

In a state of shock, Carrie sat and leaned against the bush she'd thought about harvesting. The maid knelt beside her.

"What happened?"

Carrie catatonically replied, "He tried to rape me," then collapsed in tears.

She was still sobbing when a security detail ran up the hill. They were dragging her toward the edge of the cliff, about to enact their own form of justice, when Nicolas intervened.

Enraged, he shouted, "Stop! What happened here?"

"This slut killed Sergei," the dead man's main lieutenant answered. "She's now going to join him."

"Shut up!" Nicolas turned to Carrie. "Did you do this?"

Done running from her fate, she was finished with making apologies. "Yes."

"Why?"

"He was trying to rape me!" Her anger exploded. "He said I was a distraction to you. He said he was going to throw me off the cliff when he was done and tell you I tried to seduce him."

"Bull!" Sergie's man started to pull her toward the cliff again, but the young woman's kick to his groin brought that effort to a quick halt.

"Sergei and this idiot have been grumbling about you and me for quite a while." Carrie looked at the ground with resignation. "I know how this works. You have to kill me now to maintain the respect of your crew. Don't bother. I'll do it myself."

She turned and started toward the cliff but Nicolas grabbed her. "No. I once told you that my associates value honorable behavior above all else. You've acted honorably today. You dealt out a just punishment for a dishonorable act. Let's go back to the villa and get you cleaned up."

"You can't do that!" Sergie's lieutenant yelled. "The little slut must pay!"

Nicolas looked over his shoulder disdainfully and flicked the back of his hand skyward. With that signal to his men, the lieutenant took an impromptu flying lesson off the cliff minus a parasail. On the way back to the villa, Nicolas looked down with newfound respect at his involuntary bedmate. She had more guts than most of his men.

In his line of work, emotional attachments were a detriment. Unfortunately, he had become more than attached to the young woman walking beside him. Sending Carrie out on Mosi's yacht when she disrespected him was meant to be a simple disciplinary measure to put her in line. Initially, his forcing her to wear the seductive dress in front of Omar was intended merely as a display of his beautiful possession.

What Nicolas hadn't planned on was Omar pulling Carrie onto his lap. At the moment, Nicolas thought he could handle her being a bargaining chip which could be pulled off the table later. Still off balance from Carrie being on someone else's lap, he was blindsided when Omar announced she was to be his bedmate. Watching impotently on his video monitors, he had a visceral reaction to the way Omar treated her. Tactically, the best thing he could do for his empire was give her away to settle the deal, but Nicolas was enraged by the mistreatment of his property.

Carrie's soldiering up and marching back into her abuser's room the next night without a syllable of complaint impressed him. Nicolas witnessed her treatment on his video monitors. She did it because he told her to and didn't try to flee until she felt he was going to send her away. That was closer to loyalty than he received from any of his men.

"I think it's time you send that email to one of your friends. I'll have to approve of the content, of course."

"Thank you. I'd like that."

Enough of the old Carrie still remained to compose a carefully worded message letting her loved ones know how well she was doing in her new job.

CHAPTER ELEVEN
BILL ON THE TRAIL

Mandy read the text from her friend over and over carefully. Carrie hadn't been heard from since mid-August. That just wasn't like her. No one had been too concerned until she missed the beginning of the fall semester. They had received one cryptic text about her investigating an internship opportunity in an area with limited communication. The language in the message just didn't sound like her. Now, finally, here was a text that actually read like Carrie.

Mandy called Bill from school. "She's in trouble."

"Why should I care? Carrie made it clear a long time ago that she wants nothing to do with me." He did care. He'd been a wreck since she left and cut off all contact. When he heard she was dating other guys, then went to Europe with a boyfriend, he was devastated. "What makes you think she's in trouble?"

"I just got a text from her. She says she's having a wonderful time. She said she's having just as good of a time as I did the summer before we met."

"So? She's having a good time. That's *just* what I wanted to hear," Bill said sarcastically. "Thanks for rubbing it in."

Mandy yelled into the phone, "Bill, you damn idiot! That's the summer my mom's boyfriend was raping me! I ran away and became homeless 'cause she called me a slut! Remember?"

"Oh, crap." It finally sunk in. "Where was the last place you heard from her?"

"The last time I knew it was her for sure was in early August. She was in central Greece and had just dumped her boyfriend."

"Where's he?" Bill was starting to work himself into a lather. "Do you have his name?"

"At home. We'll talk about it back at the apartment tonight."

He didn't wait. As soon as his class took a break, he ran to the parking lot and drove home. Having done the same, his stepsister was sitting at the small dinette going through past messages.

"Did you find his name?"

"Only his first." Mandy thought for a moment. "I bet her grandmother knows. We could ask her. I can get her number from Carrie's parents."

"Not yet. I don't want to worry them more than they already are. Do you have her grandmother's address?"

"Oh, yeah, I do. Carrie sent me postcards of the Long Island coastline. Want to see them?"

"No. That's all right." The last thing Bill wanted to see was visible evidence of how well Carrie was doing without him. "I just need her address."

"Are you going to write her? That seems like it would take a lot of time."

"No. I'm going there. I'm going to find Carrie one way or the other."

Bill went to the bank and emptied his account. The next morning, he hit I-90 heading east.

Kate looked up when the bell on her gallery's door dinged. The very tall, tired-looking, young man wearing jeans and a plaid shirt didn't look like her normal clientele.

"Can I help you? I'm not looking to hire anyone right now."

"I'm not looking for work. I'm looking for the lady who owns this place. Is your name Kate?"

"Yes," she said tentatively, reaching for the alarm button under her desk. "What can I do for you?"

"My name is Bill. I'm looking for Carrie."

Kate pulled her hand away from the alarm and leaned back in her chair. So, this was the young man who broke her granddaughter's heart. "She's not here, and I'm sure she doesn't want you stalking her."

"I'm not stalking. I just need to find her. Do you know where she is?"

"I wouldn't tell you if I did. She's made it clear she doesn't want anything to do with you. You should leave."

"I will, just as soon as I'm sure that she's all right. I'll disappear and she won't have to see me again."

"What makes you think that Carrie isn't all right?" Kate had also been very concerned over her granddaughter's safety. When this young man first walked into the gallery, she suspected he might be the cause of Carrie's absence.

"Can I show you something?" Bill walked up to the desk and showed her his phone. "This is a text she sent my stepsister a few days ago. Those two are thick as thieves and tell each other everything. This is the first contact from Carrie in a couple of months."

Kate read the message. "So? It says she's having a wonderful time."

"May I sit?" Bill sat down and explained the context of the message and all of the other messages Mandy had received. "I can't stop until I make sure she's all right. Will you help me?"

"What can I do?" Kate could see just how concerned he was. Carrie had never said what he'd done to break her heart, but it was obvious he still cared deeply for her.

"What's the full name of her boyfriend and where do I find him? All we have is his first name, Ethan."

"I have all of that at my house." She paused and examined the tired young man. Kate decided she could trust him. "Do you have a place to stay?"

Armed with Ethan's full name, where he and Carrie went to school, and a picture of them together, Bill scoured the university campus. Everyone who recognized the couple told the same story. Carrie ran off with some rich guy in Europe, breaking Ethan's heart. Staking out what was reported to be Ethan's favorite drinking hole, Bill finally spotted the weasel going in.

The bar was way too crowded for Bill to conduct a proper interrogation, so he waited, biding his time. After last call, Ethan came out and staggered toward his apartment. Bill followed for a few blocks, then pounced, dragging his prey into an alley. Pinned against a wall, Ethan at first denied even knowing Carrie. Bill lost patience, and the beating started. Ethan's story kept changing until finally, something he said sounded at least a little truthful.

"*Where is she?*" Bill wanted nothing more than to finish beating the sniveling bloody weasel beneath him to death. "The last anyone heard from Carrie was when you two were in Greece."

"I don't know. I don't know!" Ethan curled into a fetal position on the concrete, protecting his head with his forearms. "She told me to get lost. She said something about meeting a guy, or an internship, or something."

"Bull!" Bill hit him again. "Which is it? Make up your mind!"

"I don't know, man!" Ethan started to sob. "I don't know. They'll kill me!"

"I'll kill you right *now* if you don't start talking." Bill yanked Ethan up by the front of his shirt. With faces so close, Bill's enraged spittle spraying onto the coward's face mixed with Ethan's blood. "Last chance!"

"Okay, okay. We went out to some rich guy's private island. Then, she flew all over Europe buying art with him. When it was time to come home, she told me to get lost. She wanted to stay a while longer." Ethan left out the part where he sold her for investment capital. "That's the last time I heard from her. She was pretty adamant that we weren't together anymore."

"*Which* island?"

"I don't know. There's so many. I don't even know if it had a name."

Bill was contemplating crushing the coward's head on the curb when he heard voices coming. Ethan took advantage of the distraction and ran. Only stopping at his apartment long enough to throw his passport and a few necessities in a bag, he headed for the airport to catch the first flight out of the country. He didn't care where, as long as it was away from the enraged hillbilly, sure that when Bill discovered the truth of Carrie's disappearance, he would be dead.

Bill knocked on Kate's door. "I found her supposed boyfriend. He claims Carrie told him to get lost and ran off with some rich dude. The guy's lying, but he was scared. I think she's in real trouble. I need to get to Greece and try to find her."

"Are you sure she wants to see you?" Kate shook her head. "I think she really hates you."

"I know I screwed up and hurt her. I don't care if she hates me." Bill stared sorrowfully out the window. "I love her. If she's in danger, I have to try and save her. Once she's safe, I'll disappear and she won't ever have to see me again."

"How are you going to get there?"

Bill shrugged. "I don't know yet. Hijack a plane or something. I'll figure it out."

Kate still didn't know the exact details of how this young man broke her granddaughter's heart, but saw remorse in his eyes. She heard true love in his voice. The blood on his knuckles told her how much he was willing to risk to bring Carrie back to safety. She went to her safe.

"Here's a little traveling cash." She put her hand on his shoulder and looked him in the eyes. "Here's a credit card. Use it as much as you need to get her back here."

"Thank you for your help. I'll do my best to not let you down." He started to walk out to his old truck. Kate called him back.

"You're not going to leave that old thing at the airport, are you? It'll cost you a fortune in fees. Leave it here. You can ride the airport shuttle."

After a grueling journey, an exhausted Bill checked into a cheap hotel in the coastal village where Ethan said they had met the rich man. It was also near where Carrie mentioned in her last trusted text message. Mandy's tech geek friends in college traced the last cryptic message to a nearby cell tower. It would all be on Bill from here.

He hit the streets immediately, showing a five by eight picture of Carrie to anyone he could cajole into looking. Exhausted after two days, Bill decided to switch tactics. It had dawned on him that partying college kids were more likely to be out at night instead of daytime tourist traps. Bill went clubbing.

CHAPTER TWELVE
A TRIP TO THE MAINLAND

Arriving late afternoon in the seaside resort, Carrie showered in the hotel's presidential suite then lounged on the bed reading a book. The next day, while Nicolas conducted his business, she roamed around the town, shopping in high end fashion houses.

A trusted security detail, whose own lives were at risk if she were injured or escaped, followed her everywhere. Hovering mere feet away, carrying her purchases, they handed the clerks charge cards. That night, when the group went to the same club where she first attracted Nicolas's attention, she wore a revealing new dress.

Even though the gathering on the reserved balcony included many exotic women, it was clear only Carrie was to sit next to Nicolas. Later in the evening, she leaned over and whispered in his ear, "I need to use the restroom. I'll be right back."

A security guard started to accompany her, but Nicolas grabbed his arm. The man protested, "She may bolt. The emergency exit is right next to the ladies' room door."

"I know." Nicolas nodded toward the club's front door. "Watch from the outside. I want to see what she does."

Coming out of the restroom, Carrie glanced at the back door, but the exit sign didn't register. Back at the table, Nicolas smiled and pulled her close. His hand on her thigh, she snuggled next to him.

On the way to the airport, he insisted they ride alone in his limo. As she leaned against him, Nicolas said, "You didn't run when you had the chance."

She looked at him, confused. Then it hit her. The exit sign. It had been a test. At that moment, Carrie realized that she'd not only given up on escaping, but didn't care anymore. She was now completely his woman and had been for a while. His anger boundaries had been established long ago, and if she didn't push them, there was no reason for fear. To her, Nicolas was no longer a captor, he was her lover. If he asked her to, she would bear him children.

"Have you seen this girl?" Bill showed Carrie's picture to every person he met. Most people in the tourist town knew at least some English. If they didn't, he became adept at getting his question across through gestures. Exhausted, almost ready to go back to his cheap hotel for the night, he stopped an aloof, tall, well-dressed woman outside a nightclub and showed her the picture. She tried to ignore the impoverished-looking tall young man with the American accent—until she saw the picture.

"You mean her?" Used to being the center of attention, disgruntled at being pushed to the sidelines, the woman replied with a French accent while pointing toward a group coming out of the same door she had just exited.

Bill turned in time to see Carrie wearing a dress exposing more of her body than it covered, hanging all over some guy twice her age. Barely getting a glimpse of her through the throng of surrounding goons, he watched her passionately kiss the man with his hands inside her dress, then climb into a limo. Bill felt like puking.

"She's Nicolas's newest toy. She's lasted longer than anyone thought, but he'll tire of her soon. He always does."

"Where are they going?"

"What's it to you? You stick your nose where it isn't wanted, you'll probably lose it."

"We grew up together. I'm here to take her home where she belongs."

The woman snorted. "Well, isn't that sweet. You've come to rescue your innocent little childhood princess. She's none of *that* anymore."

"It doesn't matter to me." Bill looked pleadingly at the hard woman. "I promised her family that I'd take her home. Where are they going?"

Not sure if the woman was being spiteful or sympathetic, he jotted down everything she told him. He now had the island's name, its general location, and how he was going to die if he got anywhere near the place.

The next morning, Bill headed to the harbor. It felt like he'd talked to every fishing vessel captain in Greece before he found one willing to at least listen. After extensive negotiation, and a lot of crude sign language, the captain agreed to tow a smaller craft within sight of the island, but no closer. Getting back to the mainland was Bill's problem. With the captain's help, Bill found a small seaworthy(ish) boat with enough fuel capacity to make it back to the mainland.

Using the welder on the "agreeable" captain's boat, Bill attached a couple of extra small manual anchor winches. While making the modifications, he talked to fishermen familiar with the island. They described an impenetrable fortress completely surrounded by cliffs. The only access point was the single, well-guarded dock.

Bill decided to try scaling one of the cliffs. He and some others had spent a few summer days climbing the Scabland coulee cliffs. When they were still together, Carrie was among those trying their hands at primitive rappelling.

During the long boat ride to the island, Bill stared into the distance. He hoped desperately that enough of the girl he once knew remained that she would come voluntarily. If not, he was fully prepared to disable her and go down the cliff with her tied to his back. He was taking her home, willing or not.

After a four-hour trip, the captain woke Bill from his catnap just before midnight. "This is as close as I go." He pointed out through the mid-winter marginal moonlight at a barely visible form a few miles away. "There's your island."

Climbing down the boat's fishing net into his smaller craft, Bill asked, "Anything else I need to know? What are the tides like?"

"Fairly minimal around here, but enough that you should be careful where you anchor if you don't want to wait for them to rise again."

Keeping his navigation lights turned off, Bill motored around the island, inspecting the cliffs. Using a hand drawn map and a few rudimentary compass readings, he backtracked before coming within sight or earshot of the dock. On the leeward side of the island, wanting to be as close as possible to the cliff face so guards would have to lean out to see the boat, he anchored in an area where the rocky shoreline was only a few feet across.

Estimating the cliff to be well over two hundred feet tall, twice as high as anything he had attempted before, Bill hung both of his two-hundred-foot coils of rappelling rope around his neck. He hoped they would be enough. Slipping on his new climbing harness with an abundance of carabiners, he started the climb.

Other than the location being on the back side of the island, he chose this site for the series of small ledges along the way. Unfortunately, island ledges were primary seabird nesting areas. In his inexperience, Bill hadn't anticipated that major detail. Foot and handholds already damp from the winter weather were coated with guano. Enraged birds constantly harassed him.

Halfway up, he sat on a ledge exhausted, almost ready to give up and retreat. A curious bird landed a short distance away and watched him. Having no idea what species the odd bird was, Bill assumed it was some kind migratory thing wintering on the cliffs. Now in the bird's domain, they stared at each other. He bird watched. The bird human watched. Finally tired of the game, the creature flew away.

His determination renewed, Bill started to climb again. Twenty feet up, his grip on a dropping-coated handhold slipped. He landed back on the ledge, jarring a rotator cuff and knocking his wind out. If he hadn't landed back where his butt had already formed a dry spot on the ledge, he wouldn't have been able to hold on. While lying on his side, catching his breath, the bird landed again. Eyeing the clumsy human, it waddled up, pecked Bill's hand, then flew away.

He rolled onto his back and watched the taunting avian. "Show off."

Bruised, coated in dung, and with a bad shoulder, Bill finally made it to the top. He lay under a bush, studying the villa. From what he'd witnessed outside the nightclub, Carrie would most likely be in the main house. After concealing his climbing gear under the brush, he crawled slowly toward the compound. Hunting with his father as an adolescent, then with Carrie's dad in the Palouse, Bill knew how to stalk.

Making it undetected to one of the outer buildings, he snuck a peek around the corner.

"Hey, you!"

Looking over his shoulder, there were two men running toward him with guns drawn. "Crap."

The jig was up. Bill ran toward the main house. Surely, they wouldn't shoot in that direction—at least he hoped. He had to get close enough to let Carrie know there were caring people searching for her.

Two more men came out of the main house carrying guns, but didn't want to risk hitting one of their own in the crossfire. Tackled by four, maybe five trained guards, Bill fought with everything he had. Convinced he was going to die, he was determined to take as many of them with him as he could. Taller and stronger than any of them, he battled instinctively, dirty, no holds barred, yelling.

The world went red, then black.

CHAPTER THIRTEEN
RESCUED?

Carrie woke up early in the morning a week after their trip to the mainland. Snuggling next to Nicolas, she ran her fingers through the hair on his chest, thinking. Her verbal contract with him was close to its end, and she had no idea what her fate would be after that. Would he sell her off to an even worse master like Omar? Would she just be disposed of when he tired of her? She wanted to stay on as his lover.

Her hope was that if she bore him children, she could remain with him permanently. Carrie knew if she got pregnant without his permission, it wouldn't go well. She needed to get him in a pliable mood before broaching the subject. Getting Nicolas in a good mood was a talent she had become very proficient at.

Kissing his neck, Carrie nuzzled her way up his early morning stubbled chin. Her hand worked its way down, letting her half-awake lover know exactly what she was planning. After his needs were satisfied, she lay with her head on his chest.

"Well *that* was a pleasant way to wake up." He kissed the top of her head. "I know you well enough to know you want something. What is it?"

Twirling the hair on his stomach with her fingers, she said softly, "I want to have your baby."

Raising his head, glancing down at her for a moment, he lay

back on his pillow, mulling over her statement. Surely someone on the staff had told Carrie he already had four children, the eldest a year older than her. This whole baby request took him by surprise. None of his women had ever offered such a thing before.

He'd become quite fond of this young girl and was trying to decide what to do with her in the future. He had made her a promise to only hold her to a six-month indenture. Priding himself to be an honorable man, he was bound by that promise to release her when that period was up, but desperately wished for her to voluntarily remain. Not wanting to reveal his hand too soon, he put off answering.

"I'll think about it."

"That's all I ask."

Getting out of bed, she slipped on his favorite sheer robe and opened the drapes to see what kind of day it was. There seemed to be some sort of ruckus in the courtyard, and security guards were wrestling with a large man. Curious, she braved the blustery winter weather and stepped onto the balcony. Walking up behind, Nicolas wrapped his arms around Carrie to keep her warm, his hands fondling her breasts. Carrie leaned her head back and kissed him. She'd seen enough. After looking disdainfully at the unwelcome intruder, she turned to go back inside.

"*Carrieee!*" a familiar voice from the past pleaded from the melee, "Carrie."

She stopped and leaned over the railing for a closer look. Underneath the week-old stubble and fresh blood was the face that had given her so much pain, the face of betrayal she'd avoided for over eighteen months, the face that set in motion the chain of events which brought her to this balcony. Bill's face. Carrie huffed, closed her robe, and went back into the bedroom.

"You know him?" Nicolas called from the balcony.

"I thought I did." Unfamiliar emotions welled up inside her. "He broke my heart. It seems like an eternity ago."

"What's he doing here? How did he know you are here?"

"I don't know. I don't want to see him. Send him away."

"You know I can't do that." Turning, he called down to the guards, "Hold him. I want to interrogate him."

"Please don't kill him."

Nicolas cocked his head. "Why not? You seem to hate him."

"I do. It's not him I'm worried about." Her new view of life started to crack, letting wisps of a past ranch girl out. "It's his family. His dad died a war hero, and his mother took it hard. I don't know how she'd take losing her only son. His stepfather saved my life twice and rode a horse through two walls of fire to save my family's ranch."

"Huh."

After dressing, he went into the compound's equipment shed where Bill was handcuffed to a chair. Slowly circling the chair, Nicolas closely examined his prisoner's face . . . and those of the guards. His security force had taken as much of a beating as the boy. Finally, he squatted in front of the chair and leaned in close.

"Why are you here?"

"I'm taking Carrie home." Bill's voice gurgled a little from the blood in his mouth.

"She says she doesn't want to go."

"I don't care. I'm not leaving without her."

"Huh. I don't think you realize you haven't much say in the matter." Nicolas had to admit, the kid had gumption. "How did you know she was here?"

"Her ex-boyfriend. I beat on him until he confessed where he left her." Bill looked hard into the rich man's eyes. "I don't think he told the whole truth. He said Carrie told him to get lost and ran off with you. I don't believe a word of it."

"I knew I shouldn't have let that weasel go. He had absolutely no honor." Nicolas stood and turned to go. "Get rid of him."

"*No!*" Carrie shrieked and ran into the shed. After hurriedly dressing, she had been just outside the door listening to the conversation. "Don't kill him!"

"What? Why shouldn't I?" Nicolas asked.

"You can't kill anyone without people knowing what you did," Bill said. He wasn't going to leave here alive without his lost friend. "I told everyone where I was going and what I was doing before I left the mainland. If I don't return, they'll know what happened."

Nicolas laughed. "You don't think we have contingency plans for that? You *have* heard of something called accidents, haven't you? That rickety old boat you came here in will never make it back to shore."

"How'd you know I came here on a boat?"

"Oh, *please*, don't insult my intelligence. My informants told me you were coming days ago. The fishing vessel captain radioed after he dropped you off." Nicolas glanced toward Carrie. "The only thing I didn't know was why you were coming—until now."

"You kill him, you'll have to kill me." Carrie jumped in front of Nicolas. "I thought you valued honor above all else. From my perspective, he's the only one here who's being honorable. Certainly not me. I took the coward's way out. Not my ex-boyfriend, who you let me think you killed. Not even you, mister bigshot. How was it honorable the way you brought me here?"

Enraged that she spoke to him that way, much less in front of others, Nicolas grabbed her arm and yanked her into the courtyard. "What the hell is the matter with you? An hour ago, you told me you wanted to have my children. You hate that young man, yet you *disrespect* me in front of my men to protect him?"

"I love you." Carrie reached out and put a quivering hand on his chest. "I *do* hate him, but that doesn't mean I want him to die. He may be misguided but he *is* conducting himself with honor."

Nicolas sorrowfully looked down at the young woman. He'd become quite fond of her. Now that she had forced his hand, he had no choice. It was time for them to part ways. "Go back in the shed and wait. I have to think this over."

Carrie watched Nicolas walk back to the mansion, then went into the shed and sat in the corner. Even though she despised Bill, it still stung when he wouldn't look at her. It was as if the sight of what she'd become sickened him. When she walked in front of him, he turned his head the other way. Finally, an hour later, the helicopter's turbine started to whine. One of Nicolas's main aides came into the shed.

"Load them both up."

Carrie meekly followed as armed guards led handcuffed Bill to the chopper. Her captor for the last five months watched stern-faced from the third-floor balcony. She turned and mouthed, "I love you."

Resolutely, she sat in a back seat while they cuffed her ex-friend to the copter's floor. With the curtains drawn, she hadn't a clue which direction they were headed, but it seemed like a long time. Maybe they were being taken somewhere the currents would pull their bodies away from the island when they were thrown out?

Bill's stepsister, Mandy, was worried sick. He had kept her posted almost daily on his progress. Her adopted mother, Karen, called looking for him. He hadn't returned her calls or messages. Mandy understood Karen's concern for her son.

"Bill's not in Spokane right now," Mandy said.

"Oh no. He hasn't dropped out of school, has he?" Karen was at a loss. She just couldn't get through her son's self-imposed walls anymore.

"Uhhh . . ." Mandy stalled for time. How could she hide what was going on without betraying the trust this wonderful woman had given her over the past years? "Yes, he has. But before you go off the deep end, let me explain. He's actually found a purpose in life. He's trying to make amends."

Mandy explained her concerns over Carrie's safety and Bill's mission to find her. When she told Karen it had been a week since Bill's last message, Mandy could hear her stepmother hyperventilating.

"Where is he? Has he found her?"

"He's in Greece. I have the town and hotel written down." Mandy knew she would be asked, so she might as well let out what she'd been told. "Bill saw Carrie from a distance. That's all he would tell me. Even though I asked, he refused to say where she was or what she was doing."

"Do you think they're in danger?"

"I don't know. Maybe. There's got to be a reason he wouldn't tell me that stuff." Mandy paused for a moment. "I know how worried Beth and Randy are. They must think Carrie's just being an inconsiderate twit. Maybe you shouldn't tell them what we know for a little longer. Maybe we should give it another day or so before calling the Greek authorities and telling the Bennetts."

"One day. If I don't hear from you tomorrow morning, I'm telling Beth."

When the helicopter landed, Carrie thought this couldn't be good. Were they being sold as slaves? Were they going to be shot on the ground then loaded back on board for disposal at sea? The door opened, and Nicolas's aide pulled them out onto the airport tarmac. He threw her suitcase and backpack on the ground, handed Carrie her passport, and pointed toward the terminal.

"Don't talk to anyone. Leave Greece. Never come back."

Bill silently picked up the bags and walked to the terminal. Sitting her luggage inside on the floor, he finally spoke—not to her but in her general direction. "Wait here. I'm going to the hotel for my stuff. When I get back, I'll buy us the tickets."

She nodded, not that he saw. He was already walking away. While waiting for Bill to return, *if* he came back, Carrie inspected her gear. She wouldn't put it past some of the disgruntled lackeys on the island to plant contraband to get her arrested. In her backpack, she found a fat envelope. *Yep*, she thought, *it's a trap.* When she opened the envelope, it contained a large amount of money and a note.

Here is some money for your artwork. I'll cherish it. I would have given more, but this is all you can get through customs. You should give that young man another chance. He risked his life for someone he knows hates him. That's one of the most honorable acts I've ever witnessed.

Bill did return. On the local flight to Athens, he managed to sit elsewhere on the airplane. However, on the long flight to Schiphol airport in the Netherlands, the only seats available were together. Even though he ignored her visually, he couldn't escape her scent. Not having time to shower, she still smelled of her activities in the villa before his capture. It was a long, silent flight with him staring blankly out the window.

The five-hour layover before their flight to LaGuardia seemed more like a week. He finally spoke, interrupting the silence during a meal in the concourse.

"Next stop is in New York, then your grandmother's. I left my truck at her house. I'm going home. Do what you want. Your choice." He walked away before Carrie could answer.

The layover gave her a chance to clean up, change clothes, and charge her phone, its battery long dead from months in the backpack. In an exchange of texts with Mandy, she caught up on what had happened since she disappeared. Even though Mandy kept poking around the edges, Carrie refused to confide where she'd been or what she'd done.

Convinced she was in love with Nicolas, and wanting to be with him, she was confused. Eighteen months before, she felt betrayed by Bill. She'd been sold into slavery by Ethan. Now, rejected in Greece, she was being escorted home in shame. Carrie curled up on a bench in the airport lounge, wishing she could dissolve and absorb into the dirt. It was where she belonged. Her never-failing remedy for everything—time on a horse—wasn't going to repair her brokenness.

"Time to go. They've announced our flight." Bill stood over her and, for one of the few times since the villa, spoke to her.

"Okay," she replied but was sure he didn't hear, already heading toward the gate.

He didn't wait, boarding the plane well ahead of Carrie. He'd gotten her out of the compound and on her way home. Now that they were on the final leg of the journey back to New York, where he assumed she would stay on Long Island, his obligation was over. What had started out as a rescue mission and an opportunity to apologize to a dearly loved friend he'd wronged, was now a tedious journey with someone he no longer recognized.

Boarding quite a bit after her escort, the seat beside him was still empty. None of the other passengers wanted to be crammed next to someone his size for the long transatlantic flight unless there was no other choice. Carrie knew he didn't want to be near her. She didn't want to be close to him either. But she was emotionally lost, in a wasteland lacking a caring touch in the midst of a crush of people. When she sat next to Bill, he flinched.

During the long nighttime flight, she stared at her lap, trying not to touch her ex-friend. Knowing she shouldn't, Carrie mourned being torn from her love in the villa. She had long since accepted her irrational feelings for Nicolas. Reason doesn't control emotion.

She had loved Bill almost since they first started hanging out together but didn't want to admit it until shortly before their big blow up. Now, he was gone too. Mentally ground into dust, Carrie started silently sobbing. Convulsing in agony, she leaned against Bill and forced her arm through his.

Simply out of compassion for another wounded human being, Bill's remonstrance toward her faded somewhat. He raised his arm, and she curled up in her seat, head on his chest. She cried until she'd no more fluid left. When she felt him shift into a little more comfortable position, Carrie asked, "Are we ever going to get past this?"

"I don't know . . . probably not. I can't unsee things. I can't unknow things."

"What are you going to tell everyone?" she asked.

"Nothing. It's not my story to tell. You tell them what you want."

Carrie stared at the folded-up seat tray in front of her for a while. The weight of Bill's arm on her side made her feel safe. "I just realized what today's date was. Is it okay if I say happy birthday?"

His head jerked back. How did she remember when he didn't? What purpose did it serve to even bring it up? He grunted, "Thanks."

"If it's all right, I'd like to go all the way home."

Bill looked back out the window and said softly, "That's up to you. I got you this far. It's out of my hands now."

CHAPTER FOURTEEN
DECISIONS ON THE BEACH

Even after their conversation on the plane, Bill couldn't stand to be too close to the stranger he was escorting. It hurt too much. They had been virtually joined at the hip since they were thirteen and knew what each other was thinking by just a glance. Now, barely recognizing her shell, he was clueless what was inside.

It was a silent walk beside one another toward customs, into baggage pickup, and toward the shuttle. During the ride to Long Island, they sat separately, staring blankly in opposite directions out the windows. Kate picked them up at the station for another quiet ride to her house.

When Carrie immediately disappeared into the house and Bill threw his gear in his truck, Kate stopped him. "What are you doing?"

"Leaving. She's safe now. My job is done."

"No one has told me anything." Kate clung to his arm. "Where did you find her?"

"That's her story to tell. Whatever she says is the truth."

"Well, it's too late in the day to leave, and you're tired. You'll at least stay until morning. I insist."

Bill walked down the street for privacy and called Mandy for the first time since his initial sighting of Carrie outside the nightclub. "Just checking in. We're back in Long Island."

"First, you're an ass! How come you didn't call me?" She wasn't that mad, just relieved. When Carrie texted her from Amsterdam, Mandy knew they were safe. "How is she?"

"I don't know. I don't recognize her anymore and can't stand to look at or talk to her. I'm heading home in the morning." Bill sighed and paused for a moment. "I guess she'll be flying back. That's as much as I've gotten out of her which made sense."

"She's not driving back with you?"

"No. I don't want her to. I don't think I could stand to be near her for that long."

Mandy kept pushing for information, "Did she tell you what she was doing? Any mention of what she went through? Anything at all?"

"Nothing." Then, Bill slipped. The trauma of seeing Carrie the way she was in the villa had devastated him. His voice cracked a little. "I heard her tell the boss guy that she loved him and didn't want to leave. I . . . I've already said too much."

"That's enough. Now I know what to ask her. Talk to you later."

He barely made it through the door before Kate grabbed his arm and dragged him back outside. "Walk with me. Let's go down by the beach. It's abandoned this time of year." In the middle of winter, she was right. Even with the biting wind buffeting them, Kate was more concerned with matters other than comfort. "That's not my granddaughter up there. What did you do to her?"

"Nothing. That's how I found her."

She led the young man into a sheltered area out of the wind. "What was she doing? Where did you find her?"

"If she wants you to know, she'll tell you." Bill's phone buzzed. It was Mandy again. "Hello?"

"Are you alone? Can you talk?"

"I'm with Carrie's grandmother. She's asking me the same questions you were." Bill was getting tired of the grilling when he had no intention of answering.

Mandy asked, "Is Carrie within earshot?"

"No."

"Good. Put me on speaker phone." Mandy introduced herself to Kate, then got to the point of her call. "I just got off my call to Carrie. Thanks to what you told me about the guy she was with, I have a pretty good idea what's going on."

"What guy?" Kate looked at Bill.

"You two can talk about that later. May I call you Kate?" Not waiting for an answer, Mandy continued. "Well, Kate, I'm only a third-year psych student, but after talking to her and from what Bill told me, I have a guess. Find a computer away from Carrie and look up victim attachment disorder, specifically Stockholm Syndrome. I don't know if that's exactly what she has, maybe a variation. If my guess is correct, you need to get her professional help ASAP."

Once back in the house, Kate and Bill did as Mandy had asked. It all started to make sense to him now. For the last eighteen months, Bill had been on an emotional roller coaster. He'd gone from guilt for cheating on her, confusion when she wouldn't let him apologize, anger when she started dating other guys, and devastation when he found out she was sleeping with them. He'd tried recovery dating with Willa, not dating anyone at all, drinking, and completely losing interest in school all together.

Now, he was back to guilt. From his point of view, everything Carrie had been through was because of his immature actions. It was because of him she started sleeping around. It was his fault she was taken captive or whatever she was in Greece. He didn't know how to fix her.

Kate patted his shoulder. "I'd like you to accompany my granddaughter the rest of the way home. She really needs the company."

"I can't. I don't know if we'd survive that long trapped together in the cab of my truck."

Kate was insistent. "Leave it here and fly back. I'll buy the tickets."

"Then I'd have to come back and get my truck."

"I'll buy it from you," Kate softly said. "It's the least I can do. Besides, my gallery could always use it for deliveries."

Trapped, lost, and alone in her own mind, Carrie alternated between missing Nicolas and pining over his lost love, hating Bill for past wrongs and perceived present slights, and wishing he would talk to her again. She didn't know what she wanted. Finally, tired of staring at the wall in her room, she went into the living room.

Instantly paranoid seeing her grandmother and male nemesis conspiring at the computer, Carrie asked, "What're you two doing?"

"Just checking flights to Spokane." Kate quickly switched away from the psychiatric website. "I'm booking you two on the same plane."

"He's not driving back?" Still not sure where she and Bill stood, Carrie addressed Kate. The way he had acted since the villa, she was surprised he'd agree to be on the same plane with her again. "What about his truck?"

"We've taken care of that, dear." Kate smiled with relief. A half-expected meltdown hadn't occurred. "You should call your mother and tell her you're coming. I'm sure she'd like to hear from you."

Carrie muttered, "I can't."

Bill finally spoke. "I'll call Mandy. She can pick us up at the airport and take you the rest of the way home."

Carrie cocked her head. Even though it was the longest phrase Bill had uttered since Greece, its meaning was unclear. "Won't you be going home?"

"No. I'm staying in Spokane." End of conversation. Bill got up and left the room.

Kate drove Bill and Carrie to the airport in her gallery's van. Her granddaughter had a lot more luggage to get to the Palouse than she took to Europe. Quiet during the trip, Bill rode in the back using the baggage as an armchair. The wily older woman made sure the two youngsters had non transferrable seats aboard the aircraft beside each other. Her granddaughter needed supervision, and Kate had come to believe that no one outside of immediate family cared more for Carrie than Bill. He tried to hide it, but she could see it still in his eyes.

Conversation between the two youths through baggage check, security, boarding, and the first half hour of the flight consisted of single syllable acknowledgements or grunts. Bill sat next to the window with Carrie in the middle seat next to an elderly grandmother-type who appeared to be with a larger family group sitting behind them.

When Carrie excused herself to the woman and made her way to the forward restroom, Bill saw a thirtyish guy across the aisle lean out and watch her walk. When she returned, the man smiled invitingly, and she politely smiled back. The man was just about to strike up a conversation when he saw the death look on Bill's face. Deciding personal safety had priority over an in-flight hook-up, the man looked away.

Puzzled by the sudden break-off of eye contact, Carrie turned to squeeze into her seat and saw her traveling companion's threatening glare. For the first time in the trip, an actual sentence was uttered. "I wasn't going to run off with him, you know. You don't need to be my constant guardian."

As Bill silently looked back out the window with sadness on his face, it dawned on her that was exactly the role he'd taken on. Why he had, she didn't know. Instinctively, she patted his arm then returned to her solitude.

The bored older woman in the aisle seat struck up a conversation. "So, you look like you've been traveling."

Carrie politely replied, "Yeah, I just got back from Europe." Pretending to ignore them, Bill listened intently.

"Oh, I've always wanted to go there but never had the opportunity." The woman's interest piqued, it became obvious this was going to be a long conversation unless Carrie rudely broke it off. "Where did you go?"

"We started off in Spain for a little bit, then worked our way east along the Mediterranean."

"That must have been fun at your age. How long did you stay?"

"It was only supposed to be for a month or so." Carrie had to pause and choose her words carefully with Bill sitting beside her. "I, uh, ended up staying in Greece a lot longer than intended."

"Really? Why?"

This had gone on too long. Carrie needed to end the conversation. "Oh, something about the place just held me captive." She felt Bill flinch.

"Was this nice young man your traveling companion?"

Carrie glanced up at Bill. Acting like he wasn't eavesdropping, jaw clenched, neck veins throbbing, fingers flexing against his thigh, he stared out the window with an expression she could only describe as lost.

"No. He's an old high school friend. We bumped into each other in Greece and decided to travel home together."

"That's simply a wonderful story! It must be kismet you two running into each other so far from home." It dawned on the woman that there was a lot more to the story. Her two traveling companions' body language hinted at a Shakespearean tragedy. "Well, I better get back to my knitting."

For another hour, Carrie tried to busy herself reading every magazine and safety manual in the seat-back pocket in front of her. The occupants in the seats in front of them were either sleeping or had earphones on. Bill pretended he was napping but was actually staring at the aircraft wall, thinking. Finally, his thoughts had to come out.

"I'm sorry."

"For what?" Carrie asked.

"For what I did to you," he tried to whisper, but the older woman strained to hear while knitting. "It's all my fault what happened to you. It's my fault you're like you are."

Carrie whispered back, "What are you talking about? Yes, you broke my heart, but I got over it and went on with my life."

"Something has happened to you, and I caused it." Bill studied the back of his hand for a moment. "The girl I knew would never have taken up with that guy in Greece. She wasn't the girl I saw on the balcony."

"Just what did Ethan tell you?" Carrie whispered too loudly. "Yes, I broke up with him and dated Nicolas. I didn't know Ethan had run up an investment debt he couldn't pay and sold me. I didn't know about it until Nicolas forced me to become his indentured concubine and wouldn't let me leave."

The older woman gasped and dropped her knitting. Acting like she hadn't heard anything, she looked the other way while picking it up. Bill glanced up at her then back down at Carrie.

"It didn't look like you were unwilling at the club or on the balcony. You even told him you loved him outside the shed."

Carrie started to cry. "That was the deal he gave me. I either had to be his personal escort or be sold into a whorehouse or something. I was *trying* to keep you alive, you idiot! Everything was going fine until you showed up, running around the island like a bull in a china shop."

"I was trying to save you."

"Save me from what? My contract with Nicolas was almost over."

"And then what?" Bill asked.

"I don't know. I was supposed to be able to go on my way." Carrie stared at her knees. "He may have sold me to a whorehouse anyway. Or he could have simply killed me when my usefulness to him was over. I don't know."

"You're safe now. You'll be home soon."

"Safe from what? Who's going to want me now? You?" She glared challengingly at Bill. "You can't even look at me."

He looked at her. Bill looked at her for quite a while. Then he put his arm around his ex-friend and pulled her close.

With the conversation in the seats beside her causing flashbacks of her own troubled past, it was more than the older woman could handle. She left her knitting on her seat and went into the lavatory for a good cry. When she returned, the wounded youngsters sitting next to her had fallen asleep in each other's arms. As the passengers deboarded in Denver to transfer to their separate flights elsewhere, she grabbed Bill's arm and pulled him aside.

"You take care of that young lady. Don't let her push you away. She's going to need you." She slid up her sleeves to show Bill the long scars on both her wrists. "No one was there for me." Then she disappeared into the crowd to find her family.

CHAPTER FIFTEEN
SHE'S HOME, NOW WHAT?

B ill texted his stepsister, Mandy, their arrival info from the Denver airport. After boarding the plane for the final leg of their journey, he sat silently beside Carrie. For the moment, the tension level between them from the previous flights had lowered somewhat. She tried to break the silence by asking him about his life since they had last seen each other.

"How was school? Is WSU giving you what you wanted?"

"No. I didn't like anything there. I quit after the first year." He turned to the window and mumbled almost inaudibly, "My heart wasn't in it."

"Oh." She paused for a moment. "What are you doing now, then?"

"I moved in with Mandy. She's going to Eastern Washington University. I started welding school but quit to take a vacation in Europe."

"You didn't have to do that."

He looked her in the eyes for a moment before turning back to the window. "Yes, I did. You'd have done the same if the roles were reversed."

While he blankly gazed out the window, Carrie stared at the back of his head and thought. No, she wouldn't have. For what he had done to her, he could have been burning in hell and she wouldn't have lifted a finger. She hated him and would have been perfectly happy to never lay eyes on Bill again. When he showed up at the villa, she had to sacrifice her love for Nicolas to save Bill's life—not for him but for his family. The only reason she was near him now was because she needed human companionship, even if it was someone she despised.

"So, have you been seeing anyone?" For lack of anything else to kill the silence, Carrie asked him the same questions one would a complete stranger at a party. "How about Willa? Did you guys ever get together? You must have been popular at school."

Anger flashed across his face as he turned to glare at her. "That's none of your damn business. But, yes, we did go on a few dates at the end of summer after you made it *abundantly* clear you weren't coming back." His expression changing to extreme sadness, he turned back to the window. "I know where this is going. You're going to tell me what you've been doing. Don't. I don't want to know the guys' names you've dated. I don't want to know how many or what you did with them. *I don't want to know!*"

Carrie's mouth fell open as she studied the back of his head. It finally hit her that he didn't come after her out of guilt or family obligation. Bill risked his life because, after all this time, he still had feelings for her. She began to hate him just a little less.

When Bill powered up his phone at the Spokane terminal gate, it went berserk with text messages from Mandy. She had told his mother, Karen, about the flight. Karen told Beth that Carrie was on her way home. Beth and Carrie's dad, Randy, drove to the airport to greet their daughter. A big welcoming committee was in the front lobby.

"Crap," Bill muttered to himself, then texted Mandy back.

"What's that all about?" Carrie asked as they walked toward the security checkpoint.

"Nothing. I have to use the restroom. You go on ahead, and I'll see you in baggage claim."

Carrie was only halfway down the stairs to the entryway when

Beth, Randy, and Mandy ran up to greet her. After the tearful hugs, Beth looked back up the stairs.

"Where's Bill?"

Carrie glanced back. "He'll be along in a minute. He said he'd meet me in baggage claim."

"Bill's not coming," Mandy said softly. "He refuses to come to this side of the security checkpoint until you've all left."

"What?" Carrie turned back toward the checkpoint.

"Why not?" Beth wanted to thank him, possibly mend some fences.

"He says this is time for you guys. He doesn't want to dampen your reunion." Mandy smiled proudly up the stairs. "He says his job is done now and wishes you all the best. Don't try to out-wait him. You know how stubborn he can be when his mind is set."

Beth hugged her daughter, crying. Her opinion of that wretched boy had done a complete one-eighty, again.

Bill sat in the cafeteria area behind the security checkpoint, waiting, thinking. He had gone to Greece expecting to rescue the innocent girl he grew up with and loved. The young woman he found and brought home only resembled her physically. At the bottom of the airport stairs greeting her parents was a hardened stranger.

As much as he loved the idea of Carrie and him as a couple, he didn't know if he could accept what she had become. His heart wanted to stay with her, but his mind insisted he had to move on. His phone buzzed. After reading Mandy's text that the others had left, he ruefully looked one last time out the lounge windows at a darkening sky, then resolutely shuffled toward baggage pickup.

Already having completed his first quarter of welding school before he went on his European Carrie rescue mission, Bill returned to school. Immersing himself in classes to block her from his mind, he breezed through his next two quarters to gain certification in all the various methods. Because the program was based on competency levels, he completed the course early.

The next summer, not wanting to return home, he called Mr. Roberts again. Willa's dad had just the opening for him in Moses Lake—one hundred miles from the Bennett ranch and Carrie.

The only one in the shop and not in the field doing repairs on the farm's equipment, Bill hung an "out to lunch" sign on the door and walked across the county road to a little dive cafe frequented by locals. He didn't much care for the one size fits all menus at the chain restaurants along the freeway, and the good Mexican food trucks were on the other end of town. He'd barely started to read the menu when he felt a presence beside the table.

"I haven't decided yet," Bill said without looking up.

"That's good because I'm not here to take your order. When're you going to be back at the shop?" The pretty delivery girl from the local auto parts store scowled down at him. "You're my last drop-off before *I* get to eat lunch. I figured you'd be over here."

"I just got here, but I suppose I could go back and open up for you."

"Don't bother." She grinned and sat down. "I'll just take my break now. I'll deliver the parts when I feel like it."

Surprised at her lackadaisical attitude, he had to smile. She stopped in the shop almost daily delivering parts and always seemed to be in a hurry. "Won't your boss get mad?"

"My dad owns the parts store. What's he going to do? Ground me? He'd have to answer to Mom if he did." She reached across the table and pulled the menu out of Bill's hand. "What's the lunch special today?"

Bill laughed. "Yup. Nepotism at its finest."

Jennie immediately fell for the tall boy with good manners and started scheduling her breaks to match his. During her lunchtime fishing expeditions with him, she figured out he was unattached and put her efforts toward changing which status box he checked on forms. Her parents couldn't find any major faults with Bill when she made him come to dinner. He seemed perfect.

For the moment, his biggest flaw was his tiny bachelor pad. There was barely enough room to turn around between the microwave, refrigerator, and the bed. Tiny as it was, Jennie preferred to spend time there than her own place—a bedroom in her family home.

"Tell me about your past girlfriends." She cuddled next to Bill in his bed. "I'll tell you about my exes."

He became instantly distant. "There's not much to tell. And I'm not sure it's such a good idea."

"It can't be that bad." She kissed his ear. "I'll start. I dated one boy for quite a while in high school. He went his way, and I went mine after graduation. I've only seriously dated two different guys since. You? You're such a hunk, you've probably left a trail of broken hearts."

Bill snorted. "Boy, you've got that wrong. For a while I dated Willa after graduation. Her dad is a bigshot in the company I work for."

"Talk about nepotism. You made fun of me. What about you?" Jennie laughed and sat on his chest. "There's got to be more girls than that."

"After Willa moved on to higher tax bracket boyfriends, I had a few dates in college but nothing serious until you."

"Oh, come on! Surely you had a high school sweetheart." Jennie playfully pretended to perform chest compressions on him. "No one? Not even one special girl?"

"I said *no one*." Brusquely, but gently, Bill pushed Jennie off his chest and rolled on his side facing away from her. "No one worth mentioning."

Spooning her large boyfriend, she threw an arm over him and kissed his back. *So*, she thought, *there's an emotion destroyer lurking in his past.* It had to be at least two years ago. He was bound to be almost healed. It didn't matter what had happened. Jennie wouldn't mention her again.

CHAPTER SIXTEEN
HOMETOWN DISSATISFACTION

Life back on the Palouse was about as boring as it could be compared to what Carrie had become accustomed to. Long Island was sophisticated, filled with worldly people, and John. College had been eye opening. The island had been nirvana once she accepted and acclimated to the regimentation. Nicolas was a strong, powerful man and an excellent lover. Then that idiot Bill developed his savior complex and ruined it all.

Now, she was stuck in the middle of nowhere with her mother escorting her to weekly visits with a shrink. Psychiatrist, huh, what a joke. He didn't come right out and say it, but Carrie knew the point he was circling. He was trying to convince her that her love for the older man in Greece was false, some sort of manipulated delusion. What did the shrink know? Even though she consciously knew it was wrong, in her heart she loved Nicolas. Thanks to the actions of her family and ex-friend, she could never again be with Nicolas. Now, all she felt was betrayal and resentment.

Carrie refused to do any of the menial ranch chores. Her old friend, Charlie, tried to get her to ride horses with him, but he had his own family. Her father, Randy, somehow now speaking in a completely foreign language, just couldn't communicate with her. Her mother, Beth, finally blew a fuse when Carrie refused to help in the annual calf vaccination/dehorning/castration ritual.

"That's it! You need to start carrying at least some of the load around here! You're not going to just sit around and pout. Go get a job."

"Fine! I will!" Carrie stormed out of the kitchen.

Job opportunities in their small town were limited. The local mercantile handled mostly ranching and farming supplies. Carrie would just as soon take a beating than be anywhere near that stuff. Not yet twenty-one and too young to sell alcohol, she couldn't work at the convenience store. That left the tiny drive-in. With all older girls having left town to make their mark, and school still in session, she was hired on for the day shift.

A parade of dirty ranch and farm workers eating at the restaurant constantly asked her out. Considering herself too worldly to even acknowledge them, Carrie still smiled to get their tips. One day a well-dressed man in a suit stopped for lunch. Now *he* was flirt worthy.

"What can I get for you today?"

In his early thirties, Vern was an insurance adjuster visiting the area at least once a week. Still mourning Nicolas, discounting the psychiatrist's opinion, a bored and spiteful Carrie thought, *Why not?*

"Mom, you don't have to take a day off to bring me to the shrink's this week," she addressed Beth civilly for the first time in quite a while. "I can drive myself. I think I'll catch a movie or something."

"You sure?"

She smiled sweetly. "Yes. I don't even mind if you call the doc to make sure I attend my appointment."

After pretending to bare her soul at the therapist's office, Carrie went to lunch with Vern. Lost, searching for something but not knowing what it was, she spent the rest of the day in a motel room. Vern was married, lived in the county seat, and didn't travel at all. In her present state, Carrie didn't care, but his wife sure would.

Another person also minded—Carrie's father's cousin, Dr. Josie Bennett. After her weekly rounds at the county hospital, Josie went to a local cafe to get a bite before heading home. Walking across the parking lot toward the cafe, she saw Carrie kissing an older man. They weren't just kissing, they were going into a motel room. The next day, Josie stopped at the drive-in.

"Just what the hell do you think you're doing?"

Already carrying a heavy load of guilt, remorse, and self-doubt, Carrie feigned innocence. "I don't know what you mean."

Josie snapped, "Don't pull that crap with me! I saw you and that guy going into a motel. You can't keep doing this to your parents. You need to listen to your counselor."

"You're such a bitch! What are you going to do about it? Rat on me?"

"Yes, as a matter of fact, I will."

"Fine! I'm done with this podunk town anyway!"

Needing to get away, not knowing where, or why, Carrie impulsively decided to move to Spokane. Unfortunately, she couldn't afford to live in the city without dipping into the college fund her grandmother, Kate, had set up. The only way she could talk her parents in to giving her access was by telling them she was going back to school. She registered at the same college as Mandy and, now that Bill was in Moses Lake, temporarily stayed in her spare room.

Vern had been her first bedmate since coming back from Greece. When Mandy let it slip that Bill was dating someone, Carrie struck back in jealous anger. To hell with what the shrink said. She'd show them all by moving into a small studio apartment and getting a boyfriend.

⚔

"I'm just so happy that we've finally got our own place together." Jennie sat beside Bill on the hand-me-down sofa from her parents' rec room. "How's your dinner? I slaved over a hot microwave for at least five minutes to make it."

"It's great." Bill kissed her head. "I haven't enjoyed a home cooked meal like this in a long time."

After supper, Bill put his arm around his girlfriend while they watched a movie on her laptop. The computer was Jennie's. The coffee table it sat on was another artifact from her parents' basement. As usual, she fell asleep in his lap before the movie was over. Bill stroked her hair and wondered why they always watched a movie she chose when she never made it to the end.

Jennie woke just enough when he carried her into the bedroom to strip before climbing into bed. Because his arm was too large and heavy to lay over her while they spooned, it had become their habit for her to cuddle to his back. Bill would lay on his stomach, arm tucked under the mattress with one knee protruding from the covers for temperature control. Jennie would lay her head on his shoulder, one arm across his back, and one leg over his.

"Night, honey." She sleepily kissed his shoulder.

"Night, pumpkin," he whispered back.

Bill had never been able to force himself into using such endearments like honey, dear, or sweetie when talking to his girlfriend. He lay staring over the side of the bed at the floor, pondering why. Feeling her soft breath on his shoulder and her fingers slowly stroking his back even while she was asleep, he contemplated. Jennie was completely committed to him. If she had her way, they'd be reciting wedding vows the next day.

He knew her devotion. He knew he would probably never find anyone who would make a better wife. That was why he was with her. Bill *wanted* to be totally there for this wonderful girl. What was holding him back? What?

CHAPTER SEVENTEEN
AN AHA MOMENT

Jennie found out about Mandy's party and, thinking it was about time she met some of her boyfriend's family, insisted on going. "You must be Mandy. Bill's told me so much about you!"

"Not all bad, I hope." Mandy hugged her brother's possible new remedy for his lack of drive. "I didn't think he talked about his family at all."

"Not much." Jennie laughed. "But it's still more than he says about anything else from his past. It's like pulling nails. I visited him at work once and he introduced me to a girl he'd dated for a little while, Willa I think."

"Yeah, they went out a few times in college."

"She asked Bill if he'd seen some other girl, but he immediately shut down the discussion." Jennie shrugged. "I asked him about her later, just trying to get to know him better. He acted like he had no idea who I was talking about."

"He gets like that." Mandy outwardly laughed. Inside she knew exactly who Jennie was referring to and began to worry. She didn't think Bill would drive from Moses Lake just for a party and hadn't been too concerned when she sent out a blanket invite to friends. Mandy shrugged and went back to visiting guests. The other invited problem person rarely visited, too tied up in preparing for the next school semester and rapid exchange boyfriend tryouts.

Sitting on Bill's lap in the crowded apartment, Jennie immersed herself in gleaning information on her boyfriend from Al, Mandy's longtime companion. Bill mainly grunted and nodded. "Now that Bill and I have an apartment together in Moses Lake, it's a good home base if he decides to go full time with the industrial farm."

Feeling Bill flinch, she saw his face blanche. When Jennie turned to see what he was looking at, a pretty, little dishwater-blonde was hugging Mandy by the front door. At least a decade older, the girl's escort was already checking out other women in the room. Jennie thought she might as well have been a rug on the floor to be ignored when Bill and the newcomer locked eyes. The blonde turned, passionately kissed her date, disdainfully looked back at Bill, and went into the kitchen. Bill turned back to Mandy's boyfriend.

And that was it. Jennie immediately knew. That was the one "we don't talk about." That little blonde with the hard, tired eyes was the reason Bill was constantly distant. A foreboding shroud of heartbreak descended over the party. Deep inside, a voice nagged to be heard, telling Jennie her relationship with Bill couldn't last. It might not end for a while, but it *would* end.

She asked, "Who is that?"

Bill answered with a subdued tone, "Oh, some girl from high school. Her family's ranch was a few miles from our house."

Unsatisfied with the vague answer, she pushed, "So, you two used to date?"

"No. We hung out a little. She took off to the east coast right after graduation." Bill shifted uncomfortably in the chair. "I need to get some air. I'm going for a walk."

Jennie couldn't let it drop. A self-destructive compulsion drove her into the kitchen. Unable to stop herself, she walked up to the blonde with the hard eyes. "Hi, my name's Jennie. I'm Bill's girlfriend. I don't think we've met."

This wasn't going to end well, Mandy thought before making the introduction. "Jennie, this is Carrie. We were neighbors and went to school together."

Jennie turned and forced a tense smile at Carrie. "That's what Bill said. He said you went east right after graduation. What have you been doing?"

When Carrie spoke, her words could just as well been shards of dry ice. "I bet he did. What else did he say?"

Seeing the expressions in the room, Jennie felt like a gladiator laying in the colosseum dirt, looking up at Caesar with his thumb pointing down. "I . . . I have to get up early for work tomorrow. We should get going. Nice meeting you all."

Bill was leaning against his pickup, staring into the bed, when she came out of the apartment complex almost at a run. He blankly nodded when told she wanted to leave.

Driving west on I-90, Jennie leaned toward Bill with her hand on his arm. Watching him stare into the sunset, she knew. They were done. It may not be in a week, or even the next month, but they were done. He would never be totally hers.

Carrie had to leave Mandy's apartment early. Running into her past pain flipped an internal switch. She needed physical reassurance. She needed it now. Her last-minute male escort wasn't about to protest when a cute twenty-year-old girl wanted to hit the sheets with him.

It was the best sex he'd had in a long time, maybe ever. Then, right in the middle, she went berserk, hysterically sobbing. He jumped up and gawked at the freaky chick curled up on the bed. She may have been cute and fun in bed, but this was too much. He grabbed his clothes and ran for the door of her studio apartment.

"I'm outta here."

Carrie lay in bed sobbing, not knowing why. When she saw Bill with that other girl at the party, all she could think about was showing him how well her life was going with him not in it. Rolling over, she stared at the pile of schoolbooks on her dresser. She had pre-registered at the same university as Mandy but hadn't paid her tuition yet. With her mind occupied far away, her heart just wasn't in it.

Spending time on her lover's island, then torn away and held captive by her own parents in their misguided attempt to cure her of an infliction she didn't have, she'd missed a whole year of school. Stupid shrink. What did he know? Who was he to tell her who to love? He advised her parents to send her back to school as a "healing mechanism." Really? Heal from what? Carrie made up her mind. To hell with them all. She wasn't going back to school. Now, she had another problem. Her parents were paying for the tiny apartment so she could attend college. No school, no apartment. She needed a job.

Carrie went to every art gallery and supply house in Spokane. But, with a blank resume, her chance of getting hired was nil. She could have invoked her mother's name but didn't want her parents to figure out what she was doing until it was too late for them to intervene. Falling back on her experience in the drive-in, she found a job as an entry level waitress in a rundown restaurant with an attached cocktail lounge.

To hide from her prying parents, she rented a post office box in another area of town and dug the envelope of Nicolas's money out of its hiding place to pay first and last month's rent on an apartment closer to work. Carrie had a hard time putting the envelope away. With all the bad memories buried deeply in her subconscious, just the feel of the paper brought back good ones.

She wrote a letter to Nicolas, telling him how much she missed him. Before sealing the envelope, Carrie enclosed a picture of her family's ranch and another one of her little hometown's main street. She mailed the letter without a second thought. What could possibly go wrong with telling someone that she missed them?

⛬

Jennie watched her relationship with Bill wither. Was she pushing him away? Was it all her imagination? She could see that, in his mind, he was trying. It just wasn't enough to satisfy her expectations. Before the party at Mandy's apartment, his distance perplexed her. She couldn't put her finger on it because it just didn't dovetail with the rest of his personality. Surely, she could fix him.

When the little dishwater blonde and her older date had walked into the party, it all became clear. After witnessing the exchange of looks between Bill and the blonde, it only took Jennie a few seconds to realize that there was no cure to Bill's distance, at least in the timespan she was willing to commit to the effort.

She had to decide whether she wanted to continue. It was her decision. She knew Bill was too honorable to break it off and would stick it out because he gave his word. It was who he was. As long as times were good, her discontent simmered on a back burner. Then, when Jennie stopped in the shop to go to lunch with Bill, she overheard the tail end of a conversation between him and one of the company's owners.

"I don't think that I'm the best choice for the job, Mr. Roberts," Bill said dubiously. "There are a lot more experienced men working for you."

The man in the suit was insistent. "That may be so, Bill, but you know the layout. You worked there before. You know the area, the locals, and I trust you."

Bill shrugged. "I . . . don't know."

Mr. Roberts smiled. "Let me sweeten the pot. How's free housing sound? I'm taking off for the winter, and I need someone to watch the place. The guest quarters behind the main house are yours for the duration of your time there. Think about it."

At the little cafe near the corporate farm's welding shop, Jennie watched as Bill ate silently. She couldn't take it any longer.

"Why so quiet? Does it have something to do with your boss?"

"Yeah, I guess." Bill ran his straw up and down through the

plastic lid of his milkshake. "He offered me a job. I'm not going to take it."

She asked, "Is it a promotion?"

"Yeah."

"Does it pay more money?"

Bill sighed. "Yeah, but I'd have to move."

"Move where?" Jennie asked hopefully. There might be an upside to this after all if it was a bigger town.

"Back to the Palouse," he mumbled. "I don't want to go. There's nothing there for you."

He might as well have slapped her. The time had come to choose. Jennie had been torturing herself over their relationship since the party. She knew she couldn't keep going like this forever. She could take the long, drawn out, less traumatic path of letting the relationship fade away until there was no feeling left, or just pull the trigger. Jennie flipped a mental coin and chose the quicker, intensely painful way of jumping off the cliff.

"You should take it."

"What? There's nothing there for you to do. I can't do that to you."

"I won't be going." Jennie could barely hold herself together, already wishing she could suck back in what she'd just said. "It's time we went our separate ways. I don't like what we've become."

Bill's ears heard, but his mind didn't understand. "What are you trying to say?"

"I'm saying that we're done. Take the job." She stood to leave before completely breaking down. "I'll be at my parents' house until you've cleared your crap out of the apartment. Just go."

She ran out of the cafe sobbing.

CHAPTER EIGHTEEN
CHANGES IN GREECE

Nicolas came from inside the villa as the helicopter was shutting down. His latest errand boy pulled a canvas bag from the passenger compartment and headed toward the power generation building and its incinerator.

"Is that the mail?" he asked.

"Yes," the messenger replied. "I sorted through it on my return flight. You received nothing of consequence, so I was taking it straight to the burner."

"Give it to me," Nicolas said testily. "*I* will decide what is of no consequence to me."

"But, sir . . ."

"If you value your job, you'll give me the bag!"

Recognizing his boss was in one of his "Bad Nicolas" phases, the courier handed over the bag. Nicolas dumped the contents onto a table next to the pool and sorted through the heap of opened solicitation envelopes. At the bottom of the pile, he found a single, letter sized, unopened envelope. With no return address, the letter had a Spokane, Washington postmark.

Nicolas held up the envelope and demanded, "What's this?"

The courier stammered, "It didn't look business related. So I didn't bother. I figured it was some sort of unimportant fan mail from an unknown admirer."

Actually, the courier had a fairly good idea who it was from. If he was right, the sender had disrupted business from the first day she came to the island. At first, the young woman's presence stabilized the boss's periodic mood swings and stopped his constant flow of women. He only reverted to Bad Nicolas when she did something to displease him. Now that she was gone, his personality flips were increasingly more frequent. Echoes of uncertainty from the circumstances of her leaving still affected the crew.

"*I* will decide what is unimportant!" Stuffing the letter in a shirt pocket, Nicolas tossed the bag back in the courier's direction. "From now on, *I* will open all the mail. It would be good if you remember your place."

As his boss stormed back into the house, the courier headed toward the incinerator and caught sight of some of the other men who witnessed the exchange. Because of their occupation, they were already sensitive to Nicolas's turbulent emotional undercurrents. He had been bordering on paranoia since the Carrie banishing incident. There had been grumbling about his favoritism toward her while she was on the island. When he didn't sell off the disrespectful odalisque, sending both Carrie and her friend away unscathed, he had lost a substantial amount of fearful respect among his underlings.

Sitting alone in his personal art vault, Nicolas opened the envelope, read Carrie's letter, and looked at her pictures. With a melancholy smile, he locked her missive in the safe with his other most valued items.

It was time to go. His oldest child was due to arrive on the ferry. After the university in England and Nick Jr. parted ways with mutual dissatisfaction, the boy had expressed an interest in the family business. Nick was spoiled and bullheaded—bad traits in relationships but good for becoming a crime boss.

Sure enough, Nick Jr. wasn't alone on the ferry. A dozen half-inebriated partiers staggered off the dock and followed him up the path. Two paused to urinate off the dock. One spewed his lunch on the bow of Nicolas's fishing boat.

Watching from above, Nicolas was certain none of the group were from his son's school. Being an absentee father didn't mean his spies weren't watching. Obnoxious and entitled, Nick Jr. had no real friends. This group must all be stragglers scooped up in local clubs. A few Nicolas recalled seeing locally.

"Father!" Nick ceremoniously bowed. "My esteemed entourage and I are awed to be in your presence."

Nicolas growled, "Cut the crap, Nick. This group is nothing but passed out drunks you collected on your way to the wharf. Get them back on the boat. Now!"

Stinging with humiliation, Nick led his circus back to the ferry, "Sorry, guys. Wrong Island. Go on ahead while I establish who *really* owns this island."

Looking around to make sure none of the guards heard his faux bravado, he undertook another more respectful greeting with his father. He had to maintain a low-key presence to achieve his long-term goal of taking full control. If he had his way, it wouldn't be that long term of an objective.

"Sorry about that, Dad. I just got a little carried away on the way home."

"Don't let it happen again," Nicolas snapped. "The family name must be upheld. If it isn't respected and feared, we're done." Then he turned abruptly and headed for the main house.

Nick looked at his father's men, expecting them to carry his luggage. When they all walked off, he grabbed what he could and followed his dad. The maid took his luggage at the front door while he returned for the rest. Having only been on the island a few times growing up, he expected to be quartered in the special guest room on the house's second floor. When the maid led him to a room at the opposite end of the hall, he asked, "What's the matter with the room at the bottom of the stairs to the third floor? Shouldn't I be staying there?"

"No one is allowed into those two rooms," she replied. "Your father is the only one who has access to the vault room on the left. The room on the right has been closed to visitors for more than a year. I'm not even allowed to clean in there."

Grumbling under his breath, Nick put his stuff away. This was all going to change when *he* took over. But first, he needed to learn the ropes. How hard could bossing around a bunch of lackeys possibly be?

Quickly bored with the nitpicking aspects of bookkeeping, learning where all the company's operations were located, and risk management lessons, Nick headed for the crew's lodgings. After all, computer programs were designed specifically for such menial tasks. Playing cards with the boys was more in his wheelhouse. It was also an excellent way to snoop on the inner workings.

After being on the island for not much more than a month, even the lowest tiered workers avoided Nick's company. This whole being the boss thing was getting tiresome. He needed a good party. Besides, he had an ally's contact back on the mainland who would be getting impatient for an update.

"Say, Father, aren't you flying to the mainland tomorrow?"

Nicolas looked at his son suspiciously. Since when did the kid start taking a respectful tone with anyone? "Yes. I'm going to a couple of business meetings, then returning with a few of my top advisors."

"Mind if I tag along? I'd like to see how you work. Then, I want to look around a little. It's been quite awhile since I really explored the town."

"I suppose it would be okay," Nicolas replied. "Just remember. These people are not your party friends. They expect to be treated with respect."

"Yes, sir. I'll go pack a bag with a change of clothes." He smiled at his father. "It's one of the things I learned from you. Always be prepared for the unexpected."

Watching his son walk off, Nicolas wasn't sure if Nick was

actually absorbing his lessons or if he had simply perfected saying what others wanted to hear. After the first business meeting on the mainland, the father wasn't too surprised when his easily bored son took leave to explore.

Tired from his meetings late in the afternoon, Nicolas got out of the limo and walked toward the helicopter. Not totally unexpected, his son was still unaccounted for. With his most senior advisors onboard and the door about to slide shut, Nick came running across the tarmac carrying a gym bag. Throwing the bag under his seat from outside, he yelled above the engine noise, "I ran into a college friend in town who's touring the Mediterranean in his family's yacht. We're going to hang out. Don't worry about me getting to the island. He'll give me a ride." Nick pointed to the bag. I bought some books on business management. I don't want to lug them around all day. You don't mind, do you?"

As Nick backed away from the door, the security guard said, "I need to search the bag."

When the guard reached for the bag, fatigued Nicolas snapped, "It's just books. We're running late. Close the door and let's go."

Nick ran back around the small terminal and hopped into a limo with blackened windows. The vehicle wasted little time in heading toward the seaport.

Still angry over his son's continuing irresponsibility, Nicolas lost track of the business talk in the copter cabin. As they headed out over the water, he stared at the gym bag. Maybe the kid did have a little bit of drive. The contents of that bag may very well change the future.

CHAPTER NINETEEN
THE PALOUSE
BECKONS AGAIN

Bill taped Mr. Roberts' list of repetitive chores to the kitchen wall in the guest house: Tour the main house checking for water leaks and furnace operation once a week; feed the two horses every day; at your discretion, go from property to property repairing irrigation systems and servicing the equipment.

He'd only been there a few weeks when Thanksgiving rolled around. After spending the day with family, he returned to the cottage after dark. The lights were on, and an unfamiliar sports car was parked in front. He had a good idea whose it was.

"Finally, you're back." Willa smiled. "Did you bring me any leftovers?"

"What're you doing here? Shouldn't you be in some Bavarian ski village with friends?"

"I got bored and wanted to spend the holidays at home."

"Willlaaa . . .?" Bill hung his coat on the wall hook.

"*Okay*! If you really want to know," she pouted, "my boyfriend's a turd and we broke up. Both of my parents are spending time with their *special* friends. Everybody I know is off having fun. I had nowhere else to go, so I came home."

"Let me put this stuff away then I'll open up the main house."

"If those are leftovers, I wasn't kidding about being hungry."

Bill sighed and put the containers on the dinette table. His lunches for the next week were about to disappear. "I'll get you a fork and a plate. "I'll open up the house while you eat."

"Just the fork, please. I'm starving. I'll eat right out of the containers." Willa wolfed down the food more like a street urchin than a high society denizen. "Don't bother with the house. I'll crash here."

"Uh, I don't think that's a good idea."

"*Please?* I don't want to be in that big house all by myself. I'll sleep on the fold out couch." She poured on the charm. "It's not like you have anyone who's going to be jealous or anything."

"What?"

"Don't try to deny it. Daddy told me you had a girlfriend in Moses Lake. Since I don't see any female stuff around, I'm going to assume the prefix "ex" applies here." Willa smiled. "I'll be good. I promise."

When Bill was awakened in the middle of the night by a girl snuggling next to him, his first thought was that Willa broke her promise. Then it dawned on him: Being good had two polar opposite connotations. He remembered that the second meaning definitely applied with Willa.

But nothing happened. He waited for her to make an advance, trying to decide how he would handle it. Soon, all he heard was her contented soft breathing, deep in slumber. He woke the next morning to the smell of coffee. Willa had figured out how to work the coffee maker.

Stumbling out of the bedroom, he asked, "When did you get so domestic?"

"Don't get your hopes up." Willa pointed from where she was sitting on the sofa toward the empty mug on the kitchen counter. "That's about the extent of my domestic skills."

After filling the mug, Bill sat on the other end of the couch. "So, what's the deal? I woke up in the middle of the night with you in bed next to me, wearing one of my shirts. Then, you fell asleep without trying anything."

"Sorry for that." She stared into her cup for what seemed an eternity before continuing, "I just needed to be near someone who's kind but doesn't want anything from me in return."

"Huh, is that why you showed up without warning on a holiday?"

Scooting next to him, she placed her head on his shoulder. "I just get so lonely sometimes. You're the closest thing I've ever had to a real friend."

That shook him. He had never considered her a friend. In the past, they had simply shared proximity to each other when no one else was around. "I guess I could clean my crap out of the spare bedroom if you're going to be around for a while."

Bill and Willa became platonic roommates. They didn't love each other. A lot of the time, they didn't even like each other. But, sharing the bond of mutual hollowness, they understood each other.

Feeling guilty, Bill looked at his roommate in the mirror while he shaved. "It doesn't seem right to leave you alone while I head off to all of the town's various Christmas events. You should come with me."

Most of the small town remembered the rich, young woman from her high school days. Karen knew they'd dated a little at the beginning of their college freshman year. Beth had heard Carrie talk about Willa in high school and suspected that this girl might have had something to do with the big blow-up. Mandy knew everything but kept her mouth shut.

Beth hadn't had the chance to thank Bill since he rescued Carrie from Greece. Even though he did his best to hide on the other side of the Grange hall during the community Christmas party, she cornered him. Unable to stop herself, she trapped the surprised young man like a frightened rabbit against a wall and hugged him.

"You never gave us the chance to thank you for rescuing Carrie and bringing her home from Greece." Beth stood on her toes and kissed his cheek.

Bill stammered, "I . . . I didn't do anything special. We just kind of ran into each other and flew home together. That's all."

"And horses don't kick, and dogs don't bite when startled." Beth turned toward Willa who was confused by the conversation. "Who do we have here? Are you going to introduce us?"

At that moment, Bill would have just as soon been on the receiving end of a dog bite while being kicked by a horse. "Uh, Mrs. Bennett, this is Willa Roberts. She went to school with us. Willa, this is *Carrie's* mom, Beth Bennett."

In her own mind, Beth's suspicions of Willa's involvement in the big explosion were confirmed when the girl's face paled whiter than the snow covering the Grange's parking lot. "Willa Roberts? Isn't your father one of the owners of the corporation buying up all the old homesteads?"

"I . . . don't know anything about his work." Desperately, Willa looked for an escape route. The only semi-friendly face she recognized was Mandy's. "I see a friend over there I haven't said hi to. Pleased to meet you, Mrs. Bennett."

Beth watched Willa almost run across the room. "She seems nice."

"Yeah, I guess." Bill nervously looked around. "I don't see Carrie. Isn't she coming?" He instantly knew it was the wrong topic of discussion when a flash of despair crossed Beth's face.

"We haven't seen her since mid-summer. What happened to her over there? She won't tell us. What did you see?"

"It's not my story to tell. I'm sorry, but I made a promise to keep my mouth shut." Bill studied his boots for a moment. "I will say this. Carrie needed help when she got back. She needed counseling. Did she get it?"

"We tried for months. She went for a while but quit." Beth wasn't prepared for the influx of emotion surging to the surface, and she headed for an outside door. "I need to get some air."

Willa watched Bill and Beth's intense conversation while standing beside his sister. "What's going on over there? Mrs. Bennett acted like I was a demon or something."

"In her eyes, you are," Mandy answered.

"Why? Sure, I got myself in the middle when Bill and Carrie broke up. So? Last I heard, she was off on the east coast with a boyfriend and happy."

Mandy shook her head. "You *really* have no clue, do you? Because I want to respect Carrie's privacy, I can't tell you much. But yeah, she went to Europe with a boyfriend. I'm not going to get into specifics about what happened, but she went through some traumatic stuff. Bill flew to Europe and rescued her. Carrie went to counseling for a while but has disappeared again. Beth is worried stiff about her. I don't think Mrs. Bennett knows everything about what happened between Carrie and Bill, but I'm pretty sure she thinks you're involved."

"Oh, crap." Willa looked at Bill. "He hasn't told me any of that."

"He knows more about what Carrie was involved in than I do, but he won't tell *anyone*. He says it's not his story to tell."

Willa asked, "He went to Europe to get her? I thought she hated him now. How'd he get her to come home?"

"By force. He basically dragged her onto the plane. They've only seen each other once since at a party in my apartment." Mandy shook her head. "Let's just say it didn't go well."

After Mandy walked off to visit elsewhere, Willa studied her roommate. What kind of person travels halfway across the globe to escort someone who hates them home? It was a foreign concept to her. Willa wasn't sure her own parents would expend that kind of effort.

She also wondered what happened to Carrie that required her to be rescued. Rescued from what? Counseling? What for? Carrie always seemed to be the one in control during high school. This was all foreign to Willa.

Her "friends" were all off on their own adventures. She didn't know where either of her parents were in the world for the holidays. Willa was sure of one thing: Wherever her parents were, it was as far from each other as possible. Having every intention of raiding the wine cellar in the main house, spending Christmas day binging on junk food, and having a personal pity party, she resisted when Bill insisted she come with him to his parents' house. She knew it was only out of pity, but he wouldn't relent.

The community Christmas party the week before made one thing crystal clear to Willa. There was one taboo subject never to be brought up: Carrie, and what had happened to her. Those who knew wouldn't talk. Ones that didn't were too wounded. She was still coming to grips with Bill's quixotic trip to Europe. Sacrificing that much effort for a known lost cause just didn't make sense.

Walking into the Schmidt family's large, old farmhouse felt like entering a mythological universe. Teenagers bickered while a preschooler ran amuck with holiday fervor. An elderly couple fawned in German over each other on the sofa. Bill's grandmother and mother, Karen, fussed in the kitchen. Bill's grandfather and stepfather, Charlie, were putting on jackets, about to embark on a secretive mission in one of the outbuildings.

"Make yourself at home." Bill nodded toward the kitchen. "Maybe build up some brownie points with Mom. I'm going to help Charlie and Grandpa for a minute."

Helping in the kitchen was another foreign concept to Willa. Big dinner parties in her family had always been handled by servants or caterers. Her mother had no domestic skills and saw no need to even try with just the three of them.

Karen smiled kindly. "We've got this. It's too crowded in here right now. I'll yell when it's time to set the table. Look around. Make yourself at home."

Never having been around a blue-collar family before, Willa

took what Karen said at face value, not realizing Bill's mother meant: "Sure, pitch in over by the sink." Oblivious, she smiled and wandered around the house. In the library, she was subjected to a crash course on what made Bill who he was.

One wall was dedicated to a man she initially thought was Bill's uncle, Peter Schmidt. Pictures surrounded a triangularly folded flag. A display case held a Distinguished Service Cross, two Purple Hearts, and an array of campaign ribbons. Willa stopped in front of a wedding photo of a much younger Karen and this Peter fellow. Beside that photo were more pictures of a younger Karen, Peter, Bill, and his sister, Nettie.

Willa shrugged. Assuming Karen married her first husband's brother after being widowed, she walked over to another wall with more recent pictures. Next to the pictures of a now much larger family was another display case containing three more Purple Hearts, a Bronze Star, a bunch of campaign ribbons, and a public service award from the county Sheriff. The man in the picture was Bill's stepfather, but the caption identified him as Charlie Walden.

Bill's sister, Nettie, appeared beside her.

Willa asked, "Is Mandy coming? I thought she'd be here by now."

"Nah," Nettie answered. "She was here last week, so for Christmas, she's at her boyfriend's parents' place."

"I'm confused." Willa looked back at the pictures. "It says here that your stepdad's last name is Walden, but all of you go by Schmidt. What's the deal?"

Nettie laughed. "That's a convoluted story. It has to do with divorces, adoption, abandonment, and remarriage. The short version is that when Charlie and Mom decided to get married, it would have meant three last names in the house. Charlie and his kids all decided to assume the Schmidt name. He said it was the right thing to do."

This whole doing the right thing concept was foreign to Willa. "Is it about time for supper?"

"It's getting close. We should go and help."

"Your mother told me that they didn't need any help. She told me to go make myself comfortable."

Nettie laughed. "Have you ever been in a real-world house before? That was a test. You're *expected* to help out. You're supposed to insist and chip in anyway."

"Oh crap!" Willa almost ran into the kitchen, having no idea what to do when she got there. While breaking dishes in the sink trying to make herself useful, she observed the close-knit family. Was doing the right thing, sacrifice for others, and honor the adhesives that held them together? None of those elements were present in her own broken family.

Dinner was another major culture shock for her, beginning with the prayer. Sitting beside the elderly, and very conservative Neufelds, Willa just listened. Heather was training to be a CNA after school, wanting to enter the medical field like her stepmother and older sister. Ricky liked the farming or ranching idea. Nettie was undecided and keeping her options open. It made Willa think that she was just squandering her life.

The one topic not discussed was the Bennetts and their absence. Willa took from the body language and circular references that Carrie's parents had isolated themselves on their ranch, mourning their daughter's second disappearance.

The Christmas holiday was too much for Willa. Everyone in this little town seemed to have a purpose. They'd either done something heroic, made a contribution to help others, been so loved by others that their absence was grieved, or cared for another person so much they would travel to the ends of the earth to help if they could. She was none of those, even to her own family. Before New Year's, she packed her bags again and was about to leave, as usual without saying goodbye, when Bill walked in.

"Going somewhere?" he asked.

Willa wouldn't make eye contact while speaking. "Yeah. I'm smothering here. I need to find a party somewhere."

"That's not what's going on." Bill knew her well enough that he could read her tells. "What are you really doing?"

"Okay, if you *have* to know, I think that I need to grow up a little. I need to find a purpose."

He hugged her. "How?"

"I don't know for sure," she whispered with her arms around his neck. "But I'm going back to school. I'm going to get my MBA. Maybe take a job at my dad's company."

"So, you're off to the convent?"

She laughed. "Don't be an ass. I have no intention of becoming celibate. I just need to become useful to somebody, anybody." She kissed Bill's cheek and got into her car. "Thank you for being there for me. I mean it. Thank you."

Willa left for her version of the adult world. Returning to his own adult world, Bill went into the stables to care for her dad's horses.

CHAPTER TWENTY

TROUBLE ON THE RANCH

"It's late spring and almost haying season. I have to work on the swather's cutting head after morning chores." Randy rinsed his coffee cup and put it in the drying rack. "It'll never make it through the first cutting if I don't."

Beth asked, "Shouldn't you call Charlie to help? I don't like you doing stuff like that alone."

"Nah, he's busy making trinkets for your next art show, and Ricky's over helping the Neufelds. It'll be fine. You're going to be in your studio within hollering distance if I need another set of hands."

Randy had the swather disconnected from the head and backed out of the shop by the time Beth wandered through toward her studio. "You're going to be welding? You know I hate the fumes."

"Looks like it. I'll leave the shop door open, and you can use your vent fan." He lay on the floor attaching the lifting sling for the overhead hoist.

"I don't like using that thing. It makes too much noise." She kicked her husband's leg as she walked by. "I'll just add fixing it to your list of ignored projects."

He laughed and stood to attach the cable from the overhead hoist to the sling with a clevis. His mind elsewhere, it had been over nine months since they last heard from their troubled daughter. Randy didn't double check the clevis pin.

Just for show in case his wife walked through the shop, he sat a couple of jack stands under the fourteen-foot-long swather cutting head once he had it hoisted. With one end in the air and the other resting on the concrete, Randy sat his old, metal toolbox underneath and stretched out his welding leads.

After scooting around under the head on his wheeled shop stool inspecting problem areas, he started cleaning the rust from around the largest stress crack with the wire brush attachment on his side head grinder. Wanting to achieve a good weld, he was pushing hard when the swather head jerked.

Leaning back, he looked up. One end of the retaining pin had worked its way out the clevis. "Crap!" Randy shoved back his stool, but too late. The harness straps slid out of the clevis, and the swather head came thundering down. Although recklessly placed, the jack stands kept the head from dropping straight down, forcing it to deflect sideways a bit, but not enough.

Glancing off his shoulder, it broke his left arm and trapped him. The metal toolbox kept his torso from being crushed. Still between the swather head and the toolbox, his left leg wasn't so lucky.

Hearing the crash, Beth rushed out of her studio. Her first gut emotion was to rush to her husband's side and try to comfort him, but the blood puddling under Randy's leg overrode sentimentality. She had to stop the bleeding from his femoral artery. Grabbing a ratcheting tie-down off the workbench and a half-inch breaker bar, Beth applied a rudimentary tourniquet before calling the local clinic. Josie and Karen were much closer than paramedics headquartered in the county seat.

Julie, the clinic receptionist, took it from there. "Josie's doing her rounds at the county hospital; Karen's on her way. You get back to Randy, and I'll call 911." She set the phone tree into action.

When Karen arrived at the ranch, local volunteer firemen followed her up the driveway. Karen stabilized Randy while the volunteers repaired the hoist and lifted the swather head. Knowing immediately this was a more serious injury than she could handle locally, she called Julie.

"Get the medivac helicopter on its way. We need to send him to Spokane."

Beth looked up from comforting her husband. "Oh my god! His bone is sticking out!"

"Yeah. He's got a compound fracture. I can get the bleeding under control, but we need to get him to a hospital."

Helping Karen ready Randy for transport, Beth dug deep in her inner moxie container. "He's not coming home right away, is he?"

"No." Karen applied the emergency splint to his arm. "With a compound fracture, there's a risk of infection. They'll pump him full of antibiotics for a couple of days before fixing the break. He'll be in Spokane for a week or two."

"Oh."

"You can ride with him in the helicopter."

"No. His life isn't in danger thanks to you." Beth hugged Karen. "But if he's going to be in Spokane that long, I need to pack some things and drive up. First, I need to get someone to run the ranch while I'm gone. Everyone I know is in the middle of planting or getting ready for the haying season."

Tentatively, Karen replied, "I know someone who might be willing to help. *If* you're okay with it."

In the stables repairing tack, Bill heard a car drive up. Mr. Roberts had warned him Willa might show up any time and wanted everything ready for her in case she had the whim to ride. Figuring that's who drove up, probably with her most current boyfriend, he kept working. When someone cleared their throat, he looked up.

"Mrs. Bennett." He jumped up from his stool. "What can I do for you?"

"I need your help . . . if you want."

"It depends." *Here it comes*, he thought. Carrie's in trouble again. He wasn't inclined to go through that much pain again. "What is it?"

"Randy's hurt and will be laid up for a while. I need someone to run the ranch."

"I'll be glad to help whoever you find." This was different. Bill would do anything for the elder Bennetts. "Who do you have in mind?"

"You." Beth put her hand on his arm. "You know the ranch inside and out. I want you to do it."

"The answer is yes. When would you like me to start?"

"Now. Well, tomorrow morning. Your younger siblings said they'd handle tonight's milking."

"*Now?*" This was asking a lot. He had to give notice to Mr. Roberts. He had to button things up here. "Can I give you an answer in the morning?"

"I guess you can call me." Beth was almost begging. "I'm on my way to Spokane. My bags are in the car. That's where Randy is—in the hospital."

"Yes, I'll do it." Bill needed no convincing. It was the right thing to do. "Is the bunkhouse usable?"

"Stay in the main house. You know the layout." Beth fought the urge to pull him down and kiss his cheek.

Later, during her drive to Spokane, she thought about the young man who broke her daughter's heart. Yes, Bill made a mistake. Yes, she initially blamed him for Carrie's disappearance. But he'd been trying to atone for his sin since and was still the finest young man she had ever met. Beth wished her daughter could have seen that.

"Mr. Roberts, I hate to do this, but an emergency has come up." Bill didn't know any other way than to be direct. "I have to take some time off. A couple of months, I think."

"*Months?* What for?" He wasn't happy. "When?"

"Now. A longtime friend has been disabled, and I have to run their ranch for them."

"Let me get this straight. You want me to give you a leave of absence to do what I'm paying you for on someone else's spread?" Enraged, Mr. Roberts asked, "Where am I going to get a replacement on such short notice?"

"I'm not going to abandon you." Bill had put some thought into it before the call. "Their ranch is just on the other side of town. The only thing needing daily care here at the house is the horses. If it's alright with you, I can take them with me. The Bennett Ranch boards horses for other people. I'll keep them for free. I can button up your house and check on it once a week."

"What about my daughter?"

"She has my number. Willa can call me when she's coming, and I'll open up the house. If she wants to ride, the ranch has plenty of interesting areas. Since she's used to your tack, I can take it with me. There's not much chance of it getting mixed up. Theirs is all western, and yours is English."

"How's the company's equipment?" Mr. Roberts softened a bit. His caretaker was going out of his way to do exactly what was in the young man's title. "Is it all ready for the season?"

"Yes. The irrigation systems are all up and running. The machinery has been serviced. If there are any other problems, I can come over and help."

"Go." It was rare to have such a conscientious employee. "Your job will be waiting for you when you come back. If you move on, you can expect an excellent reference letter."

"Are you Mrs. Bennett?"

"Yes, doctor." Beth headed straight for the hospital the instant she arrived in Spokane. "How's my husband doing?"

"Right now, he's in the recovery room." The doctor pointed her to a chair. "We've repaired his upper arm and applied a cast. We stabilized his shoulder and wrapped his ribs. Those should all heal fine."

Hearing a "but" coming, Beth asked, "His leg. How's his leg?"

"That's a different story." The doctor leaned forward, trying to be comforting. "Because it was a compound fracture, we can't repair it, yet. Yes, we've put the bone back inside the leg, but we can't pin it or close the wound until we're sure he doesn't develop a deep tissue infection. I've started him on antibiotics but, from the contaminants I saw in the area, I'm not optimistic."

"What happens if he gets infected?" Beth was crushed with no one to lean on. Her free-spirited mother was on the other side of the continent. Her daughter had fallen off the map. Her closest friends were back in the Palouse.

"It depends. If it's a mild case, the antibiotics should take care of it." The doctor paused. *Here comes another "but,"* Beth thought. "If the infection becomes serious, we might have to amputate to save his life. Let's hope for the best. His primary care at the scene of the accident was excellent. Better than most I've seen in such cases."

While waiting for Randy to come out from under the anesthesia, Beth made some calls. She couldn't afford a long term stay in a hotel. This late in the ranching year, the ranch coffers were hitting bottom, and there wouldn't be any more money until the steers were sold in the fall. Having been in a slump since Carrie disappeared for the second time, Beth didn't have any artwork that was worth a damn to sell. Finally, she found an artworld acquaintance who lived nearby.

"Sure. I'm glad to help. I'm in Europe for an extended exhibit, and I've been having my housekeeper watch the place. I'll give her a call and she can bring you a key. You remember where it is, don't you?"

Her friend's house ended up being a godsend. Its one downfall was that it was along the river, a thirty-minute drive through city traffic to the hospital. Only going to the house when too exhausted to continue, Beth spent every minute possible near her husband.

Randy did develop a deep tissue infection. Spending her time trying to alleviate his suffering, Beth eavesdropped on the doctors' concerned conversations outside the door. For over a week, Randy silently endured his fever and constant probing by doctors. When he slept, Beth put her head on his good arm and prayed.

CHAPTER TWENTY-ONE
ROUGH DAYS FOR PAUL

"Oh my God, you're awake." A shocked voice penetrated his fog. "You've been in a coma so long, we didn't think you were going to make it."

The nurse's aide ran out of the room, returning with her supervisor. "You're right. He *is* awake. I'll check to see who the on-call physician is."

As his brain slowly cleared, he realized he was in some sort of medical facility—not a hospital. Maybe a rest home? He didn't have any monitors beside the bed, and no IV feeds were in his arm. Too weak to try and sit up on his own, he felt under the sheet and found a tube taped to his stomach and another one coming out of what appeared to be a diaper.

"You're awake, you're awake!" A pretty, preteen girl wearing a powder blue youth volunteer vest came in and hugged him. "I'm so glad."

The nurse he vaguely remembered seeing in his initial awakening fog came into the room, followed by a man in a sports coat. "You should get back to your duties, Mara. The doctor needs to examine Officer Taft."

He looked at the nurse then the doctor while wondering, *Who's Officer Taft?*

The doctor looked at the chart. "Can you tell us your name?"

"P . . . Peter."

"Peter?" The doctor looked at the chart again. "Oh, I see. You go by your middle name. I'll make a note of that. Can you tell us what year it is?"

Middle name? The confused patient shrugged weakly and answered, "2012?"

The shallow questioning continued for a few more minutes before the doctor looked at the nurse and said, "I think we're done here for the time being. Can I speak to you outside?"

The doctor and nurse misjudged how much faster their patient's hearing had recovered than his body. Laying in the bed, the confused man overheard the doctor tell the nurse that he was showing signs of long-term brain damage from his head wound. He was coherent but was years off with his timeline. It wouldn't hurt to start a regimen of light physical therapy to build back muscle tone.

The next day, a uniformed policeman showed up carrying a pile of magazines. "Hey, buddy, it's good to see you're still kicking. Your replacement as my partner is a real piece of work."

By now, the man in the bed had become used to everyone calling him Paul, even though he was sure it wasn't his name. He also couldn't remember being a policeman. His last memory was being a soldier in Afghanistan, if that memory was his at all.

"Just to update you," the policeman continued, "the post-shooting investigation has cleared you of all culpability. Everyone agreed the scumbag you shot should never have been included in that round of budget cut prisoner dumps. All because his boys clammed up and they couldn't prove he was the one responsible for your wife and kids' deaths."

"Karen's dead?" That last sentence, coming from the policeman who seemed to be a friend even though "Paul" didn't recognize him, got the confused man's attention.

"Karen? Who's Karen? You mean Judith?"

"Yeah, yeah, I meant Judith." Judith? Who was Judith? Did he get remarried after he found out his wife had lied and really *had* cheated on him?

"Well, buddy, I've got to get back to work." The visitor stood but stopped and turned around before leaving the room. "Oh, and don't worry. Because of those powers of attorney we signed for each other, I've been keeping your apartment and mini-storage rents up for you. It's lucky you woke up. I was just about to let them go."

Mid-afternoon, Mara, the teen volunteer in the blue vest, came bouncing into the room. Without asking, she threw her arms around his neck and kissed his cheek. "I never got the chance to properly thank you the other day for saving my life." She glanced back toward the door. "Don't tell anyone I just did that. Volunteers aren't supposed to touch the patients. Today, I'm going to read or play games with you to get your mind working again. Don't try to say no. The longer I'm needed here, the later they make me return to the group home. So, you're stuck with me."

A month passed. Physicians, shrinks, and physical therapists took turns torturing him. He had accepted being called Paul Taft even though that name seemed to fit a cousin better. In fact, that was what puzzled the professionals the most. Paul knew more about his maternal cousin's life than he did his own. It was almost as if he was viewing his life through that cousin's eyes and not his. Even *those* memories went blank nearly a decade before.

He became adept at making conversation with a daily parade of coworkers and friends he did not recognize. The only person Paul felt a connection with was Mara. He reasoned that they bonded because she was just as lost in life as he was. As she escorted him on one of his exercise walks around the facility, she broke the rules and told him how they both got to where they were.

"The guy you shot kept my mom addicted so he could pimp her out. When she OD'd, he decided I needed to take her place. He found my hiding spot and was dragging me to his car when you came along and rescued me." After her confession, they walked in silence for a few minutes. Finally, she spoke again. "I heard that he was the one you think was responsible for your whole family being killed. Is that true?"

Paul shrugged and replied, "I guess. That's what they tell me."

Re-entering the building, they were met by the man Paul had been told was his supervising captain in the department. "We need to talk." The man pointed into an office with one person waiting inside. "Have you had any further memory recall of your law enforcement training?"

Paul shook his head and replied, "No."

The captain shrugged and continued, "Yeah, that's what your doctors put in your evaluation. I hate to do this, but since you can't remember any of your training, it makes you a liability to the department. We're going to have to cut you loose. You don't qualify for full retirement, but you'll receive medical disability. I'd better get going. I have other hot irons in the fire. Feel free to contact the resource office if you have any questions."

The man left so quickly, Paul couldn't ask a single question. The other person in the room was the facility's customer relations representative. Her news wasn't much better.

"Because you're no longer classified as active duty, your billing will change. Because the therapists have noted in your file that they consider you mentally competent and physically able, I suggest you start doing outpatient rehab."

Mara was waiting down the hallway when Paul came out of the office with a lost look on his face. "I hear they're giving you the boot." Her voice cracked. "I don't want to lose you too."

"From what they tell me, I'll be back here almost every day to do rehab for a while. We'll still see each other. Right now, you're my best friend."

Her grin lit up the hallway. Mara refused to leave his side as he looked up and called his partner's phone number listed in the center's contact list. She helped pack his personal possessions and kept him company until his partner's shift ended. Forlornly waving, Mara watched them drive away.

His partner wouldn't stop talking. "Boy, it's a good thing I kept up your apartment rent. Do you want to pick up your car on the way? I put it in the same lot your mini-storage is at. It probably needs a jump by now. I'm not sure, but I think some cables are in my trunk."

This was getting to be too much for Paul. Not only was the man beside him getting on his nerves, but not a single thing along their route looked familiar. The fog of confusion was starting to set in again, so he closed his eyes and replied, "No. Just take me to my place so I can settle in again."

His partner didn't want to accept that answer from his long-time friend. "We should stop and have a beer." When Paul shook his head, the man suggested, "How about we stop and pick up a six pack? I can help you open the place back up."

"No, thank you." Paul blankly looked back out the window as the unfamiliar streets passed by. "If you don't mind, just show me which place is mine. Then, if it's alright with you, I'd like some alone time to acclimate to the outside world."

"Sure, buddy. No problem."

After his partner left, Paul wandered around the unfamiliar, cluttered apartment. It was a good thing the place was small, or he wouldn't have been able to find the bathroom. Opening the fridge, he sighed. Because of spoilage, his partner had thrown away anything edible. Backing away, his elbow struck the small counter and brushed a folder onto the floor.

Angrily gathering the paperwork and stuffing it back into the folder, he read the file title. Quickly spreading the evidence list, interview transcripts, and head investigator's name in the Pressure Washer Killer case file, it hit him like a blinding light on a dark night.

Paul knew exactly who he was and what had happened to him.

CHAPTER TWENTY-TWO
CARRIE'S SPIRAL

After seeing Bill at Mandy's party, realizing he had moved on and found love, Carrie's anger toward him boiled to the surface again. Everything not right with her life at the moment could be traced back to his initial betrayal of her trust—including the stubbed toe she acquired getting out of the shower that morning.

Her waitressing job was hard work, but had its upsides. Carrie's customer service skills garnered her a lot of tips. Being a cute, young, petite blonde got her even larger tips from the male clientele. The restaurant was also a good place to meet guys. For six months, Carrie received at least one request a day to go on a date. Resentment, the only exception to her emotional void, and needing male confirmation, she accepted more than a few.

The boss cracked down when the older waitresses complained about her overt flirting with the customers. "You need to bring it back a little with the customers. You'll give the place a bad name."

Carrie turned twenty-one the next week. For her birthday, she went bar hopping with a couple fun-loving coworkers. A new world opened up. Not much caring for alcohol, it was still fun to sip on a soda while guys hit on her. She didn't even need money—just buy the first drink and the rest magically appeared.

At first, Carrie only went to bars every now and then when depressed. Not wanting contact with her old friends and having no real new ones, her self-esteem continued its downward spiral. Her constant need for a man's attention, even if for an hour or two, drove her even lower. No one wanted to be with her more than just once.

"I've seen you around." A handsome man in his early thirties sat at one of Carrie's booths in the restaurant. "Can I buy you a drink after work?"

She smiled at him. "Sure, why not?"

"Name's Rod," he said. "What time do you get off work?"

She met Rod in the restaurant's lounge at the end of her shift. Having given up on being coy a long time ago, Carrie scooted next to Rod. Not anywhere near Nicolas's level, this guy still appeared more charming and well-spoken than anyone else she had met lately. He seemed interested in more than a quick trip to a motel room. Having to work the next day, she became impatient with the chat.

"Can we talk somewhere else? I need to get up early tomorrow."

"Well, *that* was blunt." Rod smiled. "Yeah, my place is only a few blocks from here."

"That's not what I meant." It was. "It's just that it's so noisy in here. It's hard to talk."

This man was different. He didn't kick Carrie out immediately after using her. Instead, Rod insisted she stay the night. For the first time in a long while, she had a second date with someone. Then a third and fourth. It wasn't long before he insisted she move in with him. Carrie started to smile again.

"Why don't you quit that job of yours?" Rod asked after a couple of months. "I can't stand watching all of the guys making eyes at you."

She shrugged. "I can't control what other people do. It's my job to be nice to people, and their tips are more than half the money I make."

"Nice?" Suddenly, Rod started yelling. "Nice is smiling politely and walking away. You're winking at them, patting them on their arm, and shaking your butt as much as possible to get them to drool while you walk away!"

"Whaa?"

"Don't try and deny it! I saw how you flirted with that table of guys yesterday." He slapped her. "You are *my* girl! I won't have you flirting with all those other men, trying to get them to sleep with you!"

Cheek stinging, Carrie staggered back. With a flash of anger, she returned his slap. "You can't treat me like this. You especially won't ever hit me!"

Rod's roundhouse punch sent her to the floor, striking her shoulder on the coffee table. Carrie scrambled backward into the kitchenette and sat back against the refrigerator, cowering.

"Oh my god! I'm sorry." Rod knelt and kissed the top of her head. "It just drives me insane to see you around other men."

"Get away from me." Pushing free, Carrie stood and went into the bathroom to look at her bruised face.

That isolated incident became more common, soon almost a daily occurrence. At first, she thought it was her fault and made an effort to dial back her interactions with the male customers. Her tips fell as she became brusque with customers. Less money coming in also triggered her boyfriend.

While she applied concealer makeup before work one day, Rod stood in the bathroom door. "You need to quit that waitress job. It makes me do crazy things like what I just did."

Trying to gain some breathing room to think, Carrie evasively replied, "I'll put in my notice tomorrow."

"No. You'll just quit." Rod kissed the top of her head again. "You'll do it today."

Not letting her out of his sight, Rod drove Carrie to work and watched from the restaurant's kitchen entrance. The boss wasn't in yet, so she talked to Nadine, the shift's head waitress. "Something's come up. I have to quit."

"No problem, hon," the jaded older woman answered. "We'll be sorry to see you go. When would you like your final day to be?"

"I'm sorry, but today."

"Crap. The boss ain't gonna like that," the head waitress replied.

She'd been around the block a few times and had seen just about every problem pass through the booths she waited on. Even with dark sunglasses and all of the extra makeup plastered on, there was no hiding how Carrie favored her shoulder. Then, there was the hovering boyfriend in the doorway. "You coming back for your check? It should be ready by noon."

"No. Just mail it."

"What's your address?" Nadine wasn't just going to let her co-worker become another faceless victim. "Just to make sure it's mailed to the right spot."

"My P.O. box is on file." Carrie hurried out.

"Crap," Nadine muttered to herself. Ripping off her apron, she yelled to the next most senior waitress. "Cover my station. I'll be back in a bit."

"But . . ." the other waitress was just talking to air. Nadine had already run out the back door.

Knowing the city like the back of her hand, Nadine didn't have a problem following Carrie's car. There just weren't that many intersecting arterials in that section of town. After Rod parked at an apartment complex and pulled Carrie by the arm into the building, Nadine drove through the lot and wrote down the reserved parking slot's number.

The experienced woman quickly returned to work and burst into the manager's office. "I need to see Carrie's file."

"That's supposed to be private info," the manager protested. "I can't just let anyone see it."

"I don't want to read the whole damn thing. I just want to see if there's any emergency contact numbers."

Mandy's phone rang.

After a week of Rod following while she looked for new employment, Carrie was getting discouraged. The apartment's rent would be due soon. Even though the waitress job wasn't what she had envisioned as a lifetime career, she liked her coworkers. She missed interacting with the public. She desperately wanted to be out from under Rod's constant surveillance.

Rod walked into the kitchen. "Cheer up. You'll find something that fits your skills."

"Doing what?" All Carrie wanted to do at the moment was get out of that apartment. "Just what am I qualified for?"

"You can make more money working from home."

"Doing what? I wouldn't know what to do."

"I have some ideas." Rod was interrupted by a knock on the door. He let in a mountain of a man she'd seen before in the bars. The man tried to pick her up a few times, but Carrie had the impression he was a sleazeball, below even her standards—and he scared her. "Come in. Carrie, this is Lance. He'll be our guest tonight."

"*Tonight?*" She didn't like the sound of this. It was only a one-bedroom apartment. "Where's he going to sleep?"

"Excuse us for a minute, Lance." Rod pulled Carrie into the bedroom and closed the door. "Remember the part about you working from home? Lance has the hots for you. He offered me a thousand bucks to service you."

"*What?* You made me quit my waitress job because you didn't like men looking at me." Carrie pointed at the door to the living room. "Now you say you want me to *have sex* with another man?"

"You made it obvious you want to sleep around. I don't know those other guys. Lance is a trusted friend." Rod shrugged. "Besides, we need the money, and I'll be right here to make sure you're safe."

"Well, he can keep his money. I'm not a whore. I'm not doing it!" Carrie headed for the living room door to tell Lance he'd wasted his time. Rod grabbed her arm, spun her around, and slapped her. Shoving Carrie on the bed, he bent over, holding her chin.

"You're not being a whore, baby. I really need the money." Rod kissed her forehead. "Do this because you love me."

"Please don't make me," she pleaded.

"Remember how good it feels when I give you my approval." Rod helped Carrie to her feet. "Now, go fix your makeup. Unbutton that blouse."

Rod held her from behind so she couldn't run when Lance came into the room and undressed with a sadistic look on his face. Then, both men forced her onto the bed where Rod held her arms above her head.

Wasting no time in getting down to business, Lance roughly flung his victim into different positions just because he could. Terrified, impotent to stop what was happening, she kept her eyes closed with tears running down the side of her face.

When she finally opened her eyes, Carrie saw Rod had brought in a chair and his laptop. Watching from just a few feet away, he leaned forward and locked eyes with her. While she wondered why her boyfriend was subjecting her to this brutal degradation, he grinned, ecstatically witnessing her being "thoroughly serviced."

After letting Lance out of the apartment, Rod sat on the bed next to Carrie, stroking her hair. "You *really* liked that didn't you? I saw it in your eyes. I bet you can't wait to do it again with someone else. Go clean up, and let's get some sleep."

Too numb to cry while she showered, Carrie wondered why her boyfriend had done this to her. How was it possible he could enjoy seeing her with another man? Whose idea was it? It certainly wasn't hers.

The next morning, while Rod was distracted talking on his phone, she crept around the apartment discreetly looking for her purse and car keys. Determined to get away from what Rod had become, she would make a run as soon as his back was turned.

"Are you looking for this?" He held up her purse. "You won't be needing it. I've found you a job!"

Now that he'd revealed his darker side, she knew something wasn't right. She asked, "Doing what?"

He had a huge grin. "The same as last night. You're a natural."

"No. You're not turning me into a prostitute. I won't do it."

Rod lost it. He didn't stop with just slapping Carrie around a little. He punched her, flung her into a door jam, and kicked her. He knelt over the scared, crying young woman curled in a fetal position on the bedroom floor. "I've got dates lined up for you almost every night." He kissed the top of her head. "You know I love you, don't you? Who else is going to love you like I do? Do this because you love me."

"I do love you," Carrie lied, sobbing. She would say anything at that moment to get away.

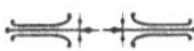

"Bill, I need your help," Mandy pleaded over the phone. "Why haven't you been answering your messages?"

"I've been busy," he answered. "With Randy laid up and Beth taking care of him, it's just been your dad and Ricky taking care of the ranch."

"How's he doing?"

"The doctors have his infection under control. They're talking about operating on his leg this week to put the pin in."

"How's Beth doing?" With all that had happened to the Bennetts, Mandy hated to add more worry to their plate. "Where's she staying during all of this?"

"She's at one of her art friend's in Spokane. Since there's no stairs in the house, she's planning to keep Randy there for the first part of his rehab." Bill became suspicious. His stepsister could have gleaned all of this from his mother a week ago. "What's the real reason you called me?"

There was no easy way to do this, so Mandy just spit it out. "Carrie's in trouble."

"Again? So, it's situation normal." Anger, resentment, loss, pity, jealousy, a jumble of emotions hit him all at once. "What do you want me to do about it?" he growled, then softened. "Where is she?"

"Here. In Spokane."

"Go talk to her. You're her friend, not me. Tell Beth." Bill almost got himself killed the last time he helped his ex-friend and hadn't received a word of thanks. Instead, Carrie blamed him for ruining her life again. The mere mention of her name was painful. "Leave me out of it."

Mandy pleaded, "I can't. I can't tell Beth. They already have too much to deal with. Bill . . . she's in real trouble. Maybe worse than she was in Greece. Please."

"I'll think about it." He paused for a moment. "If I do agree to help, it won't be for a couple of weeks. We're right in the middle of the second cutting of hay. You know how that is."

"Just come as soon as you can."

CHAPTER TWENTY-THREE
BOTTOM

Rod never left Carrie unattended while she recovered from his beatings. If he had to leave, Lance came to the apartment and "watched" her. Watching was the men's euphemism for Lance using her. When her body had almost healed, she woke in the middle of the night with Rod passed out on the bed. Quietly, she dressed and filled an overnight bag. As she reached for the front door deadbolt, the hall light came on.

"Where're you going?"

"I needed some air, so I was going to take a walk."

While healing from this new beating, Rod forced her to stay at Lance's rural house "for her own protection." Protection from what? Rod was the one hitting her. Running wasn't an option. Lance kept her locked in a room when he left to buy building supplies for a remodeling project in his basement. At least he had a fluffy little dog that kept her distracted. Carrie slept in Lance's bed because that's what Rod ordered.

Surprised that Lance, although by no means gentle, was considerably less brutal during her stay than their first encounter, Carrie summoned up the courage to ask him why. Not having *that* much courage, she waited until after he expended most of his energy on her. She didn't want to rock the boat while waiting for an escape opportunity.

"Why are you being so nice to me?"

"Rod said I couldn't bruise you while you're here." Lance lay on his back thinking for a minute. "Since no one's watching, I don't have to act all macho."

Rest time over, Carrie initiated round two, knowing what he omitted. If they were left alone and he wasn't worried about her bruising, there would be nothing stopping him from being brutal again.

Two weeks since her last beating, it was time to return to Rod's place. Her facial bruises had almost healed, but her shoulder still hurt at times. Putting on her makeup in front of the toothpaste splattered mirror, Carrie was scared how Rod would react when she told him her newest secret. Convinced he only wanted her because she was cute, young, and innocent-looking, she needed to tell him before she started showing. Bruises ruined the illusion. A bulging belly would only make it worse.

A young girl was coming out of the building as Lance escorted Carrie from his car. It appeared like the girl came out of her boyfriend's apartment.

"Who was that?" Carrie watched the strange girl walking away.

Rod snapped at her, "Don't get all in my face about something that doesn't concern you. I'm in a good mood about a sure-fire deal. Clean up around here. I'll be back later."

She wondered what his new scheme was now. He'd locked the apartment door from the outside and taken away her phone, so she sat at the dinette and fiddled with his computer. For all his bravado, Rod didn't have much in the way of computer savvy. His password was almost as simple to figure out as knowing what brand of beer he preferred.

The first things popping up on his saved list were porn sites offering money for "amateur" videos. Carrie rolled her eyes, then it hit her. She went into his saved video files and found one for every time Rod made her have sex with Lance—from multiple angles. There were more recent videos of him and that young girl.

Without considering the consequences, Carrie erased the videos. She was in the bedroom searching for the cameras when Rod came home.

"Oh, good. You're dressed and looking real nice." Rod kissed her and set down some bags from an electronics store on the table. "I'll be right back. I've got another load to bring up from the car."

She looked in the bags. He'd purchased a higher end video camera and two microphones.

"What's the video equipment for?" Carrie asked when he returned with bags from an adult toy store.

"I'm going to take videos of you posing all sexy." He walked into the bedroom. She followed.

"I'm not posing for any pictures. I don't want the whole world seeing me naked."

"Sure you will. It'll be fun." He dumped the bags out on the bed.

Carrie stared at the assortment of adult toys, some of which she could only guess what their intended purpose was. When he emptied the second bag with ropes and a gag, it was too much.

"What's that stuff for? You're not using *any* of that on me!"

"Oh, I'm not." Rod grinned. "Since you've been having such a good time with Lance, we're going out to his house later. He's built a room where he's going to really, *really* service you on film."

"No, *that's* not happening!"

"Sure it is." Rod arranged the toys on the bed. "That's why you've been at his house. He's been practicing on you."

So shocked that her recuperation time had actually been rehearsals, all she could do was mutter, "What?"

"We wanted to make sure you do everything right." Rod was gleeful. "Come on! You know it'll make me happy. You want to please me, don't you?"

"Not anymore." Beyond being crushed, Carrie was now desperate.

"It doesn't matter. Lance was trying out new stuff on you while I was auditioning your possible replacements here."

"*Replacements?*" Carrie was almost speechless. "What's the gag for?"

"He's going to tie you to a special contraption he designed and use all these new toys on you. You're *bound* to make a lot of noise." Rod was tickled with himself. "We don't want to disturb the neighbors with you screaming in pleasure, do we?"

"I'm *not* doing this!" Having sex with another man was one thing. Being tortured was another.

"Sure you are." Rod walked into the kitchen to assemble his electronic equipment. "You're so pretty, we're going to make a lot of money. In fact, if the videos with Lance work out like I planned, my next video will be you with a whole bunch of guys at the same time."

"I told you, I'm not doing it!" Regaining a tiny portion of her self-worth, Carrie put on her shoes to leave.

"You have to, babe. We need to get them done before you're too old to be merchantable."

"*Too old?*" She was dumbstruck. "Is that what that girl was doing here? Is she even legal age?"

"It's not like that at all, babe. We have to finish your video series. You're just getting too old-looking to bring in the big money."

"There aren't any videos to sell," Carrie spit out without thinking. "I found and erased them all."

"*You did what?*" he yelled.

"I erased them. I don't want to be a whore." Carrie pleaded, "Don't make me into a whore."

"*Make you into a whore?*" Rod exploded. Grabbing her hair, he flung her to the kitchen floor. "*You were already a whore when I met you, you stupid bitch! You just weren't charging for it!*"

He yanked Carrie to her feet by her hair then punched her in the face. "I took you in when no one else would have you!" Holding her by the throat against the refrigerator with one hand, he started slapping her. "This is how you pay back my kindness?" Slap. "This is how you show your love for me?" Slap. "You've been planning this all along, haven't you?" Slap. "You build up my dreams for a better future for us." Slap. "Then you destroy all my work?" Slap. "It was *my* work!" Slap. "You just laid there!"

"Stop! I want to go back to Lance's."

"No problem! I've already sold you to him. After the videos, you're *his* property. He's not going to be nearly as nice to you as I've been when he takes full ownership of you." Rod threw Carrie on the floor again and started kicking her. Curled into a fetal position, she tried to protect her head with her arms. "You worthless bitch! No wonder no one loves you!"

CHAPTER TWENTY-FOUR
AGAIN?

Bill and Mandy followed Nadine from the restaurant to the apartment complex parking lot. Nadine pointed at Carrie's car. "That's hers. She's probably in the apartment with the same number as the space."

Leaving his truck double parked behind Carrie's car, Bill and Mandy entered the ground floor alcove servicing four apartments, two on each floor. An elderly woman with a walker stood outside one of the doors with a shaking hand over her mouth, crying. Mandy showed her a picture of Carrie.

"Do you know this girl? Do you know which apartment she's in?"

The woman nodded and pointed to the door she was beside. "In there."

Bill pounded on the door. A man's voice answered, "Go away! We're busy!"

A crash and a thud came from the apartment. Bill didn't knock again, kicking the door open. Not knowing for sure if the curled up bloody girl at the man's feet was his ex-friend, he was enraged to see any woman in that position. When the young woman's arms parted just enough for him to see her terrified eyes, he lost all self-control. Seeing only red, Bill attacked her assailant.

Mandy ran into the apartment to rescue Carrie. Nadine dialed 911.

After pulling Carrie to relative safety on the building's sidewalk, Mandy checked over her friend. Not quite fully conscious, Carrie flinched every time someone tried to touch her. Nadine put her hand on Mandy's back.

"You better get in there and stop your brother before he kills someone."

For the first time, the noise coming from inside the apartment actually registered. Mandy glanced around at the half dozen apartment building residents gathering nearby, not lifting a finger to help.

Nadine nodded toward the door. "Go. I've got it handled out here."

Rod's street smarts and experience were useless against an insane bull of a young man who had a six-inch height advantage and fifty pounds more of in-shape body mass. Bill flung the older man around the apartment like he would a moldy bale of straw toward the compost pile. Mandy grabbed Bill's arm.

"Stop! You'll kill him! Stop!"

Focused on the demon before him, Bill brushed his sister aside like he would a biting horse fly from his ear. Mandy picked herself up from the floor and jumped on Bill's back. Wrapping her arms and legs around him, she tried desperately to get through.

"Stop! Please, Bill, stop," she pleaded to the back of his head. When he slowed a bit, she tried to be as calming as possible. "That's it, bro. Easy . . . eeeasy. Calm down. I don't want you heading to jail instead of that scumbag."

Rod obviously wasn't going anywhere soon. So, Bill let her lead him outside.

Kneeling beside Carrie, Nadine looked up. "I've got this. You two need to get out of here before the cops arrive."

Too late. Police cars flooded into the parking lot. Officers bailed out of their cars with unholstered weapons pointing at the obvious threat, the blood splattered young man standing over a bloody girl.

"Hands up! Get on your knees!"

"He's not the criminal!" The elderly woman moved her walker between Bill and the officers. "He's just a passerby who was trying to save this poor girl from an insane attacker."

"Up against the wall!" The first officer pinned Bill against a wall. Two others cautiously entered the apartment, weapons at the ready.

One called back, "Holy crap! We're going to need the paramedics on this one."

A bystander yelled, "The old lady's right. I saw the whole thing."

"Yeah!" another onlooker agreed. "That guy's a danger to society and needs to be locked in an asylum!"

Instantly, all half dozen of the looky-loos became witnesses. The cops smiled. Normally in domestic violence cases it was his word against hers. The woman almost always refused to file charges. With this many witnesses all pointing a finger at the guy resembling a soft pretzel lying in a puddle of salsa, Rod was at least going to spend a night in jail—after he got out of the hospital. But they at least had to ask.

A female officer kneeled beside Carrie. "Do you want to press charges?"

"No," Carrie sobbed. "I shouldn't have made him mad. I shouldn't have said no."

"When you say you shouldn't have said no," the officer put a comforting hand on Carrie's arm, "are you referring to the ropes, gag, and other paraphernalia we found in the apartment? Did you say no to him using them on you?"

"I said no to his friend using that stuff on me while Rod recorded it." Carrie looked plaintively at the officer. "I shouldn't have said no. I shouldn't have erased the videos from his computer. Now it's my fault he's hurt, and you people are all here."

Overhearing the interrogation, Mandy and Nadine hugged each other in shock. They had only met a few hours before, but both shared the common bond of the broken girl sitting on the concrete. Off to the side being grilled by other officers, Bill didn't hear.

Once Rod had been carted off in an ambulance and Carrie had been checked out by paramedics and refused further treatment, the lead female officer took Mandy and Bill aside. "Okay, you two are free to go, but don't leave the county. We'll need to question you further."

Bill apologized, "I'm sorry, officer, but I can't do that. I have a ranch to run in the Palouse."

"I could keep you here behind bars until we get this sorted out." The officer wasn't amused.

"What my brother is trying to say," Mandy put her hand on Bill's arm and took over the conversation, "is that Carrie's dad is laid up and Bill's keeping their ranch going. I live here in town so you can contact me anytime. It's only a ninety-minute drive for him to get here when he's needed."

"So, your families know each other?" Looking at Carrie, the officer asked, "What about her?"

"Our mother is a nurse practitioner and her cousin is a doctor who run a clinic together." Mandy led the officer aside. "Our two families have known each other for years. Bill and Carrie were inseparable in school. He flew to Europe and rescued her from another bad situation a few years ago. We've been trying to help her, but she's fallen into a black hole."

The officer said sympathetically, "It sounds like she couldn't be in better hands."

"We're taking her home." Mandy wistfully glanced at her friend. "We might have to hogtie her and throw her in the trunk, but she's going home."

"I didn't hear that! Yayayaya." The officer turned to walk away with her hands over her ears. Glancing back, she smiled kindly. "Good luck."

The officers stood by while Carrie's friends packed her stuff. Mandy picked up a phone on the floor and opened it to see if it was Carrie's. It wasn't. Scanning the covert photos of her friend, Mandy made a decision. Somehow, the phone was "accidentally" dropped into the toilet and flushed.

"You guys got this?" Nadine hugged Mandy. "I need to get back to work."

"Yeah, we'll get her home. Maybe this time she'll stay in counseling. Mandy hugged back. "Thank you for calling me."

"I've seen this a lot in my line of work." Nadine sadly looked toward Carrie. "It's rare that the victim has friends to fall back on like you guys. Let me know how she does. Stop in the diner anytime. There's a free cup of coffee waiting."

Mandy and Bill got into it back at her apartment while Carrie napped in the spare room. Mandy adamantly insisted, "You've *got* to take her back to the ranch."

"Me? Why am I always the one to bail her out? She hates me." He shook his head and threw up an arm. "Call her parents."

"You know I can't do that. They're already going through too much." Mandy pulled her stepbrother into the kitchen. "She needs to get out of the city. I can't keep my eyes on her all the time and also go to work. She needs to go home away from all of this."

"Crap. Load her up. It'll be after dark by the time we get to the ranch. I'll have to call your dad and Ricky to do the evening chores."

Relieved, Mandy said, "Al and I will go get her car and park it here. We'll bring it down in a few weeks when we have the time."

Bill and Carrie hadn't made it past the city limits before they started to bicker. She unhooked her shoulder belt and shifted uncomfortably in the seat. He scowled sideways. "Put that back on. I don't want to get a ticket."

"No. I hurts my shoulder," she mumbled. "Besides, I'm of age. I'll get the ticket instead of you." They rode on in silence for a while until he turned off the freeway onto a state highway heading south. "Where're you going?"

"Home."

"You're going the wrong way." She looked back toward the freeway. "I thought you lived in Moses Lake."

"No. I live on your ranch now. That's where we're going."

"*No*! *No*! Don't take me there! I don't want to see my parents."

When Carrie grabbed for the door handle, he yanked her back into the seat and growled, "You don't have to worry about that. They won't be there for quite a while yet."

"Yet? Where are they? An art show?"

"You don't know?" His mouth fell open as he glanced at her. "Just how long has it been since you talked to them?"

"Last August." Carrie watched the lack of scenery pass by her window. "Just before I was supposed to start the fall semester."

"*Eleven months*? You haven't talked to your parents in over eleven months?"

"So? What business is it of yours?" She sat silently for a few moments. "Why? Where are they?"

Bill mumbled, "Back in Spokane."

"Spokane? If they're in Spokane, why didn't you just dump me off with them? We could have been rid of each other."

"Because they don't need to deal with your crap right now!" he snapped. Calming a little, he continued, "Your dad was crushed in a farming accident almost two months ago. He had a compound fracture of his femur then developed a deep tissue infection. The doctors had to get the infection under control before they operated to put his leg back together. He broke his upper arm and screwed up his shoulder too. He's wheelchair bound until his arm heels enough for crutches. They're staying with a friend of your mom's while he does rehab."

"Take me back. I need to see them!"

"No. I told you. They don't need to deal with your crap right now." He scowled at her again. "You haven't talked to them in a year. Another month won't kill you."

"My whole life's a pile of crap because of you! You cheated on me," she sobbed.

"I flew halfway around the world to apologize to you about that. I dragged your butt home to safety. This round's all on you. Deal with it."

For the remainder of the drive to the ranch, Carrie curled up in the passenger seat, clutching her stomach in pain, quietly crying. Bill parked by the ranch house's back door to carry her stuff in. Coming out of the house after the first trip with boxes, he was miffed she hadn't even opened the door on her side of the truck.

"Get out! At least you could help pack your own junk."

"I . . . can't," she whispered. "I can't move. It hurts too much."

"Right. You're going in if I have to carry you." Roughly yanking Carrie out of the truck, he picked her up. "Crap! You're all wet! What'd you do? Piss yourself?" He looked at his hand. "It's blood! You're bleeding!"

Placing her back in the truck, he called his mom to ask what to do. Following Karen's advice, he gently packed Carrie to her room and laid her on the bed. A half hour later, Karen came back down the stairs.

"She should be okay. She just needs someone close by to monitor her."

"We don't need to take her to the hospital?" For the first time in a long while, Bill sounded concerned about his ex-friend. "She took a hell of a beating. If she's not bleeding internally, what's the matter with her?"

"I can't tell you." Karen hugged her son. "HIPAA rules won't allow me to divulge that information."

Bill pushed back from his mother. He'd been around animal husbandry almost half his life. There weren't that many ailments where a female mammal bled so much in that location and didn't need a hospital. His mother's expression confirmed his suspicion without him asking.

"Carrie just had a miscarriage, didn't she?"

Karen patted her son's arm. "Keep an eye on her. I'll be back in the morning."

CHAPTER TWENTY-FIVE
WHERE DO WE START?

Her whole body aching, Carrie woke as lighter skies began pushing aside morning twilight. The maxi-pad Karen gave her had long since soaked through, and the towels spread out beneath her were stained. She needed to pee. She needed to shower.

Rolling out of bed, she stumbled toward her bedroom door with one eye swollen shut, the other blurred. Blindly reaching for the doorknob, she tripped over a large mass on the floor and twisted her already sprained wrist. Gasping in pain, she kicked the lump on the floor.

"Stupid dog! What the hell are you doing in the house, much less my bedroom!"

What she thought was the dog groaned, rolled over and sat up. Only getting an hour or so of sleep, Bill rubbed his eyes. "It's a little early to try and sneak out, isn't it?"

"Sneak out? What the hell are you talking about? Why're you on my bedroom floor?"

"Preventing you from trying to do exactly what you're doing—running again."

"I'm not running, you idiot!" Woozy from the effort of yelling, Carrie staggered. "I need to pee."

Bill caught her. "Come on. I'll help you to the bathroom." He led her to the toilet and turned to go, but she stumbled and fell against the vanity. "Here." He held her arm. "I'll close my eyes and turn my back while you do your business."

She started to cry. "I need a shower, but I don't know if I can stand up."

"Stay seated. I'll run you a bath and help you into the tub when it's full. Where's your bubble stuff?"

"It's usually under the vanity. How'm I supposed to get undressed and get into the tub with you here?"

Bill started to say, "Since when has being naked in front of guys bothered you?" Instead, he bit his tongue, mainly because *he* didn't want to see *her* without clothing. "Just get in wearing your nightie. It looks like it could also use a washing."

After helping her into the tub, he sat on the toilet looking the other way.

Carrie needed to talk to someone, anyone. "Why're you doing this? Isn't there someone else you could delegate? What about your sister Heather?"

"Heather's busy. She's over at the Neufeld's helping Helen take care of Jacob."

"Yeah, but why you? We hate each other."

"Because you're the daughter of my neighbors." He held himself back from using the word for her that he really meant: exfriend. "That's what we do out here."

"Ow, ow." Carrie winced when she tried lifting her arms high enough to wash her hair.

"Here, let me." Bill sat on the edge of the tub and wet her hair with a cup. He gently lathered her hair with baby shampoo and rinsed again. Using a washcloth, he cleaned around her facial bruising.

"Where'd you learn to do this?" she asked but already knew. She'd seen him with that other girl at Mandy's party. It was obvious they were a serious couple. Carrie winced again. This time it wasn't from him touching her bruising. It was from the sting of Bill not using the word "friend" when referring to her, even with an "ex" in front of it. "Where's the girl I saw you with last summer? Are you two still together?"

That was it. He had to leave. "It's time to get out. I'll keep my eyes closed while I help you back onto the toilet." After helping her stand and remove her wet nightie, he handed her a towel over his shoulder. "I'll be back with some dry clothes."

Even though it hurt, she had to smile when all he returned with was a sweatshirt, a pair of her old sweatpants, and the stack of maxi pads his mother left. "That's it? I need underwear."

I didn't think you wanted to stain anything else." Returning with the panties, he grunted, "I'll be in the kitchen cooking breakfast. You shouldn't try walking down the stairs. Scoot on your butt."

Carrie silently sat at the kitchen table trying to eat breakfast. Her jaw hurt too much chewing toast, so she just squished scrambled eggs between her teeth. After watching Bill angrily cleaning up the kitchen for a while, she finally asked, "How'd Dad get hurt?"

"He'd taken the swather's cutting head off to work on before the haying season started. One end of it was suspended from the shop hoist. The clevis on the end of the cable failed, and all fourteen feet of the thing landed on him. He's lucky it missed his chest and only broke his left arm and screwed up his shoulder. Otherwise, it would've killed him."

"Oh, crap," Carrie muttered. "I thought you said he needed a wheelchair. I was so out of it last night, maybe I didn't hear right."

"You heard right. His left leg wasn't so lucky. When the head fell on him, his leg was stretched over a toolbox. His femur got a compound fracture. With the bone sticking out like that, he developed a deep tissue infection. He almost lost the leg. They had him on antibiotics for a week before they operated to pin the bone."

"I didn't know." Carrie pushed around the remaining food on her plate with a fork.

Bill almost said, "Because you were so selfishly wrapped up in your own needy world." Instead, he muttered, "I have to do morning chores. First, I have to change my shirt."

Instead of walking out to the bunkhouse, he headed up the stairs. When he returned in work clothes, she asked, "You're not staying in the bunkhouse?"

"No. Your mother wanted me to sleep in the spare room and keep the main house up. We didn't have time to get the bunkhouse ready . . . I've got to get to work."

"Can I help?"

He growled, "You even remember how?" Then, he took a softer tone. "If you can walk well enough, the eggs could be gathered. Those damn chickens still peck me."

For the first time in a long while, she smiled at him, although it was his back as he left the kitchen. It was good to know that some things in life hadn't changed, even if it was only Bill's contentious relationship with chickens.

She had just finished washing and putting the eggs in the refrigerator when Bill came into the kitchen with a bucket of milk. "Why are you bringing that in here instead of the milkhouse?"

"In case you hadn't noticed," Bill mumbled. "There's no one around here to drink it. Mom and Lynnette take some for the boys. The rest is dumped in the pigpen."

"Pigpen?"

"Oh, that's right. You're never here, so you have no clue what your family's doing." Bill poured the milk into a couple of gallon jars. "Your dad and Charlie decided raising a couple of butcher hogs was a good idea. Charlie moved the blacksmith shop to our place, and the old goat shed is now part of the pigpen."

"Oh . . ." She was about to ask another question, but he headed for the door with the remaining milk.

"Mom'll be by in a bit to get the milk. She said she'd check you over again then."

After Karen left, Carrie wandered into the stables to watch Bill muck out the stalls. "I don't see my horse. I thought I'd curry her and get reacquainted."

With her presence causing an unexpected tangle of emotions, he couldn't look at her. Staring down at the pitchfork load of manure, his self-control lapsed, and he growled, "Dead. Not that you'd care. You haven't ridden her in over three years."

She wasn't shocked even though she knew he was intentionally being cruel. The mare was old and had been on the ranch as long as Carrie could remember. The news still saddened her.

"Where did all these other horses come from?" She stood in front of her old mare's usual stall. "This one's beautiful."

"You know your dad boards other people's horses." Softening a bit, Bill started to deflect, giving a complete answer to spare her feelings, then changed his mind. Why should he care? "That one's Willa's. The one next to it is her dad's."

"*Willa's?*" Carrie hated that girl for getting between her and Bill. "What are *their* horses doing here?"

"I worked for her dad in Moses Lake until Jennie dumped me. Then I moved back here to caretake his corporate farm's properties. When your father got hurt, I quit and brought their horses here with me." He glanced sideways at her. "Unlike some people, I don't abandon others simply because things get complicated."

Starting to cramp again, Carrie walked out of the stables holding her stomach. Needing to get away from Bill, she climbed into the old dually to drive to town. The keys were gone. Keys weren't in the old two-ton truck or even the UTV. In desperation, she looked in Bill's old pickup. No key there either.

Still in pain, she stormed back into the stables. "Where the *hell* are all the keys?"

"I hid them," Bill answered, staring down at his work. "You've proven that you can't take care of yourself. So, you're not going anywhere without a chaperone."

"I'm a prisoner here?"

"That shouldn't be a problem for you." He finally looked her in the eyes. "It's what you seem to thrive on lately."

"You *bastard*!" Carrie stormed back to the farmhouse. For the first time since her breakdown while having sex after Mandy's party, she cried.

CHAPTER TWENTY-SIX

BEGINNING THE PROCESS

"Come on, hon, one more repetition. You can do it," Beth urged her husband to keep going. "The doctor said if you keep making progress, you can ditch the chair and use crutches. Maybe even go home to the ranch and do therapy there."

"Yeah, yeah, you old nag." No one wanted Randy's left arm and shoulder to heal enough for him to use crutches more than he did. Trying to maneuver that stupid wheelchair around their friend's house with one leg sticking straight out was a real pain. Almost as much pain as his leg was in. Stupid leg. Damn, that thing hurt. Drugs were out. If he told the doctor he was in so much pain, it would delay getting rid of the chair.

The next day, at Randy's weekly check-up, the nurse walked into the exam room for a blood draw and quick vitals check. "Huh. You're running a bit of a fever. It's probably nothing. This blood sample will tell us all we need to know. The doctor will be in shortly."

When the doctor did come into the exam room, he said, "For some reason, your white blood cell count is way up. We normally do an MRI on cases like this, but because of the metal pin in your leg, I'm sending you for a CT scan."

Beth festered alone in the waiting room. Since no one in the facility would venture the time of day, she called Karen.

"It's not a good thing." Karen knew she had to prepare Beth for the worst but there wasn't time to soften the blow. "He's probably developed an infection again. Hopefully, another round of antibiotics will handle it."

"The doctor's coming. I have to go." Beth started to hang up.

Karen quickly added, "Please call if you need anything explained."

The doctor had come to know the ranch wife well enough to know not to beat around the bush. "The scan showed something. It concerns me enough that I'm immediately taking him in for a biopsy."

Beth called Karen. Karen called Mandy. "Get to the hospital now! Beth's going to need a shoulder."

Running into the waiting room, Mandy sat beside Beth and gave her a tearful hug. When the surgeon came in, Mandy called Karen and put her phone on speaker. The surgeon didn't mince words.

"It's worse than I feared. As soon as I cut him open, we saw that his leg is heavily infected." He paused for a second, then continued, "As I was coming out here to tell you that he's going to need another long term antibiotic regimen, I received the lab results. Mrs. Bennett, I'm sorry to tell you this, but your husband has a severe osteomyelitis infection. He's becoming septic. We need your permission to amputate the leg immediately or he will more than likely die."

Beth gasped and started to sob. Mandy spoke into her phone, "Did you get that, Mom?"

"Yeah, I heard," Karen answered. "Beth, can you hear me?"

When Beth just nodded, Mandy spoke for her, "Yeah, Mom, she heard. Do you want to talk to the doctor?"

"Yeah. Take me off speaker."

Karen identified herself and had the doctor fill her in on all the variables. When they were done, the surgeon handed the phone to Beth.

"Tell me what to do," Beth pleaded into the phone. "Randy has always been so active. It may kill him to only have one leg."

Karen softly replied, "Yes, it may. I can't tell you what to do. What I *can* say is that if you say no, you'll probably have a dead husband with both his legs. If you say yes, he still has a chance at living a long life. It'll take a lot of work, but we're all there for you."

Beth sadly looked at the surgeon and nodded while whispering, "Yes, do it."

She collapsed into Mandy's arms as the surgeon hurried off.

Twelve hundred miles away, Paul sat in his therapist's office for his mandatory check-in.

"Well, Mr. Taft, I don't see any reason to continue our weekly sessions. I'm going to sign off on a trial once monthly visit. Any questions?"

It took Paul a few moments to reply. He was still getting used to not being addressed as "officer." Even though he couldn't remember ever being one, that was the title the long care facility, and all of the restaurants he frequented since being released, used.

"Can I travel? Maybe check in by phone? I have some distant relatives I want to visit in the Northwest."

The therapist glanced at her notes and shrugged. "I don't see why not. Just be sure to call me if you start getting any lost memories back, even if it's only a quick flash of something."

"Will do." Paul stood to leave. He knew he would never recover any of the memories everyone around him expected. They had never been there.

His next stop was at the foster group home where the state housed Mara. He had become quite attached to young girl everyone said he rescued from a life as a sex slave. Since she was always honest and sometimes brutally blunt during their interactions, he looked at her as his only real friend. Everyone else in his life were friends with what his body used to contain.

"I'm going on a short trip up north."

"You're leaving? You and the patients at the long-term care facility are the only actual humans these people let me interact with."

He laughed. "Oh, stop it! You've got school starting soon."

"Those kids, and even the teachers, treat anyone from a group home like we're piranhas looking for a fresh meal. They automatically assume we're about to do something horrible."

"Just keep your head down. I've got your back. We won't let the system get the best of us."

Mara hugged him around the waist when he stood to leave. "Don't abandon me. You're more like a father to me than anyone I've ever known."

He kissed the top of her head. "I'll be back. I promise."

As he walked out of the group home kicking himself for the reflexive kiss, Paul saw the home's daytime supervisor scowling with disapproval.

Three days later, driving through a dilapidated trailer park, he stopped in front of an old double-wide and stared at the even older single-wide two spaces farther down. The soccer ball kids were kicking in the street bounced and rolled under his car. When he exited his vehicle to help retrieve it, a suspicious elderly man came out of the old single-wide Paul had been watching.

"Can I help you find someone?" the old man called out.

"Maybe," Paul answered. "I used to know some people who lived here quite a while ago. Does the elderly woman still live in this double-wide?"

"You mean Mae? That *was* a while back. She passed three years ago." The old man tottered up and leaned back on Paul's car hood. "How'd you know her?"

"I used to live, uh, nearby." Paul paused thoughtfully. "My cousin used to live in the house you just came out of."

"You're Nurse Karen's cousin?"

The mere mention of her name, a name he had vowed to forget but was one of the things his mind refused to let go of, forced him to suck in a breath. "No, I was her husband's cousin."

"Her husband? Which one? Wait, you said 'was.' That'd make you Peter's cousin."

"Which one?" Paul repeated. This conversation was only going downhill. He asked, "She remarried? What's her last name now?"

Getting suspicious of this stranger's motive again, the old man said, "You've never told me your name. What is it? Mine's Joe."

"Paul. It's Paul Taft."

"Why don't you know any of this stuff that happened years ago?"

"Yeah, I guess it does sound kind of crazy," Paul admitted. "We've been out of touch for years. I had an on-the-job injury a while back and can't remember the last decade. I'm driving around now to see if I can reconstruct my past."

"Were you military?"

Paul started to say yes but thought better of it. "No. Law enforcement. I'm retired now because of the injury."

Accepting the answer, Joe opened up, "Makes sense. Nurse Karen's current husband, Charlie, suffered a similar injury. He can't remember anything before it happened. When he first woke up, he insisted his name was Pieter. They're all doing great now."

All he could do to not throw up, Paul asked, "What's their last name now?"

"It's the same – Schmidt. Kind of a sweet story. Since Charlie couldn't remember his past, his surname didn't mean a thing to him. So, when they got hitched, he took her last name."

"Didn't Peter, her first husband, mind?"

Joe looked shocked. "Boy you've lost a *big* chunk of your memory. Your cousin died in combat quite a while back. Nurse Karen sends me money to put flowers on his grave at least once a month. In fact, I was getting ready to take the bus to do it again. Hey, it'd save me three transfers and a walk if you'd take me. Interested?"

An hour later, Joe placed the flowers beside a granite headstone engraved with the words: *Peter Schmidt, Husband, Father, War Hero.* Paul watched, conflicted over what reaction a man should have standing on his own grave.

CHAPTER TWENTY-SEVEN
I QUIT

Bill hung up the phone. One more needed major decision had just been added to his list. Not wanting to worry Beth and Randy, he had withheld Carrie's current condition and presence at the ranch from them. They had enough to worry about. As far as her parents were concerned, Carrie was still on a carefree self-exploration trip.

Now, he had to decide whether to inform his fragile charge that her dad was going to be a cripple for the rest of his life. Telling himself it was because he didn't want to deal with more of Carrie's drama, he kept silent. Inside, he still felt a compulsion to shield her from life's bad things.

Bill pulled his keys from their hiding spot and headed for his truck. "Come on, we're going for a ride."

Carrie snapped at him, "What makes you think I want to go anywhere with you?" Realizing she hadn't been allowed off the ranch since he practically kidnapped her in Spokane and forced her to come home, she changed her mind. "Where to? What's the special occasion? Have they found room in the local convent? Or is it the state hospital?"

"The county seat." He walked out of the shop so fast she had to run to keep up. "I can't get everything I need locally to get the house ready for your dad's return. That's the closest place for building materials and a few other things to complete the job."

A few miles on the other side of town, Bill slowed and turned into a long, asphalt, private driveway leading to a mansion on top of the bluff. Knowing whose house it was, Carrie tensed.

"What are we doing here?"

"It's part of my deal with Mr. Roberts. Because I quit without notice when your dad was hurt, I promised him I'd check on the place once a week." Seeing Willa's sports car sitting in front of the stables and knowing this wasn't going to go well, he said, "Crap! I thought she was still off galivanting somewhere with her latest boyfriend."

Willa came out of the stables and walked up to the driver's side window, followed by a man Bill had never seen before. "Where are the horses? I came home for a week and thought we'd go for a ride." When she saw who was seated on the passenger side, her demeanor changed. "Oh, hello Carrie. I didn't know you were home. How's your dad?" Seeing Carrie's still battered face, Willa asked, "What happened to you? Get thrown by a horse?"

Carrie growled, "You might say that." Then she turned away.

"You need me to open up the house?" Bill could see by the rich girl's expression she'd figured out another explanation for Carrie's face.

"No. I've got that handled." Willa started to say something else to Carrie but thought it best to let it lie.

"Your horses are at the Bennett ranch. It's part of my deal with your dad. Your tack's also out there. You have my number." Bill restarted his truck. "Call ahead and I'll have them ready for you."

As he pulled back onto the state highway, Carrie finally spoke again. "So, how's *she* doing? Is she just a globetrotting society girl now? How many men has she gone through?"

Knowing what she was fishing for, he wasn't about to bite. "Willa jumped around a little in college but has finally decided what she wants. She's going for an MBA." He glanced sideways. "As for her dating habits, I don't know. I do know that, like most people, she's moving ahead with her life and isn't dwelling in the past."

Carrie turned to stare out the passenger window. Damn this place. For the second time since being dragged back here, her eyes started to leak. It must be dust from the fields.

After stopping at the lumber yard, steel yard, and discount tool store, Bill took her to a chain restaurant for lunch before heading home. While waiting for their meal, the hostess led a man, woman, and two young children to a nearby table. Bill thought the man looked like he was going to soil his underwear when he saw Carrie. He watched the man glancing uncomfortably at her. She didn't seem to care.

Sure of the probable answer, Bill asked, "Should I ask?"

"That's Vern. You don't want to know." She scooted her glass aside as the waitress brought their lunch.

"Do you want to have them box up our lunch to go?"

"No. *I've* got nothing to hide." Carrie picked up her fork but didn't take a bite. Instead, she studied its tines and said, "Anymore."

Although the rest of the meal and drive home were in complete silence, there was one minor moment of excitement when they rose to walk out of the restaurant. Carrie stopped at Vern's table and smiled sweetly at his wife.

"Those are the most darling kids. You guys live locally?"

When she sashayed to the exit, not acknowledging Vern at all, Bill thought he might have to perform CPR on the pale man at the table. Once he thought about the reason for Vern's panic attack, Bill decided maybe not. Vern had probably cheated on his wife and deserved to suffer as penance. Years ago, Bill cheated on Carrie just the one time when they were dating and was still enduring the consequences.

After paying the tab, he headed for his truck. Carrie was belted in, staring off into the distance. It hit him as he climbed in: She'd just shown a spark of her old fire. Somewhere inside the bruised but hardened young woman beside him, parts of his old friend still remained. He wondered just how much.

At the ranch, he stacked the new building materials against

the back porch. When he returned from the machine shed with a chainsaw and started taking measurements in the mudroom, Carrie exploded.

"What do you think you're doing? This isn't your house. You're *not* going to saw a bunch of holes in *my* house!"

"First," he snarled, "this isn't *your* house. It's your parents'. I'm doing what your mom asked me to do—building a handicap access to the second floor for your dad. Their bedroom is directly above the mudroom. I'm going to build an elevator into their corner closet."

"Why can't he just go up and down the stairs with his crutches? His leg should be healed soon enough to do that."

Exasperated with the obnoxious, self-centered young woman, he barked at her, saying more than intended, "He doesn't have a leg to heal anymore! They cut it off!" Angrily, he knelt and concentrated on making reference pencil marks on the floor.

"What?" Carrie's question was barely audible.

Bill's spiteful retort knocked the wind out of her. When he turned and cut off the conversation, he didn't hear her feeble plea to be heard and understood by someone, anyone. The boy who used to be her best friend and confidant now looked at her with disdain. She was only a babysitting obligation he took on because no one else would.

She wept, "I'm worthless," while running toward the stables.

She needed to escape. Since her latest captor hid all of the vehicle keys, a horse was her only transportation. Carrie ran to her old mare's stall.

"Dammit," she muttered, remembering her trusted friend had died of old age.

Then, it hit her. The Thoroughbred in the stall was Willa's. Since the rich girl stole her future with Bill away, Carrie reasoned, it was only fitting that she permanently take the horse away from Willa. Flinging the gate open, she galloped the mare out of the stables toward the ranch's upper feedlot.

Bill heard a horse gallop out of the stable.

"Crap!"

Never ridden without its bridle and English saddle, the horse didn't know what to do with the hysterical rider on its back. Carrie didn't care. Having not been on horseback since the summer at Kate's, and only wearing tennis shoes, proper gear didn't matter either. She had no intention of either of them returning alive.

"Stupid horse!" Carrie screamed. "Hasn't anyone ever taught you commands without a bit in your mouth? Hasn't anyone taught you leg commands?"

Not knowing which way to go, the mare still understood the human on her back wanted to go as fast as possible. The easiest way to comply with that input without any other comprehensible rider command seemed to be along the two-rut ranch road. Luckily for both the mare and her agitated rider, all of the barbed wire gates between the stables and upper sorting corrals were open that time of year.

Carrie's main focus was on reaching the top of the coulee's highest cliff. All other thoughts were tiny planets orbiting around a sun's suicidal goal of plunging into a black hole: *No one loves me. I'm a slut. All men are untrustworthy beasts. It's my fault Dad is crippled. This is all Bill's fault. This is all my fault. All women are deceitful bitches. Willa's horse is a pile of crap. It deserves to die with me. They'll all miss me when I'm gone. No one will care. Will they even notice? Maybe they'll put up a monument.*

The only impediment in the destroyed young woman's path was a gate beside the upper sorting corrals. It was a fight to open the access gate to the scablands open range part of the ranch. By the time Carrie dismounted to open the gate, Willa's horse was almost as hysterical as its rider. With the gate open, the mare did everything possible to keep Carrie off its back. Climbing the board rails on the corral to remount, Carrie saw grim-faced Bill galloping up the road on her dad's horse.

She yelled at the mare, "He's still too far away. He'll never catch me. It'll serve him right to see me die and have to tell everyone it was his fault."

Having never ridden bareback alone before, Bill hurriedly saddled Randy's horse. Mr. Roberts' Thoroughbred probably was the fastest horse in the stable, but Randy's quarter horse was more sure footed on rough terrain. Bill gave chase. Coming over a small rise, he saw Carrie in the distance. At least he was on the right track. She was too far ahead to hear him, but he shouted anyway.

Willa's Thoroughbred had just about enough of the delirious human's contradictory commands. Riding through a herd of cattle at full gallop definitely wasn't what it had been trained for. Seeing a chasm between itself and the opposite horizon was more than it could handle. It was not about to be ridden at full speed into thin air. At the last possible moment, the horse slid to a halt.

The Thoroughbred's rider kicked and slapped the halter rope against its sides. It looked over the edge of the precipice. Nope, *that* wasn't happening. It revolted and tried to buck the young woman off. Of the two, the Thoroughbred at least had the horse sense to head away from the cliff during the disagreement.

A safe distance from certain doom, the horse realized there was about one hundred pounds missing from its back. It stopped bucking and ran toward the stable, not caring about the rider. That insane human could walk back.

Bill witnessed the animal's desperate act of self-preservation as he gained ground on Carrie. For a microsecond, he thought about trying to catch Willa's horse and bringing it back for Carrie to ride. But when he saw the look on her face as she leapt up and limped toward the cliff, sucking for air and nursing bruised ribs, he knew there was something more going on than spitefully trying to cripple a horse.

"Stop," he cried out. "What're you doing? Trying to kill yourself?"

She didn't need to answer. Her decimated expression said it all.

He rode past to block her path. She ran behind the horse. Out of time, Bill spun the quarter horse and galloped at her.

Jumping from the saddle onto her back, their struggle rolled them toward the precipice. His leg slid over the edge. Fighting to keep them both from plummeting to their deaths, he desperately grasped at sagebrush to pull them to safety. Pinned beneath him, she fought to pull free and roll off the cliff.

"Let me go!" she screamed. "I've destroyed everyone's lives! It's all my fault!"

"Dammit, Carrie, stop fighting!" Over a foot taller and twice her weight, Bill still could barely hold her down. "It's not all about you! The whole world doesn't revolve around you!"

"What?" Carrie went limp. It was the first time she had ever heard him shout in anger.

She lay immobilized beneath his weight. The pain from her bruised ribs grinding into the basalt and sagebrush stubble poking her stomach was nothing compared to her agony caused by the rage radiating from Bill. Carrie had never seen him mad—really, really mad—with anyone, much less her.

She finally whispered, "You can let me up. I won't try that again." He rolled off but held her wrist in an iron grasp. "You can let go now. I said I wouldn't try it again." When he held on and led her toward the remaining horse, she tugged on her arm. "Don't you trust me?"

His reply hurt more than anything he had ever said to her before. "No, not anymore. I used to believe that you were the most trustworthy person I'd ever met. I haven't felt that way in a long time."

He mounted Randy's horse without releasing his grip. Then, using only one hand, he yanked her up onto the saddle in front of him. Even when he dismounted at the sorting corrals to close the gate, he used only one hand, holding the horse's reins with the other. During the ride back to the stables, he rode two handed, arms on both sides of Carrie to keep her from getting any ideas about jumping off.

Staring down at the saddle horn, she asked, "Are you ever going to trust me again?"

"I don't know. We'll see. It'll be a while, if ever."

After recapturing Willa's horse, Carrie silently helped Bill construct the elevator. Once they secured the channel iron uprights, they built a platform with large caster wheels as guides inside. Using a cheap electric winch and idler pulleys from the discount store, they soon had functional—although definitely not OSHA approved—handicap access to the second floor bedroom closet.

She made supper while Bill put the finishing touches then test rode his masterpiece. While she cooked, Carrie felt him watching, keeping track of her actions. After dinner, she thought she saw him counting knives. That night, she heard him laying a bedroll outside her bedroom door.

She tossed all night. He was right. She *had* made it all about her. When Bill started her downfall ball rolling, she had done nothing to stop it. In fact, her decisions only gave it more momentum. While she was wallowing her own miserable existence, other people she knew also had terrible things happening in their lives.

Carrie whispered to herself, "Buck up, cowgirl. You've got a job to do."

CHAPTER TWENTY-EIGHT
A HEALING HORSE

Carrie didn't have a clue how to fix herself. She hoped enough of her old relationship with Bill remained that he would help her. The next morning, she carefully stepped over her sleeping guard and went down to the kitchen. With the coffee brewing and bacon frying in the pan, she heard rustling upstairs. Soon, frantic footsteps running around checking the rooms, then Bill's thundering down the stairs shook the kitchen's overhead light. Carrie smiled weakly at his panicked expression when he burst into the kitchen.

"It's about time you got up. I didn't want you to have a heart attack by going out and starting chores without you. So, to kill time, I'm cooking breakfast first."

Only replying with a grunt, he went back upstairs to get dressed. Still, she saw a look of relief on his face. After a silent breakfast and chores, Carrie went into the stables and led Willa's nervous mare out to groom. Hearing the stall gate open, Bill ran into the building expecting a repeat performance of the previous day.

Relieved, he asked, "What are you doing?"

"Making amends to this poor horse," she replied. "I treated her like crap yesterday."

Bill watched for a few minutes. "That's good. I just got off the phone with Willa. She's home for the weekend and bringing her boyfriend out for a ride. Saddle both Thoroughbreds up for them. That English tack hanging just inside the door is theirs. Then, saddle up your dad and mom's horses. Since Willa has never ridden here before, we're going along and showing them the trails."

Carrie winced and started to protest but bit her tongue. It would do no good. For the moment, someone else held the reins and controlled her life's direction. Maybe that was best. Every major decision she had made in the last few years proved to be the wrong ones. Nursing bruised ribs from being tackled, she still managed to get all four horses ready and tied to a corral railing by the time a sports car pulled in front of the stables.

When Willa led her boyfriend up to the animals, Carrie saw her nemesis checking out the fresh scratches on her own arms and bruised face. Bill came into the stables and reached for the reins of Randy's horse.

Carrie stopped him. "I want to ride Daddy's horse."

"But I'm the biggest," he said. "He can carry me."

She insisted, "For what we're going to do today, Mom's horse will do just fine for you."

Bill shrugged and led the group out of the stables and toward the upper feedlot. When they neared the first gate, Carrie rode ahead and dismounted to open it. *Okay,* he thought, *She's going out of her way to look like the bigger person in front of Willa. Why?*

"Would you hold his bridle?" Carrie asked him. "I want to try something."

The large gelding wasn't happy with her trying to mount from the right side. Even though the horse had known the girl for years and had carried her many times, this was wrong, all wrong. After considerable dancing around, she gave up and mounted on the left.

"What was that all about?" Bill asked. "Are you trying to get hurt? Or are you just trying to show off how good of a rider you are?"

A few minutes of silent riding later, she softly answered, "You said Daddy lost his left leg. He won't be able to mount on the left anymore. I want to train his horse to be mounted from the right." Carrie paused for a bit then continued, "That way he won't have lost everything he loves."

After mulling over her plan for a few moments, he replied, "When we get to the gate by the sorting corrals, we'll try again. I'll pin his horse against the corral rails with your mom's horse. You might have better luck."

Willa eavesdropped on the conversation and wondered, *Lost a leg? Losing everything he loves?* She knew Mr. Bennett's accident was why Bill went part time with her dad and moved to the ranch as a caretaker. Now, Carrie was back, looking like she'd been run over by a truck. Willa was certain it wasn't Bill who put those bruises on Carrie's face.

If he didn't beat Carrie up, then who did? She had a lost look in her eyes. From the way Bill acted toward his ex-girlfriend—outwardly gruff but with tender actions—Willa could see he still cared deeply for her. Did any of this have anything to do with the uncomfortable community Christmas party? The rich girl watched the underlying tension in front of her. Something traumatic had happened to Carrie, and Bill was trying to put the pieces back together.

Willa looked at her boyfriend and smiled. She had lucked out with this one. Bill had been a large factor in making her own life's path more reasonable. Maybe she could return the favor and help him with Carrie.

"You know," Willa leaned over and whispered to Bill, "I've been watching what you're trying to do. I'd like to help."

"What do you mean?" He nervously glanced toward Carrie.

"I don't know the details of what happened," Willa spoke softly so only he could hear and nodded toward Carrie. "But it's obvious something very traumatic happened to her. I don't need to know. I kind of feel responsible, though. I'd like to help."

When he stared at his saddle horn with a lost expression, she could see that she was dead on.

"Yeah. Carrie's gone through some tough times in the last few years. She got herself involved in a couple of really bad situations. It's not my place to say anything more about that. I'm just trying to help her put the pieces back together."

"I've been watching her work with that gelding today. She had a look of purpose on her face." Willa glanced over to make sure that her own boyfriend and Carrie were occupied and out of hearing range. "It gave me an idea. There's a horse rescue place north of Spokane that matches traumatized horses with people. The idea is that the horse and person heal each other."

"That's too far for us to commute. I . . . I don't know if I can trust her to go by herself yet." Desperation on his face, he said, "I don't know if I can afford it."

"You let me worry about the details. Let me make some calls to find out the specifics."

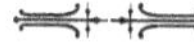

A few days later, Bill carefully addressed Carrie at breakfast. "You're making good progress retraining your dad's horse. I think the gelding will be ready when your parents get home."

She grumbled, "I've got to do something. I'm going stir crazy here."

"I, uhh, I've been talking to your mom." He could see rage forming on Carrie's face. "She thinks it'd be a good idea for us to get another horse for you to train."

"It pisses me off that you can call my mom any time and make plans for me! Doesn't anyone care what *I* want? Why doesn't she just talk to me?" Carrie festered for a few minutes, then asked, "Why get another horse? We can barely feed the ones we have. How are we going to pay for the thing?"

This next part of the conversation was not going to go well.

Judging by her reaction so far, and knowing the history between all involved, he expected an explosion. Hopefully, he could contain it. Bill stammered, "The . . . the horse is free. All we have to do is pick it up. The feed bill is paid for." Seeing her suspicion building, he knew he might as well just blurt it out. "It's a traumatized rescue horse. Willa found it and is paying for its keep."

Carrie exploded as he expected. "Willa! I'm not taking a damn thing from that bitch!"

Bill grabbed her arm as she launched from her chair. "You have no choice," he lied. "She's paying the *ranch* to stable and rehab *her* horse. The *ranch* needs income. *You* need a job to keep you occupied. The decision is final. You've been outvoted by everyone, including your parents."

Pulling her arm free, Carrie stormed out of the house. Bill called Willa and discussed the unplanned change in the narrative. Everyone needed to be on the same page if the plan was to work.

All of the horses retreated to the back of their stalls when the enraged young woman stormed into the stables and started slamming tack around. When they wouldn't come to their stall gate for a treat, Carrie knew *she* was the problem. In spite of a tasty bribe, even a horse didn't want anything to do with her when she was like this.

She sat on the floor against the stall gate of her dad's horse to calm. Finally, Carrie felt the gelding nuzzle the back of her head. Realizing Bill was right, she stood up. Working with horses centered her.

A week later, Willa drove over from college, and the three left in the ranch's crew cab dually towing a gooseneck livestock trailer. Bill desperately wished his stepfather, Charlie, could have come along for no other reason than to dilute the tension inside the truck's cab. However, It was the Bennett Ranch's turn for the fall round-up. All of the local ranchers gathered in a group and went between the various spreads to help each other out. It cut down on hiring temporary help.

Even though both Willa and Bill tried to get her to sit in front, Carrie wouldn't budge from the rear seat. From her perch, her eyes bored holes in the backsides of her two most distrusted people. They had both betrayed her, one worse than the other. Carrie had never liked or trusted Willa in the first place, so in her mind, Bill's sin was greater.

For Bill, it took an eternity to make the two-hour drive. Looking in the rearview mirror, it was an eternity he felt obligated to endure. He couldn't wait to bail out of the truck at the equine rescue center.

A friendly woman with a weathered face wandered over from a corral gate. "I'm Evelyn. You must be the people looking to adopt a horse."

"Yes, that's us." Willa led her out of hearing range to explain the subterfuge. "We have to be careful how we word things in front of Carrie. We had to tell her that this is going to be my horse and I'm paying her parents' ranch to rehabilitate it."

Evelyn was dubious. "I'm not sure I like that. It's our policy to adopt out to only committed people."

Willa explained as much of Carrie's traumatic history that she knew. She told Evelyn how watching the young woman regain interest in life while retraining the quarter horse to be mounted from the right gave them the inspiration to find a real project horse.

Bill yelled from the corral gate Evelyn had been standing near when they drove up, "Is this the mare?"

"Yeah. Why don't you see how she reacts with your friend?" Evelyn called back. Then, she turned back to Willa. "I'm uncomfortable with this whole thing. The horse will tell me what I need to know."

Carrie stared over the corral railing at the Appaloosa cowering on the far side of the pen. It reminded her of the Morgan who tried to trample her almost a decade ago. In a twisted chain of events, that incident led her right back to a similar situation. She climbed over the fence and walked to the center of the corral thinking, *This time the horse might kill me. Maybe I deserve it.*

"Crap!" Grabbing a lariat, Evelyn ran toward the pen. That idiot girl wasn't supposed to go in alone.

With its ears turned back, the skittish Appaloosa approached within ten feet and stopped. Wounded horse and wounded girl studied each other. Each saw something in the other painfully familiar—distrust of everything. Carrie held out her hand. After a few moments, the mare's ears started flickering back and forth, and it tentatively walked close enough for her nose to be touched by the outstretched hand. Then, it retreated to the opposite side of the corral where it stood with its ears relaxed to the side.

"Well, I'll be." Evelyn loosened her tense hold on the lariat. "That's the first time she's put up with anyone even being near her, much less approaching them. Those two must be kindred spirits." Turning to Willa, she said, "You can have her. Come into the office to fill out the paperwork. Then, we'll get some help to load her up."

Back at the ranch, Willa was forced to work with Carrie and the Appaloosa on weekends. Carrie did most of the day-to-day work but, to maintain the subterfuge, Willa had to put in token showings. As he watched from a distance, Bill smiled. Carrie seemed to be focused and have new purpose. Willa's blossoming maturity and sensitivity to others' needs impressed him.

The horse gained a name—Spot. A lazy name to give, but with the three constantly on edge about how the others would react at any given moment, no one had the energy to think of a better one.

It became a daily routine for Carrie. Do her chores first thing in the morning, cook breakfast while Bill finished his more extensive list, work with Spot for two hours, one hour with her dad's horse, then eat lunch. Willa would show up on weekend afternoons to help with "her" horse and, in the process, learn a few training tricks herself.

Bill asked after Willa had left for the day, "How's your dad's horse doing?"

Already knowing how the training was going, he was fishing for how Carrie and Willa were getting along. After inadvertently adding to his ex-friend's trauma when his spiteful snap revealed Randy's true condition, he was also questioning his decision to keep Carrie's presence at the ranch from her parents. Bearing the burden of shielding further hurt from everyone else had long since become overwhelming.

"I think he's about got it," Carrie answered. "He's used to me now. Why don't you give it a try?"

"Oh, sure. What you actually want is for me to bite dirt in the corral, isn't it?"

"It wouldn't hurt," she replied with a slight giggle. "Well, at least it won't hurt me."

That almost imperceptible snicker from Carrie might as well have been a freight train's horn at a busy crossing the way it struck Bill. He didn't get an answer about the two young women's relationship, but he did get another important clue. Somewhere inside the wounded young woman beside him, parts of his old friend *did* still exist. How much he didn't know, but he was determined to bring her out.

As he expected, the quarter horse wasn't very happy about being mounted on the right side by anyone other than Carrie. But acquiring a few new bruises was worth it seeing the slight twinkle of pleasure in her eyes bossing him around again. The horse picked up the concept quicker than the rider, which wasn't a bad thing in Bill's opinion. Working together on the gelding allowed him to track her emotional stability.

Another week of cooperative training having removed more of the reparations guilt weight from his shoulders, he decided it was time for a phone call. He had taken it upon himself to make everyone who knew what was going on swear oaths of silence. Now, he had to man up and make the confessional call himself.

CHAPTER TWENTY-NINE
COMING HOME

Late morning Monday Thanksgiving week, Carrie and Bill had finished working with Randy's quarter horse when they heard a vehicle pull into the ranch yard. While Carrie started to remove the saddle, Bill headed toward the stables door.

"Wait here," he said. "I'll go see who it is."

Now used to her self-appointed guardian vetting all outside contacts, she still grumbled, "Yeah, I'll be right here."

She removed the saddle, blanket, and bridle. Carrie had just started to curry the big gelding when she heard voices coming up behind her.

"Do a good job, there. I don't want my horse getting saddle sores."

"Daddy!" she squealed and spun around. Carrie wanted to run and jump into the arms of the strong man who had raised her. However, the gaunt person leaning on crutches, with a Velcroed-on left arm brace, and a sockless plastic left foot in a slip-on loafer, was not that man. "Daddy," she said softly and gently reached up to kiss his cheek.

Beth tearfully threw her arms around her daughter. "I'm so glad you're finally home."

"I've been here for months." Carrie looked at Bill, then asked, "Didn't you know? No one told you?"

Randy shifted uncomfortably on his prosthetic leg. Bill said, "Carrie, why don't you help your parents get unloaded and into the house. I'll finish up here. Later, I'll come in and show them how our access modifications work."

Carrie and Beth helped Randy up the back door steps. With him parked on a kitchen chair, the young woman and her mother carried luggage and the wheelchair from the SUV. After the last trip, Beth took Carrie's arm in the master bedroom.

"Sit beside me and tell me how you're doing."

Letting a little sarcasm slip out, Carrie replied, "What? You mean Bill hasn't kept you posted on my every failing? Surely, he's carried on about how much of a disaster I am and how big a hero *he* is."

"No, hon, we didn't know you were here until a short while ago. I don't know for sure if it was right or wrong, but Bill took it upon himself to keep radio silence about you."

Carrie snorted, "Of course he did. He's got a God complex and knows what's best for everyone." When she started to stand, Beth gently grabbed her arm and pulled her back onto the bed.

"Hold on. Did you ever think about how hard all this was on him? I know you two haven't gotten along for a couple of years, but when I asked for help, he didn't hesitate. He left his job and took over the next day." Beth leaned against her daughter. "He hasn't said anything about how or when you came home. All he'd tell me is that you were here and safe."

Carrie studied her mother for a few moments before asking, "He didn't say anything about me? Nothing at all?"

"No, dear, it was just like when you two came back from Greece. He refused to say anything more than the fact that you were physically healthy and home." They heard the back screen door slam and rummaging in the kitchen. "Come on, let's go down and have some lunch."

When Carrie walked into the kitchen and saw Randy massaging his stump, his empty, flaccid trouser leg dangling and prosthetic leg laying on the floor beside the wooden chair, she froze her in place. Her mixed anger and confusion toward Bill were thrown on a back burner.

"You just going to stand there, or are you going to help cook lunch?"

Bill's wording may have been harsh, but his delivery was tender, understanding. Carrie shook herself and headed for the range. While the Spam slices browned, she placed a cup of coffee on the table for her father.

Standing behind Randy's chair, she watched her mother, kneeling on the floor tenderly applying ointment to his irritated stump. About to burst into tears, she looked up at Bill, stirring scrambled eggs, observing with sad compassion on his face. Wiping the single tear from her cheek, Carrie walked over to remove the browned slices from the toaster. Reaching across for more bread, she had to press against him for a moment.

Bill's body was fixed, immobile, yet somehow tender. Carrie looked up, but he didn't notice, still watching Beth tending to Randy. After flipping the Spam, she buttered the toast, all while not breaking bodily contact. Watching the butter melt into the bread, she wondered how it was possible to hate someone so much yet be unable to pull away from their comforting presence.

During lunch, Bill said, "I don't want to be insensitive, but I think we should practice using the second-floor starship. Carrie put a lot of work into it."

Setting her fork down, Carrie looked at Bill, expecting a smirk. Instead, he was looking at her mother and father with an earnest expression. What was his game? Why would he say such a thing when the very day he started work on it, she tried to kill a horse and commit suicide? Was he trying to impress her parents with his perfection?

"I don't know," Randy answered. "I think I'll just use the stairs."

"No you won't!" Beth said. "I just applied salve to your leg and saw how irritated it was. You need to take it easy when you can.

That way, when *I* require your help with something, you'll be ready and able."

Seeing the look exchanged between her parents, it sank in what her mother was talking about. "*Mom*! There are others present."

"So, that topic embarrasses you now?" Beth instantly regretted the lighthearted quip when she saw Carrie's lost expression. Trying to change the subject, she looked at Bill. "So, how does this thing work? How much can it lift?"

"We installed a two thousand pound capacity winch and a double pulley snatch block system, so I'd say four thousand pounds. Minus the four hundred or so for the platform, of course." He looked at Carrie and continued, "That's about what we figured, right?"

"Uhh," she stammered, at a loss for words. Why was he doing this? Why was he telling her parents she was an active, willing participant when she had been belligerent every step of the way? "Uh, yeah, about that much."

Randy smirked. "I can see I'm not getting out of a free ride. Might as well get it over with. One death trap is as good as another."

When he saw Beth's expression, he said, "Too soon, huh? Maybe if the thing vibrates enough, it'll help me with your other demand."

"*Dad*! I said stop that crap!" Carrie got up and fled to the sink with a handful of dishes.

Beth smiled. It was the first real bit of levity her and Randy had shared since early June. She stood and asked, "Bill, why don't you show us how the thing works?"

"Sure. We're going to need one of these." Bill grabbed a kitchen chair and headed into the mudroom. "We didn't know exactly what type of arrangement we'd need, so we didn't put one in yet."

Carrie flinched while stacking dishes in the sink. She inadvertently grumbled aloud, "There he goes with that 'we' crap again."

"What's that, hon?" Beth called from beside the clothes dryer.

"Nothing, Mom. I just noticed we need more dish soap."

Bill stood on the hoist and held out a control pad. "Okay,

there's an up/down control switch hanging on this cable." Then he pointed at the elevator's fixed guidepost. "There are also fixed switches both here and on the second floor in case of emergencies. Down here, there's a little ramp we built because we didn't want to mess with the floor joists to recess the platform. Of course, we had to modify the upstairs ones to get through the first-floor ceiling, so the lift stops flush with the bedroom floor."

Beth hopped on the hoist and smiled at Randy. "Wanna gimme that ride now?"

Carrie wailed from the kitchen, "I said stop it, you two! Give the rest of us a break!"

Bill smiled inwardly as the hoist went into the second floor. Between training the gelding, the therapy horse, and now her parents' arrival, the broken girl in the kitchen was becoming human again.

After a few trips, Beth and Randy mastered elevator usage. When he sat on the bed to give his stump a temporary reprieve, Beth suggested, "Why don't you take a small nap and rest your leg? I'll check how the place is holding up."

Leaving the elevator on the second floor, she led Bill down the stairs into the den. Closing the door behind them, she asked, "How's the place doing? Where are the books?"

"It's still here," Bill answered. "With the community's help, we have enough hay for the winter. The fall cattle sale wasn't anything special. I think there's enough to get by if nothing major happens."

"That's good. You've done an excellent job."

"Thank you." Bill paused for a moment, studying the floor, then said, "Now that you're back, I should move home or at least into the bunkhouse to let you guys have some privacy. I can commute to work."

"You'll do no such thing." Beth put her hand on his arm. "You've kept the place together. I . . . we still need you. Please stay."

Searching for her mother, Carrie heard voices in the den. She flung the door open. "You two talking about me again? What have I done wrong *this* time?" Carrie ran out of the house sobbing.

"Crap!" Bill ran after her, followed by Beth.

CHAPTER THIRTY
NEW UNDERSTANDINGS

Bill and Beth chased after Carrie. At the door to the stables, he caught Beth's arm, pulled her into the tack room to covertly watch, and whispered, "Wait."

This time, instead of grabbing a horse and heading for the back forty, Carrie stood hugging her therapy Appaloosa. When she led Spot into the training corral, Bill let out an audible sigh of relief.

Beth asked, "What's this all about? What's going on?"

"Would you walk with me?" Wanting to ensure Carrie didn't overhear, he led Beth away from the corral, down the driveway toward the highway. "That's a therapy horse Willa is paying us to retrain. At least, that's the official story."

During the walk, he came clean about the incident that caused his and Carrie's initial relationship explosion. Without going into detail about Carrie's condition when Willa and her boyfriend came to the ranch to ride, too ashamed to look anywhere but toward the ground, he said, "Willa felt guilty, and this is her way of making amends. As far as Carrie knows, the horse belongs to the Roberts and we're being paid to rehab it. It seems to be helping. Between Spot and her work with Mr. Bennett's gelding, I can see glimpses of her old self coming through."

Beth jumped in front of Bill and threw her arms around his

neck, crying. Not knowing how to react, Bill uncomfortably patted her gently on the back.

"You're a fine young man," she said softly into his chest. Then, pushing back, she looked him in the eyes. "My name is Beth. My husband's name is Randy. I think it's about time you called us by our first names."

"I don't know if I can, Mrs. . . . uh, B . . . Beth."

She laughed kindly. "Never mind. Use whatever you're comfortable with. How did Carrie get in such rough shape this time? What did Willa see?" Now coming closer to understanding the young man's moral code, she wasn't surprised with his answer.

"It's not my story to tell. I *will* say that she needs those horses. They seem to center her."

Turning to walk back toward the ranch building complex, Beth asked, "What's this about her working with Randy's horse? It's about as well trained as they come."

"It's something Carrie thought of on her own. When I told her about Mr. Bennett's amputation, she decided to retrain his horse to be mounted from the right side. It accepted *her* right away. She took great satisfaction in me getting bruised as the male guinea pig."

"Let's go to the corral and check on how her project is coming along," Beth said while thinking, *And yours.*

Bill stopped in front of the equipment maintenance building. Not wanting to antagonize Carrie more than he already had, he said, "You go on. I have to service the tractor. It was acting up during this morning's feeding."

Beth knew better. The tractor either ran or it didn't. But, appreciating what he was trying to do, she answered, "Okay. We don't want something that isn't quite right preventing a task being accomplished."

Leaning against a corral railing, she watched her daughter work. From what Bill had told her, the Appaloosa was responding well. Focused on her daughter, Beth didn't hear a car door close in front of the stable. She jumped at the female voice beside her.

"The horse is coming along nicely, don't you think? Carrie's doing an excellent job."

Seeing the tall, attractive girl in English riding garb who was the cause of so much pain in her life, Beth didn't know how to react. Yet, from what Bill had told her, this young woman was also footing the tab for Carrie's new faux project.

"Yes, she is," Beth replied, still unsure of her own feelings. "Willa, isn't it?"

"Yeah, uh, I think we met a while back." The uncomfortable exchange at the community hall Christmas get-together replayed in Willa's mind before she finished answering, "At a party."

All Beth trusted herself to say was, "I vaguely remember that."

Torn with so many conflicting emotions—happiness to see her daughter, sorrow Carrie had made another bad choice, grief that her once very self-sufficient husband was now reduced to a frail near invalid needing help, fatigue from being a caretaker, anger toward Willa, anger toward Bill for falling into Willa's web, and appreciation for what Bill and Willa were doing to help Carrie—Beth turned toward the corral, stalling while figuring out something to say. Luckily, a male voice joined the conversation.

"So, this where everyone is." Randy hobbled up behind Beth and Willa. "What's going on? Whose horse is Carrie working with?"

Not sure who knew what, Willa hesitantly said, "Mine. I thought she was beautiful but has problems. I hired . . ."

Beth interrupted, "It's all right, Willa. I know." Then, she turned to her husband. "It's a rehab horse. I'll explain later. Don't ask Carrie anything about it."

Relieved someone else knew about the facade and was playing along, for the first time Willa actually looked at Randy. Just knowing about the accident didn't prepare her for how severe the injuries were. Seeing the crutches, she involuntarily looked down at the sockless prosthetic foot in the loafer.

First meeting Bill's family at Christmas dinner, and now Carrie's family and their troubles, she thought, *How can these people with all their hardships hold together?* Her parents were secure financially, alive, and physically healthy, but wanted nothing to do with each other. It was sinking in that money *wasn't* the glue that held relationships together.

Carrie finally noticed the group by the corral gate. "Daddy!" Then, she coldly nodded toward her obligatory work partner. "Willa."

Beth spoke up as a distraction, "Bill tells me you're teaching your father's horse some new tricks. Why don't you show us?"

Having calmed enough from her earlier meltdown to mention her supervisor's name, Carrie said, "It probably would be best if Bill demonstrated. Where is he?"

Her mother nodded toward the next building. "He's in the shop servicing the tractor. Why don't you go get him?"

Carrie grumbled, "Yeah. I'll go." Before leaving, she looked at Willa. "Why don't you spend some time with *your* horse?"

After her daughter walked off, Beth reached through the corral gate and touched Willa's arm and said softly, "Thank you."

Mounting the mare, the rich girl rode around the corral using simple commands. Nowhere near an expert equestrian, Willa did what she could not to let Bill down in helping Carrie. After a short time, he led the big gelding into the corral. Trying to keep both horses calm, Willa halted the Appaloosa on the far side and watched.

Bill led the quarter horse up to the railing to greet Randy. "Okay, this was Carrie's idea, and she did all the work. I'm just the human guinea pig she used when she needed a male to ride. I'll let her explain."

Beth and Willa watched closely for different reasons. The mother observed her daughter, gauging her mental state. She also watched Bill, wondering why he was putting in all this extra effort beyond simply caretaking the ranch. Was it loyalty? Guilt? Or was it something deeper, more complex?

Willa watched Beth, seemingly the family's glue who absorbed whatever came her way. Though recently crippled, Randy was still cheering on his daughter. She didn't know everything their daughter had endured but had seen the physical wounds and witnessed the change in personality. And then there was Bill. His loyalty to Carrie had been unwavering for years. Even though he outwardly feigned disdain, Willa saw through his facade and knew there was an attachment unfathomable to her.

Carrie explained to her father, "I know you need to ride as much as you need to breathe. I couldn't stand the thought of you giving that up." She turned to Bill. "Get on."

The horse acted as if everything was normal when the rider clumsily mounted from the wrong side. For a few moments, Randy leaned against the corral railing watching, then spoke, "Let me try."

"Daddy, I don't think . . ." Carrie's protest was cut off when Beth placed a hand on her shoulder.

"Let him try. He needs something to take his mind off everything else."

With Bill holding its halter, the big gelding stood patiently still while Randy leaned his crutches against the corral railing and started to swing into the saddle. It was as if the man and beast had done it that way forever. Then, the ill-fitting prosthetic leg came loose and smacked the quarter horse's left flank. Used to immediately responding to the minutest rider input, the horse launched into a gallop, knocking Bill to the ground.

When Randy's artificial leg fell, he slid half off, hanging onto the saddle horn. Without thinking, Willa spurred Spot in front of the gelding, causing it to stop and rear up. Randy slid to the ground on his back. While she grabbed the quarter horse's reins, the rest of the group ran to Randy's rescue.

Carrie screamed, "Daddy, Daddy!"

Bill took the reins from Willa to control the horse. Jumping over the corral fence, Beth was the last to reach her husband. Kneeling beside him, panicked, she asked, "Are you okay?"

Momentarily gazing up into his wife's eyes, Randy broke into laughter. "Yeehaw! Can I do that *again*?"

Relieved, Beth sat beside him half laughing, half crying.

Carrie shouted at her insane parents, "What the hell is the matter with you people? He could have been killed!"

Randy lifted up on one elbow and grinned at his daughter. "But I wasn't. Isn't that the point of living life to the fullest?"

Returning the reins to Willa, Bill went back to Randy. "If you want back on, we can help. Maybe we should leave the leg off until we figure out how to glue it on better."

Fuming, Carrie stood beside Willa and the Appaloosa while her father pulled the protective sock back over his stump. Bill put his arm around her father and helped him hop back to the corral railing with Beth leading the gelding.

Finally, Carrie looked up at her female nemesis. "Thank you for saving my dad."

"Hey, it wasn't me," Willa answered. "It was your training. Thanks to you, Spot reacted instantly. I had no idea what I was doing."

For the first time ever, the two young women shared a smile—weak, but still a smile.

With Bill's help, Randy remounted sans the leg. While he rode slowly around the corral, Carrie went up to her mother. "How could you let Daddy get back on? He could have been killed."

Beth smiled at her daughter. "You're right, but look at his face. This is the first time since last spring I've actually seen him happy." She put her arm around Carrie and watched for the reaction when she said, "You and your friend are doing a fine job on that Appaloosa. It shows good teamwork."

Carrie sighed and reluctantly looked in Willa's direction. "Yeah, I guess."

Randy and his old friend, the quarter horse gelding, became reacquainted. Until its rider was fitted with a decent prosthetic leg, the horse needed to learn what to do without near side leg commands.

Bill dug through a friend's stock car junk pile for a used five point racing harness. Using Beth's sewing skills, he engineered a prosthetic attachment harness which Randy could uncouple in an emergency by just hitting the release button. He had to wear jeans with one leg cut off and the harness fit over his clothing. But he could ride safely until the family could afford one of the higher tech prosthetics.

CHAPTER THIRTY-ONE
SAVING MARA

During the drive back to the trailer park from the cemetery, all Paul had to do was ask Joe how he met Karen. Now accepting his visitor's story, the chatty elderly man went into every minute detail about the homeless camp weekly clinic and the nurse practitioner. He told of Charlie's military history, his overdose, and Karen bringing him back from the dead. Joe became wistful when he described Karen's reaction to Charlie staring at her children's photos on the wall and asking how she got pictures of his children.

"That threw her over the edge. She ran screaming from her own home and drove away. The next day, she refused to go back into the house, hooked her old pickup up to an already loaded rental trailer, and headed for the Palouse to start her clinic.

"Charlie changed after that. He refused to be called by that Pieter guy's name anymore and spent the next couple of months in her library reading. He said that he needed to learn how to be in today's world. Isn't that the craziest thing you've ever heard? Learning how to be in a world you grew up in? Oh well, things worked out for the best when they somehow ran into each other a year later. They've been inseparable since. You gonna pay them a visit?"

Curtly, Paul replied, "Probably not. I have other important matters to settle."

After exchanging contact info with Joe outside the elderly man's single-wide, Paul drove to the closest freeway truck stop from the trailer park to eat and reason with himself. He needed to go back to California. He needed to accept his life now. He needed to move on. His hands and feet, ignoring what he needed to do, pointed his vehicle east for the four-hour drive to the Palouse.

After a sleepless night in a marginal motel, he drove to the small town Joe told of. He pulled into the only mini-mart in the area to get a soda, snacks, and directions. Climbing out of his car, Paul realized he needn't bother with the directions. Diagonally across the highway, covered with Thanksgiving decorations, was the small medical clinic the elderly man described.

While paying the cashier, he saw an old pickup pull in front of the clinic. Two men, one tall and young, the other in his early forties, went inside. Shocked, Paul dropped his wallet and fumbled to recover. Stumbling, out of breath, back to his car, he leaned against its roof for a moment to recover before climbing in. He had just glimpsed a face he hadn't seen in a long time—a face almost identical to the one he used to view in the mirror many years before.

A short time later, the two men, dressed in work clothes, came back out accompanied by a woman wearing a lab coat. She kissed the young man on the cheek and the older man on the mouth. As the men drove away, she waved then glanced in Paul's direction.

There she was. The woman he had loved more than life. The unfaithful woman who broke his heart. The woman who, even though she didn't use her own hands, killed him.

The older man was probably her new husband. The tall, young man was obviously her son—the son Paul joyously watched her give birth to.

Emotionally lost, he started his car and headed back to California. There was no family here for him to reconnect with.

The first thing Paul did upon his return from the northwest was stop by the group home to visit Mara. She came into the visitation area making an obvious effort to hide one side of her face. He gently brushed her hair aside to see a black eye and bruised cheek.

"Get that here or at school?"

She mumbled, "School."

"How?"

"A couple of kids figured out that I live here. They said I was a tramp and bound to end up working in a whorehouse. It's in my DNA."

"Did you give as good as you got?"

"Yeah, but I'm suspended now."

Trying to restrain his outrage, he asked, "Did any of the others get suspended?"

"Nah. Their parents threw too big a fit." When she saw how worked up he was getting, Mara tried to calm Paul. "Don't do anything stupid and get yourself banned from here. I can't keep going if I don't get to see you every now and then."

He stood up and hugged her. "I won't. But I can't stand by and watch you live like this."

Leaning into his chest, she whispered, "Please don't abandon me."

After she left the room, he stormed into the group home's office. "I want to talk to Mara's caseworker."

His California family was all dead. His Washington family seemingly had forgotten him and moved on. Needing someone to love, he was determined to make the young orphan girl his new family.

The caseworker was blunt. "I'm sorry, Mr. Taft, but it takes almost eighteen months to get approved as a foster parent."

"Who said anything about being a foster parent? She's more of a family to me than I've had in a long time. I want to adopt Mara."

With the help of officer Paul's past co-workers and their connections, his apartment passed inspection within a month. Thanks to a sympathetic caseworker, testimony of victims he'd helped in his body's law enforcement past, and a family court judge it had appeared before many times as part of its official duties, the girl he saved in the alley became Mara Taft by the time school let out for summer vacation.

"Come on. Let's go for a drive."

Mara looked up at her new father from a bowl of breakfast cereal. "Where?"

"We're going RV shopping. You and I are going exploring this summer."

Having never been out of the city, the young girl didn't know how to react. "Exploring? Where to? Why?"

"*You* need to see how people live away from this hellhole. *We* need to find a place to live where you can grow up like a normal human being." Paul hugged his new daughter. "Now that the adoption's finalized, there's no legal restraints where we live anymore. We're going to look for a place where we can breathe."

What he didn't say was, "As far away from the woman who's incapable of fidelity. I don't know if I can keep myself from putting Karen and her bedmate-of-the-day in the ground for good."

CHAPTER THIRTY-TWO
A DATE

Bill tucked his phone back into a shirt pocket after the call ended. Mr. Roberts had just offered him a job surveying the equipment at all of the corporation's intermountain west properties. If he accepted, he would spend the summer not only in Washington's Columbia Basin, but also traveling to Idaho and Montana deciding what actually needed to be ordered before the next planting cycle. Local foremen tended to exaggerate their needs just to get the newest trinket on their machinery.

This would take some thought. Even though Randy had recovered enough to handle the ranch's management, Bill still felt obligated to remain nearby just in case some heavy lifting was needed.

Carrie walked up behind him in the stables and asked nervously, "Would you take me to a movie? Just the two of us?"

He laughed. "You've had your keys for months. You don't need a babysitter anymore. That's why I moved back home. Do what you want."

She stammered, "That . . . that's not what I'm asking."

He turned, leaned the pitchfork against the stall, and studied Carrie for a moment. "Are you asking me to go on a *date*?"

Red faced, she deflected her eyes toward the Appaloosa. "Yes."

He was torn. Their whole downward spiral came when they tried to move their relationship beyond very good friends. She now had again almost returned to the girl she used to be. It was the troubled young woman in the middle he didn't know if he could forget and get past. Still holding love in his heart for Carrie, he had to take the chance.

"Okay. Do you want me to pick you up? Maybe go to dinner?"

"Yes, please, to both."

After work, he rushed home and showered. Snuggling on the couch, Karen and Charlie leaned forward to watch Bill rush out the door in his Sunday-go-to-meetings. It had been years since they'd seen him show that much anticipation of anything. Carrie's parents had an identical reaction when she ran to the back door in a dress as he pulled up.

Bill didn't have the chance to open the passenger door for her. She was in his truck almost before it stopped. Surprised when she scooted to the middle of the truck's bench seat, he asked, "Spokane?"

"Spokane would be nice, but it's a pretty long drive this late in the day. How about the county seat?"

He flinched. The last time he went to a movie at the county seat was the night he made the biggest mistake of his life with Willa. He just couldn't trust his guilt reflexes there.

"I think Spokane would be best. It's got the biggest variety, and I don't mind the drive."

Carrie shrugged. "Sure."

Reflexively leaning her head against his shoulder, they quietly drove to dinner. She didn't know why she showed such initial intimacy, but now that she had, Carrie was reluctant to withdraw. Confused, not wanting to send mixed signals, or even worse, false ones, she remained uncomfortably frozen in position. At least Bill couldn't see her face, tortured with confusion.

Bill was just as lost with how to handle her head against his arm. So close, he couldn't escape the scent of her shampoo, he wasn't sure if the butterflies in his stomach were from affection or revulsion. For five years, her nearness was comforting. Then, he mourned her absence for a year and a half. During her first rescue and the two following years, he choked in disgust.

Swerving to miss a deer bounding across the road gave them both a reprieve. Carrie took advantage of Bill's maneuvering and scooted to her side of the truck. That little bit of physical distance reduced the tension inside the truck's cab enough for the rest of the drive to be pleasant, almost hopeful for them both.

At dinner, she sat next to him, laughing and joking. In the theater, she leaned against him when he braved an arm around her. During the ride home, their comfort level reached the point where her sitting next to him seemed like old times in high school.

Each passing mile marker elevated the intimacy tension inside the pickup one more notch. His hand went to her thigh. Hers slid to his chest and toyed reflexively with a button. He would laugh or she would giggle nervously at virtually anything the other said.

Finally, a few miles from the ranch, it became too much. Violently turning the truck's wheel, he dove into a slightly off the main road scenic overview. She was in his lap kissing while he still struggled to turn off the ignition. His hand slid up the back of her quivering leg. The fingers on his other hand fumbled with her dress's zipper.

When Bill opened his eyes a bit to look at the zipper and choose a better position on the seat for what they were about to do, he saw it. In the moon's reflection off the windshield, Carrie was on Nicolas's island compound balcony. They were kissing with the rich man's arms around her, hands inside her sheer robe. Bill froze. Instantly out of the mood.

It took Carrie a few more moments of passion to realize she was kissing what felt like a slab of petrified wood. Seeing his frozen gaze, she turned to see what had caused the sudden change of mood.

"What?" She looked out the windshield at the view. "What do you see?"

Rattled by the vision, without thinking he stammered, "I . . . I saw a man pawing you in your slut days."

"*WHAT*?" It was as if a nuclear device had exploded the truck's cab. Frantically pulling her dress down, she tumbled more than climbed off his lap. "*What did you say?*"

"That's not what I meant. I shouldn't have worded it that way. I . . ."

"But it's what you *did* say. Now I know how you *really* feel. Take me home *now!*"

"But I . . ." Bill stopped. He knew by the look on her face there were no words that could counteract what he let slip.

For the last few miles to the ranch, the deafening sound of silence within the pickup's cab drowned out the noise of tires on asphalt. Outside the ranch house's back door, he tried to apologize again, but the scene played out just as it had the night of the graduation party. Carrie held up her silencing hand and jumped out of the cab. Before slamming the door, she said, "Don't call or come over. I need to think."

Bill called Mr. Roberts first thing in the morning, "If that job offer in Montana still stands, I'll take it."

CHAPTER THIRTY-THREE
VISITOR FROM EUROPE

"I think we need to diversify into the western hemisphere," Nick said to the head man. "I believe I have an area which might warrant your attention. It's not our usual type of business investment, but that's the point."

A grunted reply came from the villa's balcony, "Which areas?"

"As usual, hiding money under the radar of the financial watchdogs," Nick answered. "I have something agricultural in mind along the same lines as our olive groves here. I've been doing some research and think it's time for me to make an investigatory junket."

"Go. Just stay lowkey."

Nick knew exactly where he was going. When no one was looking, he had rummaged through the vault room and took the one thing his father seemed to cherish the most—a well-worn envelope containing a letter and two pictures. Using the pictures for reference and the postmark for a starting point, he had done extensive online research for his cover story.

He conceded a begrudging respect toward his father for one thing: Nicolas employed very efficient legal investigators. By the time Nick landed in Seattle to meet the contracted advisor, he had a briefcase full of agricultural corporations, their holdings, and what crops they grew.

The trick was to narrow down the search area. To increase his chances of locating his target while using the investment junket as his cover, he searched out the seediest private investigator he could find. He was determined to figure out just what kind of person could have had that much of a hold on his father.

After examining the pictures and letter, the PI drew an oval on a map. "Here's the most likely area these pictures were taken. I'm tied up for the next month with a divorce case. After that, I can go out there and give this Carrie Bennett person my full attention."

Map in hand, Nick later showed the map to his contracted advisor. "Here's the area we're most interested in. It seems to have the greatest potential for the type of growth my company desires."

During a boring meeting his advisor insisted on with some corporate farm types, he showed the little town's picture to the company president.

"Where did you ever get that picture?" Mr. Roberts asked. "It's a tiny town almost not on the maps. I maintain a house there to hide in when I want to get away."

"Really?" This was even better for Nick.

"Yes. I chose the location because it's not only a charming little town but it's also close to some of my properties."

"It sounds wonderful. I'd like to see it someday when I have the time." Growing up, Nick had learned a lot about how to get what he wanted out of his mother and remote father by making it seem like it was their idea.

Mr. Roberts leaned back in his chair. It would be a double score to get a fresh capital infusion in his company while at the same time finding new foreign markets for his products and land buying prospects in Europe. *Hmm*, he thought, *a vacation house in the Mediterranean.*

"I have an idea. Why don't you and your associate stay at my Palouse house while you're checking out properties? From what you've shown me, it's about as central as you can get for the region's vineyards and hop growers, also. The whole area is permeated with wheat, barley, and potato farms. Everything a beverage conglomerate needs."

Nick smiled. It was the exact offer he had been fishing for. "I don't know. I don't want to put anyone out."

"Nonsense. The least I can do is offer a little hospitality to a possible future business associate."

A few days later, as Mr. Roberts showed Nick and his advisor around his Palouse property, Nick asked, "You have nice stables, but they're empty. Where are your horses?"

"I've been away more than usual lately. The man I had watching the place was called away, so I'm boarding them on the other side of town. My daughter goes there to ride now." Willa's car pulled into the yard. "Oh, here she and her boyfriend are now."

Willa Roberts was hot, Nick thought. His time in Eastern Washington might just have benefits beyond his initial mission. Now, just to get her away from her boyfriend. When she stuck out her hand, his shake was closer to a caress.

"Your father said you like to ride. It's been a while, but maybe you and your friend could show me your horses some time." Nick sensed her boyfriend wasn't inclined to let her out of his sight, a mere inconvenience which hadn't stopped him before. "Although, I'm not too familiar with all of this cowboy stuff. I learned in Europe."

"Well, since tomorrow's Saturday, you may get your chance if my dad doesn't have anything for you." Willa smiled at her boyfriend. "We were planning to go to the Bennett ranch tomorrow to ride. I've been practicing using a western saddle on a horse I'm helping to retrain. You can ride my horse and use my tack."

When she said the name Bennett, it was all Nick could do not to laugh. Was Karma somehow smiling down on him? He held back. It may all be a coincidence, but wouldn't it be great if his target was that easy to find?

"I'd love that. I'm just the PR guy here. My advisor and your father will be busy talking shop."

Mid-morning Saturday, Carrie just finished saddling up the three horses Willa asked for in her phone call the previous night. Her nemesis, her boyfriend, and someone she didn't recognize walked into the stables.

"Isn't it getting a little hot for you to go riding?" Carrie asked. "I mean, it *is* June in the Palouse."

"We're just home for a week or so before taking off to Europe," Willa answered. "I need to put my time in on Spot, don't I?"

Carrie half grinned. "So, we're still maintaining that charade, are we?"

"I don't know what you mean." Willa rolled her eyes. "Where's Bill? Aren't you and him going with us?"

Peevishly, Carrie said, "You didn't see him? Your father has him off on some job." Wanting to deflect from that sensitive subject, she looked at the third person in Willa's entourage. "Who's this? Does he know how to ride?"

"Hi, my name's Nick, and yes I do, but it's been a while." The visitor spoke with a heavy British accent. "I only see three horses. Aren't you coming too? Being a third wheel makes me uncomfortable."

Carrie studied him for a moment. He was young, very handsome, and somehow strangely familiar. "I suppose I can go since my chores are done. Give me a minute to saddle my mother's horse."

As the ride progressed, Willa and her boyfriend got farther and farther ahead. Too busy chatting with the first new male in a long time who seemingly wasn't trying to change or fix something in her, Carrie didn't notice.

"So, who's this Bill that Willa asked about? Is he your boyfriend?"

"I wouldn't call him that," she answered. "I don't know what we are anymore."

"Is he dependable? Does he know the region around here?" Nick asked. "I overheard you say that Mr. Roberts called him for a job. I assume he's the one chosen to escort my advisor around looking at properties."

"That's highly probable. Bill has worked on most of the local Roberts properties."

"I understand those holdings are almost all field crops north of here. That's my advisor's expertise." Nick looked sideways at Carrie. "I'm wanting to check out vine crops—hops and vineyards. Aren't most of those south of here?"

"Mostly. A few are northeast."

"To save time, I thought I'd check those out while your friend and my advisor are off in the other direction. Uh, what do you do for work?"

"Right now, nothing," she answered. "Why do you ask?"

"I need a guide. Would you be interested? I'd pay for your time."

Carrie studied her saddle horn. She had been a virtual captive on the ranch for a year. The last few months, she'd had more freedom and started venturing farther afield. Her and Bill became more relaxed and even went on a date, sort of. Still having a long way to go in the process of accepting each other again, it started uncomfortably but went much better as the night went on. Then, he pulled back and said what he did. It devastated her.

Now she thought just getting off the property without a watchful escort would be liberating. With Charlie picking up the slack at the ranch, she felt comfortable spending more time away from home. "How much? When do I start?"

"Is Monday too soon? We can do a short day trip to the vineyards north of here. If you prefer, we can keep the arrangement just between us so your friend won't get jealous."

"That won't be necessary. His opinion isn't important right now."

Riding up with her boyfriend, Willa asked, "What are you two talking about?"

Nick replied, "I was just trying to talk Carrie into showing me some local vineyards."

Willa's face lit up. "That sounds like fun! Can we go too? We can make it a foursome."

"Sure, why not?" Nick answered. This would be perfect for his plan. The other couple could be used as buffers so he didn't appear to be a stalker. "Speaking of foursomes, it's been great getting back on a horse again. Is it possible to do this again tomorrow?"

Carrie shrugged. It was nice to talk to a new person, especially one this handsome and educated. "My family's in Spokane for the weekend, so I have nothing better to do."

Willa grimaced a little and glanced at her boyfriend. "Sorry, but we have somewhere we have to be Sunday."

"Oh, well I guess that kills the idea then." Nick looked hopefully at Carrie.

Wanting a distraction from her ongoing conflict with Bill, she decided a ride with the young man beside her would do just fine. "Nonsense. I don't think you'll try and kidnap me or something. Just the two of us can go out tomorrow."

Willa studied her father's guest and Carrie for a moment. There just might be a spark there. Maybe introducing the two would gain her some more redemption points. "Well, you two have a good time. We'll all get together Monday to start our vineyard tours."

When the other couple rode on, Nick leaned over to Carrie and whispered, "Don't worry. You'll still be on the clock during the tours."

CHAPTER THIRTY-FOUR
TOUR GUIDE OR ESCORT?

The next day, Carrie had Willa's horse and Spot saddled when Willa and her boyfriend dropped Nick off on the way past. Willa called out her window, "Can you get him back to our place when you're done?"

"Sure. If he doesn't behave, it's only a ten-mile walk."

Enjoying a day getting to know a male more world traveled than any other man in the vicinity, she relaxed in his presence. Back in the stables after the ride, Nick pressed up against her from behind to help her remove the saddle. His closeness somehow familiar, Carrie paused and leaned into him, savoring the moment. Shaking herself back to reality, she put her hand on his back as he threw the saddle on its rack.

"You need to be fed. After we brush the horses down, do you want to get something to eat?"

Having been called back into town by Mr. Roberts, Bill saw Carrie's car out front of the tiny, local drive-in. Wanting to check on her, maybe try to explain again feelings he didn't understand himself, he spun around in the road and drove into the parking lot. Just as he pulled his keys from the ignition and reached for the truck door's handle, he saw her through the window, sitting at a table, talking and laughing with a guy he had never seen before.

With a blank expression, she locked eyes with Bill. He restarted his truck and backed away.

Nick saw Carrie's angry expression and turned to see why. As a tall, young man sitting in an old pickup backed away from the drive-in's front window, he asked, "Who's that? An ex-boyfriend?"

"If you want to call him that. He works for Willa's dad."

Nick studied her for a moment, then turned and watched Bill's truck disappear out of town. The old boyfriend might cause some complications. He'd have to keep him away while wooing Carrie.

Monday, Mr. Roberts introduced Bill to his company's possible new associates. "These are some foreign businessmen I'd like you to show my various properties to."

Bill replied reluctantly, sizing up the guy he'd seen with Carrie. "I can do that. We can start looking at the closest today and tomorrow. Later, we can go farther out."

"That's great." Mr. Roberts dug in his pocket. "Here are the keys to my condo in Moses Lake. It's only two bedrooms, but you can stay as long as you need."

Nick smiled. "If it's alright with you, sir, I'd like to remain here. I'm going to check out the vineyards and hop growers in the region. In fact, your daughter and her boyfriend volunteered to be my guides until they are off to Europe. They've invited Willa's horse trainer friend to come with us to make it an even number."

Bill almost choked. He and Carrie's relationship had been strained since he so inarticulately tried to tell her he needed more time to sort out his feelings. Now, this handsome rich dude with a self-satisfied condescending smirk on his face was planning to take her to the fanciest places in the area. What Bill didn't see was while he, Mr. Roberts, and the advisor talked, Nick was sticking a magnetic tracking device in the wheel well of his truck.

During the two days Willa and her boyfriend were along, Nick did his best to act business-like but charming. He needed Carrie to relax in his company enough to continue alone with him on the tours. Driven to find out what had made her so special to his father, he was determined to get to know the little blonde—especially between the sheets.

When Mr. Roberts' daughter left on her junket, Nick maintained his charming best behavior. Somehow, this Bill fellow remained a large roadblock. Whenever his name came up in conversations, Carrie became distant. It was time to move him further out of the picture. Nick called Mr. Roberts.

"I've been examining your land holdings. You have extensive grain production in Eastern Montana, don't you?"

"Why, yes we do," Mr. Roberts replied. "I didn't think you were interested in anything that far inland."

Smiling at himself in the guest house bathroom mirror, Nick said, "I think we are. I'd appreciate it if your man could show my advisor those properties."

"I'd be more than happy to send him that way. I imagine it'd take a week or two to travel over there and go between the various properties. If they left next Monday, would it be okay?"

"That'd be great." Nick was having a hard time disguising his glee while on the phone. "I'll tell my advisor to be ready for your man to pick him up."

These Americans' fixation on vacations was working out wonderfully. With Mr. Roberts off somewhere and Willa in Europe, Nick was going to have the Roberts' place all to himself for weeks. It was time to make his move.

Saturday, they headed back to town in his rental car after touring the last local winery. Sensing she had relaxed in is company enough, he asked, "I'm all by myself tonight. Would you like to stay and eat some take-out with me? I mean, you already have to drop by to fetch your car. We could examine some maps and you can show me where the concentration of hop growers and vineyards are south of here."

At that very moment, they drove past Bill walking out of the small mercantile in their town. He and Carrie made eye contact. She gave a fake laugh just to rub it in, then turned back to Nick and answered, "Okay. Pull into the drive-in and we'll get something."

This Nick guy was hard to pin down. Sitting beside him reading the maps and eating, he seemed so familiar. From the first time they rode together, when their hands brushed, it was no big deal, even pleasant. Now, starting to feel a longing tingle in his presence, she battled to suppress it. Then, he leaned in and sniffed her hair and acted like he was about to kiss her. It was time to go.

Sunday dinner was strained for both Bill and Carrie when their families gathered at the Bennett house. While the others visited, the two of them barely acknowledged each other with more than a grunt. When Carrie wasn't looking, he would look in her direction longingly. When he was focused elsewhere, she alternated between hurt and anger in her glances toward Bill.

Virtually the only words spoken between them was when Bill, trying to figure out what Carrie and Nick's relationship was, asked in a private moment, "How were the vineyards?"

She answered curtly, "Fine."

His words came out all on their own, "So, are you two dating now?"

She snapped, "That's none of your business. You gave up the right to ask that weeks ago."

"I take that as a yes," he mumbled. Unable to stop himself, he said sadly, "I guess that means you're sleeping with him."

Carrie's temper flashed. After finally sorting through her mistrust issues with him and the way he basically held her captive, she had worked hard at restoring their relationship. It was *him* who had rejected *her.*

"*That* is even less of your business." Turning away, she stomped off.

The dinner broke up early. Carrie's parents had to travel to Spokane and stay overnight for an early morning adjustment of Randy's artificial leg. Bill needed to head for Moses Lake and stay the night so he and the advisor could leave for Montana at first light. Alone, bored, even madder at Bill, Carrie decided to take her British boss leftovers.

When Nick opened the door, he smiled at the pretty girl in a dress and heels, holding a sack of food. "Well, food delivery couriers are getting better looking each day."

She blushed. "I thought you could use a nice home cooked meal. Since we've both been abandoned for the evening, I thought we could be social orphans together."

From the first day riding horses, Carrie's mind swirled with comparisons. Always the consummate gentleman, every time Nick did something nice for her, she wished Bill could have been even a tenth that attentive during the last few months. As time wore on, her resentment toward Bill supplanted the comparisons.

Angry from his assumptions earlier in the day, Carrie had spitefully put on a dress she knew Bill liked and, for the first time since leaving Europe, wore heels. After they ate, Nick led her to the sofa and handed her a glass of wine.

Sitting with his arm on the rear of the couch, he leaned toward her and said, "Let's discuss our inspection tours around Yakima and Walla Walla."

This time, Carrie realized he definitely was going in for a kiss. She pulled away slightly, allowing just a peck, then giggled to make him feel more comfortable with the half-hearted rejection. But still, the fact that a man was interested in her aroused feelings she hadn't felt in a long while. She hadn't been with a man in a mentally "good" way since her enslavement in Greece.

"I should leave now. We have a long day tomorrow." Reluctantly standing, she reached for her purse. "We have to drive all the way to Yakima and back."

Nick took her hand and pulled Carrie back down beside him, causing her phone to drop on the carpet. "Don't rush off. We still have plans to make."

Unrelentingly, Nick persisted, not trying even a little to hide what he wanted. Constantly rubbing against her, putting his hand on her thigh made it hard for the young woman who had been out of circulation for so long to concentrate. With him snuggling her neck and cheek, even a few light pecks on the lips, her body kept contradicting what her mind said. Each time he kissed her, she let him linger a little longer.

The ratio of time spent on making plans and time spent kissing inexorably shifted away from business. Finally, when they were doing nothing else but pressing their lips together, she pushed him away.

"I don't feel comfortable . . ." Yes, she was. She knew exactly what he was going to try. As disappointed as Carrie was with Bill, all this attention from another man was welcomed. It was why she dressed up.

"Well then," Nick cooed. "Let me make you as comfortable as I can."

He pinned Carrie's head against the sofa back and *really* kissed her. Instead of pulling back, she pushed against him willingly, passionately. Nick pulled her into a seated position on his lap, and their tongues danced. Now it was her kissing *him* forcibly. Nick grinned inside. He was about to find out just what it was about this girl that drove his father to the edge. His shirt removed, her outfit's straps down off her shoulders, he started to lift Carrie's dress over her head.

She froze, realizing she was about to take out her frustration and hurt over Bill's rejection by having revenge sex with Nick. Aware this was almost a clone situation that trapped her on the island, she pushed away and stood up.

Staring down at his uniquely tattooed chest, she panted out, "I . . . I have to go. Sorry." Grabbing her purse, she ran to her car, leaving everything else on the living room floor.

Monday morning, Nick lay in bed smiling. He had found the girl who had captured his father's heart. Even though he hadn't shagged her on his first try, he was convinced he would soon. One of his three primary objectives had been accomplished. Finding agricultural holdings to use for money laundering for the company was so low on the objective list, it was just an afterthought, a cover story to fund the trip.

Looking at Carrie's phone and bra laying on the floor where she left them during her hasty exit the night before, he thought, *She soon won't be needing those. As my broodmare, she'll either be naked or too pregnant to screw. Then, I'll party with other hotties until Carrie squirts out another of my many offspring. I'll show everyone how to treat a woman back on that island.*

Back on the island—that was his main objective. He wanted to get her back on that Island and show everyone how much more of a man he was than his father. To do that, Nick knew he had to be beyond his best behavior. He needed to be a gentleman and lover above all others in history. Believing he was already the latter, he smiled again. It was being the gentleman which would tax his acting abilities.

Barely showered and dressed by 9 a.m., much earlier than he was accustomed to back home, Nick heard a knock at the door. When he opened it, there stood his contrite target.

"I'm sorry about last night." Carrie held out a to-go bag from the town's tiny drive in." I brought you some breakfast as an apology."

The game was still on. *With her so skittish, I still need to be extra careful,* he thought as he invited her in. "Come in. I wanted to call you and apologize for my unprofessional behavior but," he walked to the coffee table and held out her phone and bra, "you left these here when I drove you away with my forwardness."

Carrie blushed and sheepishly grabbed the bra. When their hands touched lingeringly, she almost lost her self-control again. Pulling herself back together, she said, "It wasn't your fault. I've had a couple of bad relationships and am so confused about what I want. I can be a bit flighty because of it. But, just so you know, it's never going to happen between us."

"That's perfectly understandable." Hiding a flash of anger behind a smile, he changed the subject. "I think it's about time we look at the vineyards and hop groves south of here. I had an idea. To save a lot of useless travel time, we can just stay at . . . what do you call them here? Motels?"

Carrie laughed. "That might be pushing the business arrangement a little."

"Nonsense." He smiled at her. "We have a working relationship, nothing more. Last night we proved that we can pull back and be professional. Separate rooms of course. But . . . you might want to pack a couple of nice outfits in case we're asked to go somewhere fancy. Something like last night's dress."

"I guess I could try that."

The rest of the morning, they spent planning out their route. That night, Carrie's parents returned from Spokane while she was in the middle of packing. Beth walked into her room after making Randy a pot of coffee.

"You know, for the last six months, your father's been doing so much better. I think it's about time we got Bill out here to remove his elevator. I'd like my closet back." Then, she noticed her daughter was packing for a trip. "Going somewhere?"

"Yeah, Mom, Mr. Roberts' buyer wanted to visit a bunch of vineyards south of here. To save driving time, we're going to stay in motels. It'll make the whole process quicker."

Beth didn't like this at all. Quick day trips to wineries north of their house was one thing. Overnight stays held completely different hazards. "Are you sure you're up for this? I mean . . ."

"I'm fine, Mom. I need to learn how to handle things myself, or I'll never amount to anything. I refuse to be an emotional cripple anymore."

"Of course, dear, just be careful. That's all I'm saying."

Beth silently watched her only child for a while. Her daughter had let adventure be the gateway to traps before. She prayed this time wouldn't be a repeat. Having never met him, Carrie's family assumed Nick was a middle-aged businessman giving their daughter her first real job in a year and a half. It distracted her from festering over Bill.

Tuesday morning, Carrie parked in front of the cottage and stowed her suitcase in the back of Nick's rental car. When he climbed in, she smiled and said, "Two rooms, right?"

He grinned back. "Of course. This is purely a platonic business trip."

Knowing the way, she drove southwest while he stared out the side window, pretending to admire the scenery. In reality, he was plotting, firming up his game plan. He had no intention of letting Carrie be in a bed without him on top of her. He was going to spend the day being a fawning gentleman. When he got her back to the island, she was going to learn what a true master was.

After a carefree day of touring wineries in the Yakima area with a perfect gentleman, Carrie said, "We should get checked in to a motel."

At his insistence, she drove to an upscale motel. He hopped out and grabbed both of their luggage. "I'll get us checked in. Why don't you park, make your calls, and find a nice restaurant?"

After dinner, he handed her a room key as they rode the elevator to the top floor. When she opened the door and turned to say goodnight, he followed her into the room. "What are you doing? Don't we have separate rooms?"

Taking her around the waist, Nick kissed her ear and whispered, "Yes, but you're so hard to resist."

She giggled and playfully shoved him back into the hall. "We've been good until now. Let's not spoil it."

"Drat! Foiled again." He laughed as she closed the door. Accidentally turning the opposite direction from the elevator, he paused on the first stairwell landing, fuming. After angrily slamming his fist down on the metal railing, he collected himself and stomped the rest of the way down to the front desk and actually got a second room.

In the morning, Carrie heard a knock on her door. When she opened it, Nick stood in the hall sheepishly wearing the same clothes from the previous day. "I suppose you want your suitcase. I saw it was accidently left in my room."

"Thanks. I'll see you downstairs for breakfast." Impatient over not yet claiming his prize, he was still making progress. Nick later looked over his meal. "You know, I heard there are quite a few vine-yards in Oregon's Willamette valley, and my allotted budget can stand a little more time on the road. We could tour there before working our way back."

In no hurry to get home, Carrie shrugged. "Sure, I don't have anything better to do for a while."

They headed west, the opposite direction from home. Working their way back two weeks later in Walla Walla, Nick rented a vine-yard's guest cabin, vacant due to a last minute cancellation. Even though they still had separate bedrooms, it was getting harder for her to keep him at arm's length. They stayed an extra day tour-ing wine aging cellars. Carrie couldn't shake a troublesome feeling that Nick had already decided on what he wanted and was just kill-ing time to be with her.

Enjoying their extracurricular activities, she took it for what she felt it was—a vacation to dull the pain from Bill's latest perceived slight. There was still something about Nick she couldn't quite put her finger on. Not that it mattered. As soon as they were back at Mr. Roberts' house, she fully intended to go her separate way.

The trip was yielding more benefits for Carrie than just the wage. She became comfortable with male companionship again. During the attempt to rekindle her lost relationship with Bill, it was constantly nagging in the back of her mind. Now she knew that she could, and it brought her joy.

Impatient Nick saw things differently. He sat mulling, *This whole seduction thing is taking way too long. I haven't put this much time and effort into anything. It's time for me to make a play. I should just pin her down and take what's mine. No, that wouldn't work. Carrie needs to be willing get her out of the country. I have to destroy any reason that my target has to stay in this tiny town.* Assuming everyone had a strained, distant relationship with their parents like he did, that meant the reason was the ex-boyfriend.

Carrie had never confided what Bill had done to her to make him her ex. In Nick's world, there were very few things that would cause a girl to have such resentment. One was killing a relative or friend. He hadn't heard of any corpses lying about. Another reason was stealing from them. He hadn't seen any evidence of that either.

That left only betrayal. Judging by the ferocity in Carrie's eyes whenever the bumpkin who was escorting the advisor around Montana was mentioned, Nick could only fathom that betrayal had to be cheating with someone else. Bill's demeanor during every interaction Nick had with him shouted jealousy. The ex was trying to make amends and was threatened by other men.

Nick started subtly mentioning suspected triggers. "Look how that idiot is staring past the woman he's with at someone else." Sometimes, he'd mention a movie or book in a conversation where the lead male was unfaithful. When they passed a herd of cattle, he asked, "I wonder how many cows one bull can service?"

By the time they were almost home, he could tell his subliminal reminders of her pain were working. Carrie was agitated, squirming in her seat, allowing the car to wander around in the lane of traffic. He was either going to succeed in finally bedding her or she would drive away enraged.

"It's awfully late, and you seem really tired," Nick said when they pulled in front of the Roberts' farm guest house. "Stay the night in the guest room. Tomorrow, I have to leave and talk to my backers."

She involuntarily yawned. "I guess." Proud of herself for resisting her urges, Carrie followed as he carried the suitcases toward the house. Overly confident, she let down her guard. "We've hung around for weeks now and nothing has happened."

"Sure. Go inside and get warm. I have a phone call to make."

Nick didn't know the full story of Carrie's departure from the island, only that apparently some highly trained operative took out the guards. His father released her to stop the assault. This Bill person could not possibly have been her rescuer. He was much too mild and passive. It would have been a hired mercenary.

Deciding there was no threat of physical harm from such a weak person, Nick had to make the hick believe there was never going to be a Bill and Carrie. In order to cut Carrie's ties, he had to make her ex despise her. Having done it before in college, Nick knew exactly how. Even though he considered the girl in school to be a gargoyle, he did it solely to break her up with a guy he hated. Nick called his adviser.

"Has your guide left yet?" Nick asked. "I need to give him a message."

"Yes. He left about an hour ago."

"So, he's about an hour away from the Roberts house then, isn't he?" Nick quickly finalized his plan. "I need to give him a message, and I don't seem to have his number. Could you forward it to him for me?"

"Sure. What is it?"

"There seems to be something wrong with the guest cottage back porch." Nick could barely contain himself. "Would you have him stop by and check it out tonight? I'll be back from my vineyard inspection tour tomorrow, and I don't want to have any problems with it."

"No problem."

Nick paused outside the front door for a moment before entering. He had to time this just right. The actors must be appropriately costumed and the stage properly set when the curtain rose for the audience of one. He walked in and smiled at his target. His plan was to have Bill pass by the bedroom window on the way to the back porch and see Carrie having sex with another man.

"Would you like a glass of wine?"

"You should know by now that I don't care for alcohol," she answered.

"Not even a sip or two?"

"Oh, okay."

Standing beside the refrigerator with his back to Carrie, Nick dropped a heavy dose of Rohypnol into her glass. Hoping it was enough to knock her out and not question her actions in the morning, he handed her the glass of burgundy and sat beside her.

"I thought you'd like to try something different from what you've had for the last few weeks. I'm determined to expand your horizons."

CHAPTER THIRTY-FIVE
PASTS COLLIDE

Sitting in a middle booth of the truck stop cafeteria with his newly adopted daughter, Mara, Paul choked on a bite of his bacon cheeseburger when a tall, young man took a seat at the counter.

"What's wrong, Dad? You look like you've seen a ghost."

"Nothing," Paul gagged out. "I just swallowed wrong."

Hearing the coughing behind him, the young man at the counter turned and glanced at the commotion. That's when Paul and Bill's eyes locked. Confused, somewhat irritated that a complete stranger was looking at him with what appeared to be a sorrowful expression, Bill asked, "Something wrong, mister?" When the older man continued his lost look, mouth moving but nothing coming out, something about the familiar expression hit home within Bill. "Do I know you? You look vaguely familiar."

Mara spoke for her new father. "You'll have to excuse us. We've had a long drive today. This is my father, Paul Taft. We're passing through looking for a new home."

"Paul Taft? I knew you looked familiar. My name's Bill Schmidt. Didn't I see you at my dad's funeral? Aren't you his cousin?"

Having only known her drug addict mother, then living in the foster home, the thought of an extended line of relatives instantly excited Mara. "*Cousins?* Would you like to sit with us?"

Bill shrugged. "I can for a bit. I'm waiting for a corporate big-wig I've been showing around." Then, he scooted in next to Mara.

Paul remained silent, watching his new daughter pump the tall, young man for family information. Focusing on Bill's hands, scarred and calloused from hard work, he listened to the strong, well-spoken young man. Paul wondered how this seemingly confident young man would react if he knew he was sitting across the table from his father. Paul's left hand, involuntarily trembling from stress, bumped up against a water glass.

Mara, seeing Bill's questioning look, explained when her father remained silent, "Dad got shot in the head protecting me from a pimp. He still has bone fragments in his brain that cause his hand to shake now and then."

Paul kindly chastised her, "You don't have to tell our whole history to a stranger within the first five minutes."

"He's not a stranger, Dad. Bill's a relative. I've never had a relative before." When her dad shrugged, Mara started digging in to her new cousin's life. "Got any brothers or sisters? I've never had any."

Bill checked his phone for messages. "The guy I was supposed to meet is running late, so why not? I have a sister who's five years younger, a one year older stepsister, her younger brother and sister, and a half brother who just turned six."

Paul moved his even more violently trembling hand under the table and squeezed it between his legs. *Six-year-old younger brother?* He couldn't stop himself from asking, "So your mother remarried? What's her last name now?"

"It's Schmidt, same as before. I guess it's kind of a sweet story. Since all of Charlie's kids were adopted by someone else while he had PTSD and was homeless, we would have had three last names in the house. He and Mom decided to adopt back his kids, and they all took the name Schmidt, even Charlie. When Mom later had my little brother, they named him Peter after my dead dad."

"That's so cool! You have *five* brothers and sisters. I'd really like to meet them!" Almost jumping up and down in the booth, she pleaded with Paul, "Can we, Dad? How far do they live from here, Bill?"

Both of their minds occupied elsewhere, the two males at the table blankly stared at each other. Bill, fixated with Carrie dating this new guy, didn't know if he had the strength to bring more complicated distractions home. Paul desperately wanted to see his daughter from a previous existence but didn't know if he could handle seeing his unfaithful wife in her new, apparently happy, life. She had killed him, not with her hands but by completely removing his will to live.

Bill sighed. "I'm getting ready to drive home tonight. However, the closest motel is in the next town."

Mara ecstatically replied before her father had a chance to speak. "We don't need a motel. We only need somewhere flat enough to park our motorhome."

As surely as an oncoming train headlight in a dark tunnel, Paul felt impotent to avoid what he saw as another impending heartbreak heading his way. Before he could stop them, Bill and Mara were entering each other's contact information into their phones.

Bill stood and waved at a man heading their way. "Here's the guy I'm supposed to show around. There's a rest stop south of Ritzville where we can meet up when I'm done. I'll call you later."

Resolutely paying the tab, Paul followed his giddy daughter across the parking lot. She had lost so much in her young life, suffered abuse, and degradation. He just couldn't deprive her of this chance to meet a new family, even if it meant his own torture.

Having a visceral reaction when he sighted his now restored, beloved, old pickup sitting in a lean-to, Paul almost sideswiped an outbuilding. The RV had barely rolled to a stop before Mara leapt out and ran toward the farmhouse. Jumping back and forth between each person coming out, she grabbed their hands and squealed, "Are you my cousin? Are you my cousin?"

Paul couldn't help but be caught up in the joy his adopted

daughter showed upon meeting an actual extended family. Then, Karen came through the door and stood on the porch. With his left hand shaking more violently than ever before, he careened between reaching under the driver's seat for his service revolver to put a bullet in her cheating heart, and running up to passionately kiss his lost love.

If Mara was still in the vehicle, he would have swung it around and sped away when what obviously was her husband put one arm around Karen and placed his other hand on the head of a young boy. Trapped with no avenue of escape, he felt like he was standing on a land mine in the center of an emotional battlefield, impotent to do anything but guess which would tear his body apart first— love's bullets or scorn's shrapnel. When Mara and Bill urged him out of the RV, Karen inflicted an even worse wound than any he had feared.

She reached to shake his hand, blank non-recognition on her face. "Hi. Welcome to our small piece of heaven. What brings you to our area?"

His words wouldn't come. Unable to look in her eyes, Paul instead looked at her youngest child. "How are you, young man? My name is Paul. What's yours?"

Unsure about the strange man with a trembling hand, the lad hid behind his father's leg. "My name is Peter."

That initial meeting was just the beginning of Paul's suffering. His hosts insisted on him joining them for dinner. While his delighted daughter sat at the dining room table absorbing her new cousins explaining how they were all distantly related by blood, he did his best to endure the torment of watching his wife and her new husband's outward display of affection toward each other.

Finally, unable to withstand the agony anymore, he excused himself. "It's been a long day. If you don't mind, I think I'll retire to the RV for the night."

As he passed through the kitchen, a beaming Mara asked, "Can

I stay in the house tonight? They said I can share a bed with one of the other girls."

After he nodded and shuffled out of the house, Karen looked up at her husband from under his loving arm. "That man sure is a strange one. Something is definitely off kilter there. If my first impression counts, I don't think that I like or trust him."

The next morning, Karen knocked on the door of Paul's motorhome. Trying to discount her mistrust of her new guest, she wrote it off as him being fatigued from travel. Maybe they could start anew over breakfast.

"Come in. I'm in the back. Make yourself at home while I search for a decent pair of shoes."

While she waited just inside the door, Karen critically examined the inside of the RV. There was the expected amount of early teen girl souvenirs from an extended road trip cluttering the living area. A couple of dirty dishes lay in the sink. What caught her eye was an official-looking open folder laying on the dinette table. Her heart almost stopped when she slid a paper aside and read the title tag on the front cover: Pressure Washer Killer.

Her mind raced through multiple scenarios. *Why does he have this report? What does he know? Is this why he's here? Does he suspect I had something to do with the killings? Is Paul in contact with Detective Thompson? Does Paul know that the man she cheated on Peter with was Lamont, the actual serial killer? Did Lamont send Paul a letter the same time he mailed one to her husband?* Whatever the cost, Karen decided he must never find out that Lamont's body was rotting away eight feet under the ground less than seven miles away—with five .44 magnum rounds from Peter's old revolver still in it.

"Is there something you want?"

Karen jumped. She hadn't heard the bedroom door open. Quickly closing the folder, she stammered, "I . . . I came over to see if you want breakfast. Everyone is gathering in the kitchen before I have to leave for work."

"Sure, I'll be right over." He glanced toward the folder. "As soon as I tidy up a bit around here."

Watching through a window as his hostess almost ran across the farmyard toward the house, Paul wondered, *Why was she acting so guilty? Was there something in the folder that set her off other than the fact that it was from a time when she was busy screwing someone else instead of being my faithful wife?*

CHAPTER THIRTY-SIX
NICK'S REVENGE

Sitting beside Carrie on the sofa a few minutes after she started sipping the drugged wine, Nick feigned a worried expression. "I had a chat with my advisor. Did your friend live in Moses Lake for a while? Is that how he knows where all of the Roberts properties are?"

"Yeah." Carrie scowled. She had just about purged her need to get revenge on Bill from her mind and was ready to move on. Why did Nick have to bring him back up again? It set her off. "He lived there for over a year."

"Oh, that explains it, then." He studied her reaction, waiting for the drug to kick in.

"Explains what?"

"It appears your friend and my advisor have been back in Moses Lake for a few days." Nick almost couldn't believe how well his plot was thickening on its own, but still modified the facts to enhance his narrative. "The two of them were in a restaurant on their first night back, and your friend knew some of the other diners."

"Yeah, well, Bill interacts easily with strangers."

"My advisor said that it didn't seem like they were strangers. In fact, your friend left with a young lady, and my advisor hasn't seen him since." He barely could restrain his glee as Carrie's anger and hurt instantly boiled over.

Her face clouded, and she reached for her purse to leave. "I should go. I won't be good company for anyone tonight." Carrie staggered when she stood.

No, Nick thought, *that would ruin his whole plan.* "Here, here, I can't let you drive like this." He grabbed Carrie around the waist and pulled her to him. Kissing her forehead and cheek, he cooed in her ear, "Retaliation . . . revenge."

But, thoroughly under the drug's influence, she didn't hear. Swooping his prey into his arms, he took Carrie into the bedroom. Placing her on the bed, he opened the drapes so Bill would clearly see her naked with another man and what they were doing. "I've wanted you from the instant I laid eyes on you."

Lusting for the all but comatose girl on the bed, he removed her clothing to finally have his will with her. He had just finished taking off his own clothes when his phone buzzed.

"Hello?"

"It's Bill Schmidt. I've already passed through town and had some complications pop up. I won't be able to come by until morning."

Nick thought quickly on how his plan could be salvaged. "That's too bad. With the noises coming from the rear of the cottage, I'm nervous that if it's left unattended, some real damage could happen. The earlier in the morning, the better."

"I can be there at seven if that's not too early."

"No, that's fine. I'm sure Mr. Roberts will understand if the damage increases."

Not wanting to take any more time than necessary away from achieving his goal, he went into the living room naked and staged it with the clothes he'd just removed from Carrie. So there would be no questioning his story, he placed her underwear on the floor within plain sight of the front door. The scattered clothing would only reinforce his narrative.

The taunting of her ex-friend gave Nick a moment to reflect at the bedroom door. The laws in this country were different from what he was used to. Not sure what the consequences were of having sex with a comatose girl, he considered waiting until she was completely ensnared. It would only be a little longer. *Like hell,* he thought. *I've already waited way too long for this, and I have until seven in the morning.* Grinning evilly, he climbed onto the bed to fully enjoy his prize.

Afterward, he lay back on his pillow smiling at the ceiling and thought, *This should put an end to any hold this area has on the little slut. Those two will never talk to each other again. Now, I just have to get her on that plane.*

Carrie awoke naked next to Nick, her body telling her what she had done. Confused, she slipped out of bed and robotically made coffee. Intending to get on with her life with no one the wiser, she started to leave a note on the kitchen counter by the coffee pot. Having second thoughts, thinking it was the coward's way out, she decided to shower.

Hearing the water running, Nick hopped out of bed and installed a tracking app on her phone. Having barely finished matching his phone to hers when the water shut off, he jumped back into bed and acted like he just woke up.

Her hair still wet, Carrie came into the bedroom wearing just a towel. She handed him a coffee mug and sat on the edge of the bed. Running her fingers over his chest, she stroked the sizable tattoo dead center of his sternum.

"You know," she said, not wanting to admit she had no memory of it. "Last night was just revenge sex. It didn't mean anything. I was just getting back at someone."

Excellent! he thought, *I've gotten away with it!* Rolling on his side to spoon her, he reached around and tried to remove the towel. "It was still great. I'd love a second helping."

She stood to get dressed. "Sorry, I need some time to figure this out. I need to think it through."

Nick's phone screen lit up with a notification. Bill's truck was coming up the driveway. "I put your suitcase in the closet. I'll give you some space."

When he saw Carrie's car parked off to the side of the guest house's front porch, Bill told himself she had left it there because it was broken down. He felt the hood. It had been there a long time and was cold. Leaning against the car's fender, he futilely tried to convince himself there was another, innocent, explanation other than the obvious.

Walking in front of the car toward the front door to knock, he realized the front room was unlit. The only light from the building came from a side window. Bill knew what room it came from—the bedroom he slept in when he was Mr. Roberts' full time caretaker. He knocked on the front door.

The living room light came on, and a disheveled Nick answered wearing only a towel. "Oh, is it seven already?"

Using every bit of self-control he could muster, Bill said, "I'm here to look at the back porch."

"When you said that you couldn't come until this morning, I went out and checked it last night. Everything looks fine. You sounded tired, and I didn't want to disturb you again."

His whole body shaking, Bill asked, "So you don't want me to check it?"

"No, that's all right. It was a long day yesterday. Carrie was exhausted and wanted to go to bed." Nick smiled and motioned toward the scattered undergarments on the floor. "Then it became a *very* physical night. I *really* should get back to her."

Right then, half dressed with wet hair, Carrie came out of the bedroom searching for her shoes. Frozen in place, she and Bill stared at each other. Nick grinned smugly at his competition and closed the door.

Bill staggered off the porch. Knees buckling, he collapsed, curled up on the ground, retching violently. Unable to stand, he crawled back and lay beside his truck sobbing. Emotionally spent, he climbed behind the wheel, spun a doughnut, and headed back down the long drive.

After gleefully watching through the door's peephole, Nick

turned back to his prey. "I need to catch up with my advisor. I'll be back in a week with your pay. Maybe after you're no longer on the payroll, we can see where this goes."

"Maybe. We'll see." A contrite Carrie hurriedly finished dressing and gathered her stuff to leave. While Nick showered, she passed by the refrigerator and noticed for the first time the almost full burgundy wine decanter on the counter. She mumbled to herself, "I *had* to drink more than that to lose all memory of what I did." Then, she saw a tiny clear plastic bag with a blue powder residue carelessly left near the splashboard. Not quite comprehending what it meant, she walked out of the house.

Heading toward her car, she saw the puddle of vomit in the gravel near her car. Then, there were drag marks where Bill had crawled to his truck puking. His pickup had spun a doughnut in the parking area and sprayed gravel down the driveway.

"Oh my god! What have I done?"

Speeding through town toward his parents' place, Carrie saw Bill pulling away from the little town's mercantile. She gave chase. Trying unsuccessfully to get him to pull over, she attempted to pass and almost caused a wreck. Rather than see someone get killed, he stopped on a field access apron.

He growled when she ran up to his window, "What do you want?"

"Why did you drive off in a huff?" Carrie knew full well why. "I wanted to discuss our employer."

"My boss is Mr. Roberts. I don't know who yours is or *what* your job is. I hope you're well paid to do it."

Staggered back, almost into traffic, a passing car horn froze her. Carrie wasn't very sure herself what she had been doing the last few weeks. Bill jumped out of his truck, led her to the ditch embankment, and forced her to sit.

"Stay there until you stop being hysterical."

When he turned to go back to his truck, Carrie shouted, "Just where do you think you're going?"

"Home. It's obvious you don't want to associate with the likes of me."

"What? You idiot! Why do you think I chased you down the road like a maniac?" Carrie started to cry. "Why are you being like this? Are you *jealous?*"

"You're *sleeping* with him!"

Knowing what he had seen from the doorway but still uncertain what she had done, she deflected with her reply, "I know what it looked like, but I was tired from the long day and drive home from Walla Walla. I fell asleep."

"You two have been constantly hanging out. For weeks, you've been traveling together. It's obvious you're dating."

"I don't know why you'd care, but yes, we've gone out a few times."

"So, you *have* slept with him."

"That's none of your business," Carrie snapped. Then, she said spitefully, "You already knew that by spying and dropping by unannounced. You made it abundantly clear months ago you weren't interested in me, so what's it to you? In fact, where have you been the last few days? Nick's advisor said you ran off with a girl and he hasn't seen you for a couple of days."

"What? No! We just got back from Montana yesterday morning. I ran into my dad's cousin and his daughter. I left the advisor at the condo and drove home with the cousin."

"If you weren't spying, why were you at the guest house so early this morning?"

"Nick's advisor called me while I was driving home. He insisted there was a problem with the back porch and wanted it checked before you got back *today.*"

"*What?* There must be some mistake." Carrie was having a hard time comprehending any of this. "Nick talked to the advisor as soon as we got to the house. That's when he discovered you were chasing your ex-girlfriend."

"Huh?"

Staring at the grass covered with a thin layer of dust, she questioned, "Why would the advisor lie to Nick?"

Bill sat beside her. "Maybe he didn't. The guy was tired from traveling. Maybe there was just a communication problem. Besides, I called Nick last night and told him I wasn't coming. I told him I'd be there this morning."

"I don't think so." Things just weren't adding up for Carrie. How was Bill conveniently at the front door when she was getting dressed? Why was she blacked out when she drank so little alcohol? Maybe Nick planned it? Was the open packet of powder on the counter somehow associated? If so, why? "Maybe Nick was jealous of you? I don't know why he would be."

"I don't know what you mean," Bill said. Then, he looked at the ground and mumbled, "He's a guy. If he's into you, of course he's jealous of other men."

"I don't know why he would be. I told him from the start I wasn't interested." She looked at him sadly. "I lied. I don't remember last night. If we did anything, it was a one-time fling. When I heard you were with another girl again, it drove me over the brink. It would have been revenge more than anything. He's leaving anyway."

"It was *just* a fling? What is that supposed to mean?"

"I need a social life. I can't stay cooped up on that ranch forever. *You* were the one who pushed *me* away. I was angry with you. You really hurt me when you said I wasn't good enough to be with anymore."

Bill sighed. "That's not what I said. I'm just having a hard time figuring out what we are to each other now."

"Well, you *need* to. I'm not going to be here forever."

"Oh. I guess that's it then." He started to get up, but Carrie grabbed his arm.

"Figure it out."

"I know. I just need some time to think."

"I understand that." She leaned against him, her own tortured emotions over her actions during the last weeks ricocheting inside her head. "But you need to. We both do."

Bill stood and held out his hand to help Carrie to her feet. "We good now?"

"Yeah. I think I'll spend some time working with Spot." What she didn't say was she needed time to figure out if her sleeping with Nick had actually been about revenge, if she was romantically interested in him, or if it even happened. And what were the warning flashers in her mind over him all about? What was in that small packet of powder? "See you later?"

"Yeah, sure." His heart aching, Bill wanted to spend time with Carrie, but Mr. Roberts kept him busy. Believing she had sex with that Nick fellow tormented him. But, after his jealous outburst, he didn't want to push things.

CHAPTER THIRTY-SEVEN
CONFRONTATION

Carrie's pay for being Nick's tour guide wouldn't come until he returned in a week after his meetings, so going shopping was out. She spent quite a bit of time alone, riding the Appaloosa around the ranch's dry summer rangeland, thinking.

She loved Bill, really she did. But what kind of love was it? They didn't have the chance to figure it out after high school graduation, and life became complicated. They had both been through a lot and changed so much.

Late spring when she finally had her head clear again and was willing to try, it was Bill who had pulled away. Knowing it was a mistake to have done whatever she did with Nick, Carrie still felt liberated. For the first time since Ethan, she had pulled back, knowing it was her own decision and she was free to make it. As she rode, she talked. Spot nodded her agreement to everything Carrie said.

Bumping into each other at the town's mini-mart, Bill tentatively walked over to Carrie. "How've you been? My dad's cousin and his daughter have kept me busy."

"Fine. I've just been working with Spot and wishing I had a social life."

"Well, Mr. Roberts is hosting a big birthday bash for Willa this weekend. He's invited my family. He's also invited anyone important in the area. I hear the heads of the investment group employing your friend are coming. Were you invited?"

"Yeah. My family too." Carrie could envision all kinds of possible ways the evening could go wrong. Bill and Nick in the same room? She *really* didn't want to go, but it was when she was supposed to receive her pay.

Another person who didn't want to go was Paul. He and Karen had butted heads more than once since Mara insisted they stay. His previous body's widow went ballistic when she caught him examining her beloved old truck. He wanted to leave immediately, but his daughter wanted to spend one more night with her new-found relatives without their parents.

His motorhome was packed, everything stowed and ready to leave in the morning. He just needed to silently endure one more night in the presence of that woman and her new husband. Sullenly, he agreed to the party, but only if he could ride in Bill's pickup instead of Karen's SUV.

The instant she walked in, Willa snared Carrie and led her to the massive fireplace where Nick and Mr. Roberts stood, talking. "Nick has invited my boyfriend and I to visit his family's island villa in Greece. Isn't that great?"

Instantly, the crowded room's din was drowned out inside Carrie's head by the sound of a submarine's klaxon dive alarm. "Villa? Greek island?" She stared at Nick. "I thought you were from Britain."

"Oh that." Nick took her arm and led her to the house's front door. "It's complicated. I grew up in England and attended boarding schools there. Come on, I have your pay out in the guest house." While they walked, he smiled at her. "We make a good business team, don't we? How would you like to make it permanent? Get your passport, and we can see the world together."

"I don't know. I did have a good time with you but . . ." Her voice was overridden by a helicopter landing beside the stables.

Carrie turned and watched the copter passengers get out and walk into the house. Passing by close enough that she could see their faces clearly illuminated by the yard lights, she knew them even with burn-scarred faces. But they apparently didn't recognize her. She started yelling at Nick.

"*Those are your backers? Just who the hell are you?*"

He grabbed Carrie's arm and pulled her into the guest house. It was then, when she saw the look in his eyes, she knew what it was about him that she had been trying to figure out.

This was an exact replay of how she'd become entangled in Nicolas's web. The young man beside her was almost an exact twenty-year-younger clone of the person who had enslaved her. Carrie became enraged. She was not about to fall into that trap again.

"Calm down. Calm down," he said, still trying to maintain his cover. "Here, let me get your pay. Then, we can go get your passport while no one is paying attention."

"I'm *not* going anywhere with you! Especially if those men are involved." As Nick counted out her pay in cash, Carrie saw a bubble pack of Rohypnol tablets laying on an envelope in his suitcase. Picking up the tablets, to read the label, she saw *the* letter. It was her letter to Nicolas. "Where did you get this? Who are you really?"

Nick knew his cover story was blown. Instead of charm, he was going to have to use coercion to accomplish his goal. "I think you know who I am. Let's go get your passport. You're my family's property, and you're coming with me."

"You're Nicolas's *son?*" It all fell into place. Those internal alarms all made sense now. "Why is your last name different?"

"Oh, that." He shrugged. "I've always used my mother's maiden name. It keeps things uncomplicated in social circles."

She still had an emotional soft spot for her ex-captor even

though she had come to know and accept the abuse he had put her through. "I'm still not going with you, but how is he?"

"That fool's no longer with us." Nick couldn't disguise his evil delight over his father's death. "His helicopter blew up over the Mediterranean. No one thought to search his own son's luggage. It was a good thing I stayed on the mainland for one more night talking with *my* financial advisors."

"How'd you find me? *Why* did you even look?"

"I found your letter in his private vault. I just had to see for myself who his own personal Helen of Troy was that brought him down. Let's go."

"I'm not going anywhere with you!"

Nick leaned down close to Carrie's face and snarled, "You will or I'll go in that house and tell everyone just how big of a *whore* their little princess is."

She shoved him and ran out the door.

Bill had been beside the helipad operating the delineation lights. Broken-hearted when he saw Carrie and Nick hurry into the guest house for what he assumed was a romantic interlude, he shuffled toward his truck to leave. He didn't care what his boss thought, he just couldn't stay. The party was just going to have to go on without him. Then, he saw Carrie run from the cabin, Nick grab her, and pull her toward a car.

"Hey!" Bill shouted. He was sure it was only a lover's quarrel but still couldn't stand by, even if it was a girl who broke his heart. "Leave her alone!"

Nick's momentary distraction was all Carrie needed. She ran for the main house with her wannabe new captor pursuing. Now, Bill was chasing them both. She burst through the door and tried to get everyone's attention. Nick grabbed her arm again. Bill grabbed Nick. When Nick took a swing, Bill decked him.

The room fell silent, all eyes turned toward the tussling young men. A cauliflower-eared security guard went to intervene, but Carrie had other ideas. She hopped up on the Hord 'oeuvres table and shouted, "Can I have everyone's attention, please? I just thought you all should know the type of people you're associating with tonight!"

Willa tried to coax her down. "Come on. Let's go outside and talk about this."

"No!" Carrie shouted. Looking down at Willa, she said, "You need to hear this most of all." She pointed at Nick, nursing his chin, standing next to the men who arrived on the helicopter. "That slimeball's dad held me as his personal sex slave for almost six months. At one point, he sold me to Mister Burn Face there who brutalized me, then had his men gang rape me! Mister Cauliflower Ear was the leader in that rape! You don't recognize me with my clothes on do you, Omar? To you I was just one more flesh-colored mattress pad you could take out your inadequacies on."

Omar, now recognizing the enraged girl, grabbed Nick's arm and hissed, "Just what have you gotten us into? That little slut got my yacht blown up and gave me these burn scars."

Carrie looked down at Willa again. "I've never liked you, but I can't let you go to that island. There is nothing but men like these there." Pointing at Nick, she continued, "I held that slimeball at arm's length, trying to maintain a business relationship. Last weekend, he drugged and raped me while I was unconscious!" She looked at Mr. Roberts. "I thought you were an honest businessman. If you're in cahoots with the likes of these criminals, I guess you're not. Nick over there just told me he *killed* his own father. He said that I belonged to his father and now in some sick way he's inherited me."

Karen rushed to help Willa get the enraged girl off the table. Carrie's dad, Randy, limped toward Omar, but a security guard pulled a gun. When Bill's stepfather, Charlie, slapped it away, the pistol discharged and blew out a picture window. The tussle knocked over the table Carrie was standing on, sending her and Willa to the floor in each other's arms. Cauliflower-ear pulled his weapon and pointed it toward Carrie, Willa, and Karen.

Paul had been standing off to the side, sullenly wondering why he allowed his daughter to talk him in to staying one more night. Now, he was forced to watch what had been the love of his life enjoying everyone's company but his. Seeing Karen on the floor, he instinctively dove on top to cover the three women and didn't hear the gunshot.

Holding Nick as a shield as he headed for the door, Omar snarled, "You're coming with me!"

Bill tackled the middle-aged advisor he had been showing the Roberts company holdings. In the tussle, they knocked over a lamp. Bill's leg went into the fireplace and scooped a burning log out onto the hardwood floor. Using his prosthetic leg, Randy managed to kick the burning log back toward the hearth. Charlie jumped in, helping restrain the advisor.

The helicopter took off carrying Nick and all of the Turkish men. Carrie's mom, Beth, dialed 911.

CHAPTER THIRTY-EIGHT

THE AFTERMATH

Karen shoved her human shield off and, after glancing suspiciously at Paul's strange expression, stood to attend to everyone's minor wounds. Bill went out to his truck for some baling twine, and with Charlie's help, tied up Nick's advisor. Immediately calling his legal team, Mr. Roberts' animated phone conversation overrode the gossiping din in the room. Beth helped Randy readjust his leg, then knelt beside Willa and Carrie in the corner clinging to each other.

No one payed any attention to Paul, quietly sitting against the wall on the other side of the young women, legs under the half collapsed refreshment table. Finally, Willa shifted positions to stand. Her foot slid on something wet. Thinking it was spilled punch, she grabbed a napkin lying beside the collapsed table to wipe her shoe off.

"Oh my god! It's blood!"

Karen looked up from cleaning a guest's minor abrasion. "Hurry! Get the table off of him!"

A quick examination only confused her. The bullet wound on his thigh was only a flesh wound deep enough for some medium bleeding but not enough to cause unconsciousness. While Beth held pressure on the wound, Karen felt for bumps on Paul's head. Lifting up the hair off his forehead, she saw a scar right at the hairline.

"Bill, do you know anything about this scar?"

He glanced over from holding down his prisoner. "Oh yeah, that's where Mara said he got shot saving her from a sex trafficker. She said it has to do with his hand shaking. Bone fragments or something."

When Paul's eyelids fluttered open, Karen's concerned face was only inches away, her fingers softly sliding through his hair. His heart leapt. His love was about to kiss him. When she pulled back and flashed a light in one eye then the other, reality came crashing back. Her concern was no more than for any person she would pass on the street.

Her statement of his condition was matter of fact. "You have a minor flesh wound on your thigh. I could stitch it up in my clinic, but because you lost consciousness and with your history of a head wound, I'm just going to tape it. They can do a more thorough job at the county hospital where I'm sending you to get your head scanned. We don't want to risk a roaming bone fragment causing further damage."

There just wasn't much more Paul could say. He lay silent while being temporarily patched back together. Then he studied the room until the ambulance crew loaded him up. At least Mara was with family, such as they were.

After the police took their initial statements and collected evidence from the main and guest houses, they left with the handcuffed advisor. Bill watched from a distance as Carrie locked her car and left in her parents' SUV. His own mother gave him a questioning look from her vehicle, but when he shook his head, Karen and Charlie drove away. He needed to think.

Driving out to a roadside viewpoint pullout above a deep coulee, he sat and stared out over the late summer moonlit precipice. What was he doing? What was Carrie doing? She just spent weeks dating the son of a man he had traveled halfway around the world to rescue her from.

Only knowing what he had witnessed in person and what little she told him on the plane ride home, he was shocked by what he heard earlier that night. For the last year he had blindly helped her work through issues without knowing how deeply they affected her.

When she finally opened up and made the effort to forgive his initial transgression, Bill hadn't been able to force himself to kiss her decently. Could he ever give the girl he loved so much what she needed? Remorseful, hurt, and confused, he drove home in the early morning twilight.

Two days later, giving Paul a ride from the hospital, sheriff detectives showed up again. Only this time as mere tour guides for an FBI team accompanied by a female Interpol agent. They had already interviewed Paul, the Roberts family, and other guests, saving Bill and Carrie for last.

Nervously sitting at his parents' dining room table surrounded by agents, Bill recoiled when the lead FBI investigator placed a photo of a very bloody naked man in front of him and asked, "Do you recognize this person?"

"How am I supposed to answer that?" Bill asked. "There's not enough face to recognize. Who is it supposed to be? What happened to him?"

"I'll ask the questions here," the agent said firmly.

"Allow me to intervene for a moment." The Interpol agent, a fortyish, attractive woman wearing a well pressed pantsuit with her hair in a bun, sat at the table across from Bill. "I'm Agent Popov. We aren't accusing you of anything. In fact, we've already accounted for your whereabouts during the timespan this happened."

Bill calmed somewhat but could see the FBI agent bristling at the interruption. The Interpol lady continued in an accent Bill couldn't quite pin down. Maybe Eastern European?

"We have a good idea who this is, but we need confirmation," she said, pointing at the picture. "Do you recognize this tattoo on his chest?"

"No," he replied. "Did you ask the guy we turned over to you? I'm not that stupid. This obviously has to do with the confrontation the other night. I think he'd know everyone."

The lead FBI agent stepped in. "We did. It appears he didn't know any of the other men very well. He was a hired financial consultant. He *has* turned State's evidence and is telling everything he knows. *That* is what brought us to you. Apparently, you had a disliking toward his associate."

Bill looked back down at the picture. "Are you saying this is *Nick*? I'm sorry but I never saw him without his shirt. The only person . . ." He stopped himself. He didn't even want to think about Carrie, much less her seeing another guy naked.

Popov leaned closer. Putting her hand on Bill's forearm, she asked, "Who's name were you about to say? Is it that young lady who started the melee at the party? Has she been intimate with one of those men?"

He stared down at the table and mumbled, "From what I understand, almost all have been with her at one time or another. Although, I'm still not sure if she was willing or not with that Nick fellow."

"That was our understanding also." Trying to be gentle with the tormented young man, agent Popov pushed. "Are you sure they were intimate?"

Almost choking on what little food he had eaten in the past few days forcing its way back up, Bill gagged out, "Yes. I saw them."

"Thank you." Agent Popov stood up. "I think we have all we need from you. Stay close in case we think of anything else."

"But . . ." Not satisfied with leaving until the witness was emotionally stripped bare, the lead FBI man started to protest.

"We can always come back." The Interpol agent gave him a hard look and headed for the door.

"Agent Popov," Bill called after her.

She turned back. "Yes? Is there something else?"

Bill looked at her sorrowfully. "Just be gentle with her. Carrie's been through a lot of abuse, and not just with those foreign thugs."

"I will." She smiled kindly and walked out of the house. Seeing the deputies and FBI agents confronting Paul Taft beside the RV, she asked, "What's going on?"

Paul glowered at the lead FBI man. "He's trying to tell me I can't leave." Looking past the agents at Karen heading down the drive on her way to work, he continued almost desperately, "I *really* need to go somewhere else. I just *cannot* stay here."

Intuitive alarms sounding in Popov's head, she stalled while thinking of a solution. "We need you to stay close by for a bit longer. Your living arrangements would make it hard for us to find you in case we have further questions. As an ex law enforcement officer yourself, I'm sure you understand."

Paul sighed, then answered firmly, "I'll give you today. After that, you're going to have to throw me in a cell to keep me here."

The county's sheriff detectives went their own way investigating parts of the case not having international implications. The lead FBI agent, getting the hint his brand of interviewing witnesses was going to be a continual source of conflict with the international agent, returned to his regional office. Now that she was familiar with the area, a lower level local FBI agent accompanied Agent Popov to the Bennett ranch.

Sitting across the kitchen table, the female agent asked, "Are you comfortable, Miss Bennett?"

"No, but I don't have a choice, do I?" Carrie shifted uneasily. "I'd rather be out riding. Is there some way we could do this on horseback?"

Agent Popov smiled. "I'd actually love that. It's been quite a while since I've gone riding. However, I don't think my recording device would work well with the wind noise today."

"It was worth a try."

Thoughtfully pausing to glance out at the large area between the ranch buildings, the Interpol agent asked, "I'm trying to keep Mr. Taft from disappearing into the wilderness. I'm sensing some real conflict between him and the Schmidts. Would your parents mind if he parked his RV here for a bit?"

"After he shielded us girls and took a bullet, they'd be insulted if he didn't."

The FBI agent, acknowledging Popov's glance, said, "I'll give him a call."

Popov turned back to Carrie, knowing she had to be careful if she was going to keep this fragile witness talking. "I understand you worked with one of the men at the party. Can you describe the nature of your relationship?"

Even though her parents were off getting Randy's leg repaired after the fireplace incident, Carrie still reflexively glanced toward the living room. "If you're asking if I slept with Nick, the answer is yes."

"Oh, well I wasn't going to be quite so blunt about it. But yes, that was my question." Agent Popov studied the young girl. She had been warned this young lady had suffered trauma at the hands of the men she was investigating. Usually, victims were more withdrawn. Carrie Bennett had spunk. Still, Popov treaded lightly. "Can you tell me about the others? Feel free to stop if you need to take a minute."

"Do you mind if I start with Nick?" When Popov shrugged, Carrie continued, "From our first meeting, I sensed something was off about him. But I still accepted his job offer. And yes, I slept with him, but I don't think it was willingly. I hadn't drunk that much, I don't remember any of it, and the next morning I saw an empty packet of powder laying on the kitchen counter. Since I saw a package of blue/green tablets in his suitcase the night of the party, I'm pretty sure I was drugged."

With her witness still so compliant, Popov held back the pictures, believing they would probably end the conversation. "Tell me everything you can remember about all of the men you recognized at the party."

"You mean how we met?" A look of sadness crept into Carrie's eyes. "I should start from the beginning for it all to make sense."

"I've got nothing but time," Popov said, giving the FBI man a *knock it off* look when he rolled his eyes.

Carrie began with the chance meeting in the club and how Ethan had sold her out for personal gain. She detailed Nicolas's personality quirks, her observations of his business associates, and how she met Omar and his henchmen.

The FBI agent interrupted, "Can you give us this Ethan's full name and contact info?"

After supplying her ex-boyfriend's last address, Carrie shrugged. "I don't know if you can find him though. I think Ethan realized he was in trouble with both my family and Nicolas. He's more than likely hiding somewhere overseas." She then continued with her observations on the island.

Sensing the young woman was nearing her emotional limits, Agent Popov reached for the pictures in her briefcase. "I think you've given us enough for the moment."

"Wait. I need to tell you something." Pausing for a moment to collect herself, staring at the table, Carrie said, "I killed someone."

Popov closed the briefcase with the pictures still inside. This case just got more complicated. "Go on."

"Sergie, Nicolas's top aide on the island, trapped me on the edge of a cliff. He held me down, stripped, and said he was going to rape me then throw me into the sea." Nervously shredding a napkin, Carrie described the whole incident. "I managed to stun him with a rock. I lost it, stabbing him a bunch of times before I knew what I was doing. The island's security team showed up and were going to kill me in retribution. Nicolas stopped them and had Sergie's top lieutenant thrown off the cliff instead."

"What were their full names?" Popov asked even though she had a good idea. Interpol's Eastern Mediterranean unit knew the men had dropped off the radar and were trying to figure out where they disappeared to. However, knowing this witness had already seen dead, naked bodies, gave her an opening to show the pictures. "I hate to do this after hearing your story but . . ." The agent placed the pictures on the table in front of Carrie. "Do you recognize this person?"

Surprising Popov, the young woman across the table picked up the photos and looked at them. When Carrie shrugged, the agent pointed at the tattoo. "How about that? Have you seen it before?"

Carrie studied the picture again. As it sank in exactly what she was looking at, her face paled. "Oh my god. That's Nick. What happened to him?"

"You seem to be taking this awfully well," the FBI agent sarcastically quipped. "I thought you two were in a relationship."

"I've spent my life growing up on a ranch. I've seen plenty of dead carcasses." Glaring at the man, Carrie's eyes narrowed. But still, tears from her confused emotions fought to come out. "Yes, seeing the body of someone I know bothers me. You forget, this man's father held me captive for five months. Nick lied to me and tried to lure me into the same trap. I don't know why, but knowing he's dead is somehow a relief."

Popov stood and looked at her adversarial escort. "I think we have all we need for now. We should let this young lady get back to her day."

Walking out to their car, the FBI agent asked Popov, "We *are* done here, right? I need to get back to our Spokane field office and file a report."

Paul had pulled into the farmyard and was walking toward the agents and Carrie standing on the back porch. A glint on a small rise to the east caught his eye. Instinctively, he shouted, "Get back inside, *now!*"

CHAPTER THIRTY-NINE
A CLOSE CALL

Popov shoved Carrie back into the house, then ordered her partner, "Let's go. Head down the road and stop beside that rise."

By the time the two agents drove down the long driveway and made it to the hayfield access apron behind the hill, all they could find was churned up mud near an irrigation pipe and black peel out marks on the pavement.

Examining the evidence, the FBI agent said, "It appears that someone was surveilling the house. How did you know?"

"Paul Taft saw a glint from this knoll when we were leaving the house. I suspected it was the afternoon sun reflecting off of some kind of optics."

"Binoculars or rifle scope?"

"I don't know."

He asked, "What do you want to do?"

"Take me back to the house." On the Bennett ranch house back porch, she identified herself, "It's agent Popov. Please come to the door."

Carrie tentatively opened the door a crack. "Yes?"

"Is Paul Taft in there with you?"

"No. He told me to stay put. He said he was going to do a perimeter check. Did I say that right?"

"Does your car run?"

"Yes, why?" Carrie asked.

"Hold on." Popov turned to her associate. "Get back to Spokane and file your report. Bring a forensics team out to that knoll first thing in the morning. I'll monitor the witness." Pushing Carrie back into the house, Popov asked, "Do you have another vehicle?"

"Yeah, my dad's crewcab dually. Why?"

"Someone was watching your property. Do you know how to drive that vehicle?"

"Yeah. I've been driving it since I was thirteen." Carrie cocked her head. "We get hunters out there all the time. It was probably someone looking for coyotes."

"Maybe you're right, but considering recent events, I'm not willing to take that chance." Popov was insistent. "You need to pack a bag. I'm taking you to another location and keeping my eye on you. That's why I want to use a different vehicle than you're usually associated with."

"Okay, I'll pack an overnight bag." Stepping into the kitchen, Carrie looked back at the Interpol lady. "Don't you have extra clothes?"

"Crap! In my rush to make sure you were safe, I sent my FBI companion back to his field office before grabbing my emergency tote and briefcase out of the trunk."

"You look about my mom's size. Maybe we can find something to fit you upstairs."

Following the young lady, who only a short time before had been a witness being questioned, Agent Popov started to get a better picture of what gave Carrie so much grit. While trying on more appropriate clothing to be less conspicuous in the area, the agent questioned everything. Bill's elevator into the closet, Randy's accident, and Beth's artwork on the walls. As far as she could tell, everyone associated with the family were from strong roots.

Watching the agent change, Carrie noticed she wasn't packing a weapon. "Where's your gun?"

"I'm not a U.S. citizen, so like most Interpol agents, I accompany resident law enforcement in an advisory capacity. In extreme circumstances, I can be deputized by the local authorities. Then, I can legally carry a weapon."

Carrie found this ludicrous. "How're you supposed to defend yourself against the type of men you think are after me without a gun?" Carrie reached into her mother's nightstand and pulled out a semi-automatic pistol. "Here. My dad bought this for my mom just in case."

Popov held her hands up defensively. "I'm not allowed to possess a weapon in this country."

"You're not possessing it. I am. You're just holding it for me." She handed the weapon and a box of shells to the smiling older woman. "Besides, Mr. Taft also pulled a gun out of his RV when he went to look around."

"We should go." The agent glanced at her watch. "Where's the closest motel?"

"The county seat but, uh, the Schmidt place is a lot closer, and they have a bunkhouse." Carrie hesitated. Looking at the floor, she said softly, "Although I don't know if I'd be welcome there with everything that's happened between me and Bill."

"Do you trust them?" Popov thought back to her interviews with the Schmidt family and their oldest son. At the time, she thought they were just a nice family. By the way he answered the questions, Bill seemed to have some sort of unrequited attachment to her current charge. It hit the agent that she never found out how Carrie broke free of the Greek crime syndicate's leader. Maybe there was an unfollowed path in her investigation? There might be more clues to reveal in that bunkhouse's vicinity. The agent realized her briefcase containing the Schmidt's phone number was still in a car heading for Spokane. "Do you have their number? I'd at least like to call and ask a few more questions on the case."

Carrie pointed out the kitchen window. "Mr. Taft is coming around the stables now. Are you going to tell him where we are going?"

"Sure. I think he pretty much wants to be alone right now, anyway."

Twenty minutes later, Popov and Carrie were sitting at the Schmidt dining room table having supper with the family. The agent found it hard to maintain a professional distance in the open family's home. The mother, a nurse practitioner with an established clinic, was married to an artistic blacksmith working as a ranch hand. One high school aged boy, two college aged girls, and a six-year-old boy constantly interacted during the meal. Even Paul Taft's adopted daughter was the epitome of cheerful chattiness. Through it all, she still noticed a definite tension between Bill Schmidt and Carrie Bennett.

After supper while the older teens and Carrie did the dishes and Bill fled to the living room, Popov said, "You have a lovely home, Mrs. Schmidt. It's such nice architecture."

"You just ate a meal at our table, agent. It's Karen." Bill's mother smiled. Pointing at her oldest son and husband, she said, "Why don't you two go clean out the bunkhouse and put fresh towels on the shelf?"

"You know, Karen, watching your family and Miss Bennett interact, it occurs to me that there is more to the story than what I've been told." With her arms folded across her chest, Popov lifted one hand and stroked her chin. "Could I persuade you to give me the backstory?"

"I guess. Would you care to go for a stroll?"

"Sure. I'd like that." Popov stuck her head in the kitchen and looked sternly at Carrie. "Stay inside. I'm going for a perimeter security check."

During their walk, Karen filled the agent in on Carrie and Bill's complicated history from when they were both thirteen. "None of us know for sure what happened between them to cause this chain of events, only that it happened the last week of high school. There are some other issues complicating Carrie's recent history with violence, but I can't tell you due to HIPAA privacy regulations."

"Oh, so you're her physician along with her mother's friend." Popov walked silently, mulling, while scanning the horizon for trouble. She thought back to her own small village before corruption and war destroyed it. "It's been quite a while since I've been in such a tight knit community."

Sleeping on the bottom bunk in an old Palouse farm bunkhouse was a new experience for the agent. Yes, her job had taken her to some very primitive locations, but this was right out of one of those American west cowboy novels. If it wasn't for the demands of travel in her job, she could see herself becoming right at home here.

The next morning, at the breakfast table, Popov's phone buzzed. Stepping out into the late summer air, she answered, "Yes?"

"You can rest a little easier today, agent," her FBI escort said. "I saw a mud-covered car with Seattle area license plates fueling up at a quick stop. It looked out of place so, with the help of a couple of sheriff's deputies, we pulled it over. It was a private investigator snooping around to find the Bennett girl. Even after being hauled in, he wouldn't divulge his employer. That is, until I showed him the pictures and told him the name of the dead guy. When he realized the rest of his paycheck was never going to come, the P.I. came clean and coughed up names."

"Good work," Popov said. "Did he give any further leads?"

"The guy was a real sleazeball. He didn't know any more about that Nick guy other than his impression was our flattened Greek friend might have covered his bases elsewhere. Do you want me to send a car for you?"

Popov thought for a moment. "No. I think I have some more background work to do here on the overseas aspects. I'll check in later."

When the agent walked back into the house, everyone else had finished eating and left for other activities. Karen refreshed her cup of coffee and said, "Well, Agent Popov, you have a more relaxed expression on your face. Was the call good news?"

"Technically, I'm not supposed to answer that, Mrs. Schmidt." Popov smiled slightly. "But, since you've been so hospitable to my presence, I'll tell you that it wasn't *bad* news."

Bill's mom sat across from the agent. "Using Agent Popov is an awfully formal and cumbersome way to talk to you. What's your given name if I'm allowed to ask?"

"Using first names is frowned upon. It removes the air of authority we're supposed to maintain."

Karen laughed. "Air of authority. Agent, may I remind you that you're wearing borrowed clothing, sleeping in a bunkhouse, and are the safety umbrella of one of my dearest friend's daughter. I think we're past that. And again, my name isn't Mrs. Schmidt. It's Karen."

Popov smiled. "It's Katarina. Katarina Popov." Then quickly added, "But don't tell anyone. I still need to maintain my mystique."

"Mystique my butt, Katarina. You don't have to be all serious around here to be tough. You may not have noticed, but everyone around here is overly friendly and I'll guarantee there isn't a wimp among them. You should have figured that out when you interviewed the one-legged man and my husband who took on an international criminal popping off rounds in a birthday party."

"Well, Karen, you've given me the overhead view of the young lady's experiences during the last few years. Is there any way I can get her to open up a little more?" Popov sipped her coffee, pondering why Karen left out the guy who took a bullet defending her. Her investigator instincts insisted she ask, "I've noticed some tension between you and Paul Taft. Why is that?"

"I don't know for certain, but he creeps me out. I'm not sure if he's a stalker with a fixation on me and the kids or what."

"Yeah, but didn't he jump on top of you and the girls as a shield?"

"Possibly. Or maybe he saw it as an opportunity to get a quick grope." Karen frowned. "One minute I catch him looking at me with an almost longing expression. The next, he glares like he'd just as soon strangle me. Then there's my daughter, Nettie. He's been constantly hovering near her."

"Huh." Filing that bit away as a possible tangent that might need exploring, Popov went back to her main train of thought. "I'd like to get Miss Bennett to go into a lot more detail about her experiences in Greece. I want to get as much usable information as I can on these criminals. She seems to be a one stop shop where that's concerned."

"Carrie's most relaxed on horseback. Do you ride, Katarina?"

Right that moment, the topic of conversation walked into the kitchen followed by Paul's energetic daughter. "I need to go home and do the chores. Is that all right?"

Katarina glanced at Karen, then replied, "I think we can allow that. I'd like to observe your daily routine. It would help me formulate a more thorough protection plan for you."

Mara jumped into the conversation. "Can I go too? I've never been on a ranch, and I want to see how dad's doing."

Gathering the eggs went a long way toward getting Carrie to relax around the Interpol agent, especially with Mara tagging along constantly asking ranching questions. Popov had a similar relationship with chickens as Bill. The ranch girl couldn't resist a giggle when Katarina yelped then cussed in a foreign language when pecked.

Chores in the stables went better. Watching the agent work, Carrie asked, "You seem comfortable around the horses, do you ride?"

Popov shrugged. "I competed a little in dressage before all hell broke loose in my country. Due to my job's demands, it's been a few years."

"After chores, you want to go out? It's pretty dry but . . ."

"I'd love to," Katarina interrupted. "It would give me a chance to survey the area for security weak points."

"That excuse is as good as any." Carrie headed toward the tack room. "I assume you want English tack. That limits you to the two horses belonging to the Roberts family."

Carrie saddled the biggest Thoroughbred. When she threw a blanket on the Appaloosa, Popov pointed at a different saddle. "That one has a rifle scabbard. Is there a weapon that goes with it?"

"Sure, but that scabbard can be put on any saddle. We take it when hunting coyotes. You want to bring it?"

"Yes, and the rifle that goes with it."

When Carrie saw Mara longingly looking at the horses, she asked, "You know how to ride?"

The young girl replied, "This is the closest I've ever been to a horse. I've already asked Dad, and he said he hasn't ridden since high school."

Carrie pointed toward the tractor shed. "My dad's UTV is over there. Why don't you and your father explore the ranch on your own? Be sure to tell him not to drive off the edge of a coulee cliff."

As they rode, Popov used her unfamiliarity with the ranch to loosen up her protectee's emotional shield. As it turned out, recent events primed Carrie for a release. She showed the agent where Charlie saved the ranch by leading the herd off the cliff. Nearby, she pointed to where she tried to commit suicide with Willa's horse and told the events leading up to her attempt.

In the upper feedlot, they paused as Carrie went deeper into her abuse on the island. Unbeknownst to them both, they stopped their horses eight feet above where the corpse of another internationally wanted murderer lay. The serial killer Bill's mom shot and Carrie's parents helped bury—a body that would have closed another cold case file in Interpol's database.

The two women rode along the fence line in the upper hayfield. Carrie was describing how Charlie saved her from a drug fueled would-be rapist there when a shot rang out and the Appaloosa dropped to its knees.

Reaching for her pistol, Popov scanned the horizon. Without looking down while searching for the threat, she asked, "You hurt?"

"No, but I think Spot's done for."

Identifying a silhouette on the same knoll Carrie had just told her was her attempted rapist's overlook, the agent shouted, "Keep behind the horse. Spray that hilltop with bullets."

Pulling her father's lever action carbine out of the scabbard, Carrie did as told. Not aiming, she held it over the quivering horse and fired in the general direction. While jacking in another round, she saw the Interpol agent galloping toward the barbed wire fence. Without breaking stride, Mr. Roberts' horse gracefully cleared the fence and headed into a depression beside the neighboring property's hill.

Carrie muttered before popping off another round, "I didn't know that horse could jump."

Heading up the side of the hill, Katarina almost collided with two men running toward the Bennett hayfield. One was carrying a rifle and the other a plastic one-gallon jug. The armed man raised the rifle to shoot the agent, but just as he went to pull the trigger, his big city street shoes slipped on the desiccated grass slope. The shot went wild, but Popov's didn't. He fell dead.

The second man dropped the jug and reached for his pistol. Popov dropped him with one shot just like she'd done with his cohort. With him still alive, the agent leapt nimbly from her steed and kicked the weapon from his trembling hand. Rolling him over, she knelt on his back and applied the cuffs.

Pulling out her phone to call for backup and seeing no bars, Katarina mumbled, "Crap! No reception." She double checked the first man for a pulse, then pulled the second to his feet. "Come on. You need to make it to the fence line before you bleed to death."

Prisoner in one hand and leading the Thoroughbred with the other, the agent headed back in the direction she'd come from. Almost back to her fence line, agent Popov heard the report of a rifle. Dropping the horse's reins, she forced her prisoner into a trot. Pistol drawn when she came within sight, the only other human within view was the crying Bennett girl, hugging the neck of a deceased Appaloosa.

Popov called out, "Are you all right?"

"No," Carrie answered. "Spot's dead. I had to put her down."

"Have you seen anyone else?" Katarina cautiously scanned the vicinity. "I don't have any cell reception. You?"

"No. There's none up here on the backside of the ranch. You have to get almost back to the house to get reception."

Agent Popov glanced at her wounded prisoner, the only horse left, and the ranch girl. She was going to have to stray from protocol if she was going to keep the prisoner alive for interrogation. Even with a bullet hole in him, she didn't want to leave Carrie to guard him.

The UTV carrying Paul and Mara came roaring over the crest of the hayfield. Holding his daughter down and out of sight, he asked, "Is everything under control? Has the threat been neutralized?" When Katerina nodded, he looked at Carrie. "Can you get that big pickup up here to take this man to medical care?"

Popov negated the idea. "I don't want to contaminate the scene. It's going to be complicated enough to explain as it is. I think I have it all under control. Why don't you find some phone reception and call 911? And here . . ." Reaching in a pocket, she pulled out a business card. "Call this FBI number and tell them what has happened. Tell them we're going to need a forensics team and a coroner."

When Paul drove off, Carrie asked, "What about the horse you jumped the fence with? Are you going to jump him back?"

"I don't want to risk it in these conditions, but I guess we have no other option." Katarina forced her prisoner to kneel by a fencepost and handcuffed his arms around it.

Seeing the barbed wire clicked a memory in the ranch girl. "Help me get the saddle bags off Spot. We usually carry a pair of fencing pliers in there just in case we see a down fence while riding."

Not having spent much time on an actual farm or ranch, the Interpol agent didn't question when Carrie cut the top wire a dozen feet from the handcuffed man. When the taut wire leapt and curled itself around him, Popov recognized a sadistic grin of retribution on his would-be target.

As Carrie led the horse over the down fence, she looked at the kneeling man and snarled, "That's for killing a perfectly good horse."

By the time Paul made it back to the house, Carrie's parents had returned. When Paul and Randy returned with the UTV, the first sheriff's SUV had found the criminals' rental car behind the knoll. Authorities knew the vacant property next door, which was in receivership. They followed the tire tracks on a service road to within one hundred yards of the firefight.

While Randy and one of the deputies were removing the saddle from the dead horse, Popov put her hand on Carrie's shoulder. "I hate to do this, but would you look at the other man and see if you can identify him?"

Following the paramedics carrying the wounded prisoner to their ambulance parked behind the knoll, Carrie asked, "Why do you think I can identify the other guy? I didn't know the one you captured."

"Just a hunch, that's all." The coroner and two sheriff detectives arrived at the corpse just as Carrie and Popov walked up. The agent introduced herself even though the detectives recognized her. Then she said, "I have a witness that may be able to identify the body."

Carrie looked into the dead man's vacant eyes. She glanced down at a unique ring on his burned, scarred hand. "Yes. I've met him. He's one of Omar's men who gang raped me on that island."

CHAPTER FORTY

A TEMPORARY GOODBYE

That night, Agent Popov stopped at the Bennett house. "I've been able to question my prisoner a little further now that he's out of surgery." She stuck her hand out. "Give me your phone."

"Why?" Carrie asked as she pulled the phone out of her pocket.

"What's your passcode?" Katarina scrolled through the apps, made a few adjustments, and handed the phone back. "Someone added a tracking app to your phone. That's how those men ambushed us this morning. Can we talk privately?"

"Is that necessary?" Carrie asked. "My parents have found out everything else. I don't think I have anything left to hide."

Sitting at the kitchen table, Popov explained while her FBI cohort stood by the door with a dour expression, "Those men weren't out to kill you. They shot your horse intentionally to stop you and hopefully trap your leg under it. The jug they were carrying was acid. Their instructions were to disfigure your face and body so no one would ever want to look at you again."

Shocked, Beth looked back and forth between her daughter and the agent. "How are we going to stop this? Is there anything we can do?"

"First, Mrs. Bennett, I'm going to suggest that your daughter comes with us to the county seat tonight. My American equivalents want to question me more about the shooting. They don't think the sheriff dug deep enough into my involvement." Katarina glared at the FBI agent when he coughed. "It wouldn't be official, but she can stay with me while I get a better handle on what our Turkish and Greek friends are up to."

Surprised, Carrie looked at the FBI agent. "But they were shooting at us."

"It'll be fine." Katarina patted the young woman's hand. "You should pack a bag."

Looking down, picking at her fingernails, Carrie said softly, "I want to bury my horse first."

"Charlie, Paul, and . . ." Beth's voice tapered off when she almost said Bill's name. "Uh, a crew is coming out tomorrow just for that purpose. We'll take care of it. You go with the agent and be safe."

That night in Popov's motel room while eating takeout, she asked Carrie, "I didn't want to ask you in front of others, but when I saw the look on your face when I said someone added a tracking app to your phone, it appeared you had a good Idea who it was."

"I do." Without waiting for Katarina to push further, Carrie volunteered her suspicion. "I think it was Nick. He must have installed it the night we slept together."

No longer surprised by the young lady's blunt honesty, the agent decided to change the subject away from the investigation. After all, the Bennett girl seemed to offer up the most relevant information to the case when discussing something else. The Schmidt boy might be a good place to start.

"What about Bill Schmidt? You've mentioned him tangentially when discussing other things but, other than the fact that you used to date, you avoid him like the plague. I noticed everyone around you also tries to avoid mentioning him."

Carrie took another few bites. This Agent Popov was a blank slate when it came to sharing feelings. Katarina was so empathetic, it was almost as if she hovered between a trusted friend and a secret diary in which anything could be written. Sitting on the bed in their nightclothes, Carrie shared her complete history with Bill.

Just to make Carrie comfortable, Katarina would confide a youthful indiscretion of her own now and then. After the young woman went into detail of her last date with Bill, how it ended, and why it made her so blind to Nick's manipulations, the agent knew Miss Bennett needed to make some major life decisions. But was it her place to suggest them?

Agent Popov's phone rang. "Hello? Yeah, fill me in. Uhuh, yeah . . . *really*! Okay, keep me posted. I'll see what Miss Bennett wants to do. This is unfortunate, but maybe it could be beneficial in the long run."

When Katarina hung up, Carrie asked the pensive agent, "The call was about me?"

"Yes. There were parts not directly about you, but still . . ." Popov paused. "First, I have some bad news which isn't connected with the case. Your parents called the office. Your grandmother has had some sort of an accident. It isn't life threatening, but she's in the hospital."

Carrie jumped off the bed and started to get dressed. "I have to go home. I need to find out how bad it is."

Katarina grabbed her arm. "Wait, wait. Let me finish. Remember, I said her life isn't in danger. The other part of the call may affect how we go about this."

Still holding her clothes, Carrie said, "I'm listening. What is going on?"

"The wounded man is talking, trying to save his own hide. He's desperately trying to negotiate being sent to a prison here instead of back in Turkey. He claims that just the two of them stayed behind when boss Omar took off in his jet. According to sources, the jet made more than a few stops on its way back to Turkey. When the police met it at Istanbul's airport, it was empty. Omar's in hiding."

"So?"

"Well, between our two songbirds and the leads you've provided, my team has uncovered enough evidence to issue warrants for his arrest." Popov had Carrie sit beside her. "There doesn't seem to be any direct threat left toward you, but just to be safe, I think it would be a good idea for you to drop off the radar."

"You mean witness protection?"

"Not exactly." Katarina shrugged. "Most of the case building against these men rests overseas. You were only a minor player who has already supplied what you know and won't be needed for testimony. What I think you should do is go be with your grandmother until she heals. Break off all contact with others on your own. The only reason anyone would have to harm you now is just to garner favor with Omar. With him about to lose his empire, why would they bother?"

"That might be a good idea. I could use some time away, and I haven't seen Gramma in a couple of years."

"It's really none of my business," Popov patted Carrie's hand, "but now might be a good time to have a talk to straighten things out with that young man. Spending time apart, where you're not constantly bruising each other, might help you both in the long run."

"I guess. I just hate taking long flights on my own."

"Maybe not. My superiors in D.C. aren't very happy that I was involved in a shooting. I'm being called back for a hearing." Katarina sighed, then smiled at Carrie. "I'll have the local agent take us back to your place after my interviews tomorrow. I can stall my flight long enough and accompany you if we leave in a day or so—long enough for you to gather your things and get everything in order.

Carrie sat on a hay bale beside Bill in the ranch's stables. "Gramma's had an accident. Her gas range exploded and almost burned down her house. Instead of hiring someone, I'm going there to take care of her for a while."

Bill was dubious. "You sure that's wise? Didn't you say the people who might be looking for you are dangerous?"

"That's a good reason *for* me to go. None of them know about Gramma. All they had was the picture of our little downtown. I only talked about the Palouse when I was on the island. If I stay off the radar, they won't be able to find me."

Bill wasn't convinced. "With today's technology, all they have to do is track your phone calls home."

"The Interpol agent said that Nick had a grievance against me. He's the only one they think would spend the time to go after me because, with him, it was personal. He's dead now. I don't know enough about the rest to be able to be a dangerous witness."

"Well, they could still be chasing you just for revenge. You have to be careful. Aren't you tangentially responsible for that Omar guy's face getting scarred? Isn't that why those men killed your horse?"

"That's what I mean. I have to cut off all contact. Nick put a tracking app on my phone. I'm going to turn it off and leave it here." Carrie put her hand on his arm. "Who knows what else they've done? So we can't make any contact until the authorities say it's safe."

"How long?"

"They say Gramma's rehab and making her house livable again will take six months to a year." She looked pleadingly at Bill. "I don't care if they say it's safe or not. After a year, I'll come home."

"I guess I can find a job there to make sure you're alright."

What Carrie hadn't been saying was that she needed time away to think. She cared deeply for Bill but somehow, he had an impenetrable barrier she couldn't get past. She had forgiven him for what he had done with Willa. In fact, she had even forgiven Willa, and a tentative friendship had developed.

It was Bill who she didn't think could move on. Whenever they seemed to be getting close, she could see that look in his eyes. The look he gave her in Nicolas's shed, the look he gave her on the long plane ride back to the States. Between that and having to be rescued again from Rod, she had become eternally tarnished in his eyes. The whole Nick fiasco made it even worse.

"No, Bill. You have a life and responsibilities here." Carrie hugged him. "I'm better now. You made sure of that. Yes, I worked for a guy that I shouldn't have. But when I saw warning signs, I pulled back. I couldn't have done that before you rescued me and helped me recover. Look at it this way—it'll give us time to sort out our feelings. It might even be better for both of us in the long run."

His protective instincts still in full force, he wasn't pleased. "If that's what you want. I guess I could give you a ride to the airport."

"No, Bill, saying goodbye here is hard enough as it is. Your cousin Paul and his daughter have been cleared to leave so they've volunteered to get me to Spokane. Since Agent Popov has to report back to her headquarters, she's going to escort me as far as LaGuardia Airport."

"I guess you're right," Bill sadly admitted. "It'll do you good to walk without your goofy, overprotective crutch for a while." He paused contemplatively for a seeming eternity. "I guess you think of me as a jealous buffoon since I've been acting like that Aesop guy's Dog in the Manger."

Carrie pulled him down and kissed his cheek. "You need to decide what you *really* want. Then, you have to think about actually living with that decision. I'll miss you."

CHAPTER FORTY-ONE
TIME FOR RATIONAL THOUGHT

Following their talk, Bill got into his truck and drove to the Roberts place. After the big blow-up with the Turkish (or was it Greek?) investors and then the sheriff's department, FBI, and Interpol searches, no one had given the house a close inspection for damages. Bill was almost done with his note taking tour when he heard a car pull up. It was Willa's father.

"Oh, good. I hoped I'd find you here. We need to talk."

Bill answered, "Yeah, I was just doing a walk through to see what repairs I could do."

Mr. Roberts smiled. "Don't bother. I'll get some actual contractors out here for that. No one will be here for a while anyway. Willa and her boyfriend are back at college, and I have to straighten out the mess your little friend caused."

"I . . . I'm sorry about that." Bill hadn't talked to his part-time boss since the confrontation. "Carrie was pretty messed up with what happened on that island."

"You don't need to apologize to *me*." Mr. Roberts put a hand on Bill's shoulder. "You two saved us all from a lot of grief. A few people in my vetting department are now looking for jobs."

"I didn't mean to get anyone fired."

"Trust me," Mr. Roberts said with a big grin. "They deserved it. Your friend speaking up and you backing her saved my corporation from being tied to some very unsavory people. God only knows what would have happened to my daughter if you let her go to that island."

Bill self-consciously looked at his feet. "We were just doing what was right. Anyone would have done the same."

"No, they wouldn't have. What you two did shows character. Walk with me." Mr. Roberts turned and headed back to his car. "With my daughter at college and me so tied up repairing damages to my company, no one has the time to come here for a while. I'm selling the horses and leasing the house. Don't worry. You're definitely *not* out of a job. I'd like you to be in charge of revamping the irrigation systems on our properties around Columbia Basin, maybe even those in Montana. There's a big raise in it for you."

Bill was confused. "I . . . I don't know what to say. There are a lot more experienced men working for you. Why me?"

"Because you're smart and by far have the most character. I can trust you to do the right thing and speak up when something isn't right. Want the job?"

"How long will this take?"

"I'm guessing all winter until planting season." Mr. Roberts smiled, sensing he had filled the position. "After that, we'll see. I'm sure my company has use for your skills somewhere."

Bill didn't have to think long. His stepdad, Charlie, pretty much had the ranch under control during the off season. His other fixation—whether she needed his supervision anymore or not—was going to be gone for the same amount of time.

"Sure. I'll do it."

"Great! I've even offered your cousin, Paul Taft, a job checking our security protocols. After what he did at the party, it was the least I could do." Mr. Roberts smiled and shrugged. "He's a good negotiator. He wants to settle in one spot so his daughter can have stability. I think he's going to base himself in North Idaho, so he'll be central to our properties here and in Montana."

Bill drove home and packed. After throwing his clothes and tools in the truck, his first instinct was to drive to the Bennett ranch and tell Carrie where he was going. It was all he could do to turn the opposite direction when pulling onto the highway. They had already said goodbye. Their deal was to cut off all contact for a while, and he was determined to honor her request.

The next day he reported to work at the company's Moses Lake shop. He hadn't been in it since he and Jennie ended things. Nervous about seeing her in person again, he dreaded the first time her dad's parts house sent a delivery. While searching through the shop's storage racks for a replacement pump impeller, he heard a female voice.

"Can you sign for these parts, please?"

When he turned, the girl wearing a shirt with the parts company's logo wasn't Jennie. He asked, "Are you new? I haven't seen you before."

She cocked her head. "No, I've been making the deliveries for quite a while now."

He thought for a second. "Oh, I guess that's right. I haven't been in the shop for a long time. Are there two of you doing deliveries now?"

"Nah, just me. Why?"

Bill shrugged. "The last time I was here, there was another girl doing the deliveries. That's all."

"Oh! You mean the boss's daughter." The delivery girl smiled. "She left over a year ago. She's off somewhere, I think the coast. I guess she got engaged. I heard the boss talking to her on the phone last week about setting a date for an upcoming wedding."

Watching the delivery girl walk from the shop, Bill hoped Jennie had found someone who could fully commit to her. He had tried, but at the time his mind was emotionally hydrolocked, seized, incapable of moving forward because of Carrie.

The year and a half working with Carrie on the ranch had been cathartic for them both. Her old self was starting to shine through. He wasn't quite there yet but was getting close when he made his latest blunder of pushing her away. Maybe the person he remembered as the perky ranch girl had a point. It was time for everyone to remove their training wheels and figure out what they wanted out of life versus what they could live with.

Bill drove to his first irrigation system overhaul project north of Moses Lake. The field's access apron off the road was blocked by another vehicle with its trunk open. Impatient to start work, he got out and walked to the front of the strange car to tell the driver to move. Trying to change a flat tire, a young Hutterite woman was having a dither of a time locating the jack properly.

"Need help?" he asked.

Nervously, she shook her head.

"No, really. I don't mind." Bill smiled sympathetically. "I'm already wearing work clothes and don't mind getting dirty." When she refused to make eye contact, he added, "Besides, you're blocking the entrance to my work site. I can't get anything done until you get out of the way."

He thought he caught her smile. She silently stood aside and let him place the jack. While he worked, Bill made small talk. "Most people don't know that you need to loosen the lug nuts before lifting the wheel completely off the ground. Tire shops use impact wrenches then a torque wrench on the nuts to make sure they're tight. Customers take a dim view of their wheels coming off on the freeway."

He caught a small giggle. When he looked up, she was making a point to look the other direction. Even so, he got a good enough look at her face to recognize her from his time previously working in the area.

He continued, "It was as I thought. These nuts were really on there. You would've had a hard time breaking them loose. There, all done." He stood and put her tools and flat tire in the vehicle's trunk.

"Your car smells good." He looked in the back seat. "Are you delivering baked goods somewhere? By the way, my name is Bill."

She finally spoke with a slight German accent. "I'm not supposed to talk to outsiders without a chaperone. It's not considered proper. Thank you for your kindness." She got in her car and headed toward town.

Bill shrugged and drove into the field a short distance to the irrigation pump. A couple of hours later, lost in concentration, he heard a vehicle drive up behind him and a car door shut. When he pulled his head out of the inspection hatch, there stood the Hutterite girl.

"Thank you for helping me." She shyly handed him a small sack of day-old rolls and headed back to her car. Before closing the driver's door, she said, "It's Sarah. My name is Sarah."

Two days after the flat tire incident, Bill had almost completed the first irrigation pump's upgrades. Sarah's car pulled into the field. Getting out, she held up another sack of day-old pastries. He wiped his hands on his jeans and reached for the bag.

"Really, changing your tire was nothing. You don't have to keep bringing me treats, Sarah." He thought for a second. "Uhh, am I allowed to call you by your first name? I don't want to get anyone in trouble."

"No, it is my actions which will cause trouble." She looked nervously down the road toward her colony. "Although, I'm already in disfavor for falling behind and making late deliveries this morning."

He looked at his watch. "Late deliveries? It's only mid-morning. How late are you on getting to town?"

"I'm on my way back with the day-old leftovers. I was late preparing the baked goods for delivery earlier."

"On your way back?" Bill calculated the driving time to town. "How *early* do you get up?"

"Four. Today, I had oven troubles which set us behind." Sarah looked nervously down the road again. "I should go. I don't have a chaperone with me."

Bill became curious. "Why are you going out of your way to be nice to me if it'll get you in trouble?"

Sarah actually made eye contact. "Because you have kind but somehow sad eyes. I thought by doing a little bit of charity for you, I might be able to take away some of that pain."

Whoa, Bill thought, *she cuts right through to the point.* "You're a very nice person. I'd like to be your friend if it's allowed."

"It isn't. Well, it *is* okay for me to make polite conversation while in a group or in the context of business."

"That's it then." Bill glanced toward the colony. "I guess I'm just going to have to become a regular customer. How do I schedule deliveries?"

Sarah blushed and pulled out her phone. "I would need your business contact information. What is your business name and address?"

"Let's go with Billfix." He gave her his number.

"And your business address for deliveries?"

"That's a tough one," Bill answered. "I'm mobile. For the next few months, during the off-season, I'm upgrading the Columbia Basin irrigation systems for the company I work for. I'll be moving around between our various fields."

"As long as they aren't too far out of the way, I can still make deliveries." She again nervously looked toward the colony. "I just don't want to stray too near one of our other colonies. Word moves fast in our world."

"How many other colonies can there possibly be in the area?"

"Right now, five," Sarah answered.

"Holy crap! Oops, sorry," Bill apologized.

Sarah smiled. "Well, at least you didn't take anyone's name in vain like outsiders are prone to do."

Bill mulled out loud, "You know, I set my own schedule. Maybe we can just set up a spot in town where I can get a delivery for breakfast. Umm, someplace where it wouldn't look out of place for you to be."

"I will text you."

As she drove off, Bill had the distinct feeling that Sarah also had something deeply troubling behind her own kind eyes. Meeting for breakfast almost every day except Sunday, they became good friends. He sensed there was something excitingly dangerous in it for her. Because their societies were so different, there was seldom a lack of things to discuss.

Sarah became Bill's best platonic female friend since his and Carrie's early days. Both considering a romantic entanglement so far out of the question, they openly confided in each other.

CHAPTER FORTY-TWO
THE MOVE TO
LONG ISLAND

Agent Popov accepted Paul Taft's offer to take her and Carrie to the Spokane airport. The young woman sitting in the rear of the motorhome playing cards with Mara had way too much luggage for a mere automobile to handle. Sitting in the front passenger seat, unable to stop herself due to her years of training, Katarina made casual, but probing conversation.

"So, how did you and your daughter become Asphalt Nomads?"

"I had to get away from the city. When I adopted Mara, I just couldn't imagine raising her in an environment like that jungle."

"Adopted?" This was news to the agent. "I don't recall seeing that in any of our interviews. How did you two meet?"

Paul laughed for the first time since meeting Katarina, or even arriving in Washington. "You'd have to ask *her* that. I don't recall anything before waking up from my coma with her hovering over me."

The two made pleasant conversation, sometimes pushing flirtatious as they got to know each other. Then, she made the big mistake of asking the wrong question. "So, what's the deal with Karen Schmidt? There seems to be a lot of tension between two people who've only met a few times."

The motorhome strayed out of the lane onto the rumble strips. Veins stuck out Paul's neck and temples. The knuckles on his right hand turned white, and his left hand trembled violently. Staring down the road with an expression vacillating between extreme sorrow and rage, he finally replied, "She cheated on m . . . my cousin. Then, she lied to his face about it. He sacrificed his whole future to make her happy. Anything she wanted, he did his best to give it to her. He discovered the truth when her ex-lover sent him a letter while he was deployed. He lost the will to live and lost focus. I guess you can say she killed him."

Katarina uncoupled her seat belt and knelt beside him, placing a comforting hand on his shoulder. "I'm sorry that I stuck my nose where it didn't belong. You seem to be a very kind man with a loving heart."

"Yeah, yeah, get back in your seat before the cops stop us and I have to endure interrogation—again."

After sharing her private number with Paul at the airport, Katarina and Carrie sat next to each other during the flights and layover to LaGuardia. Even though the agent was a hardened international law enforcement officer, to the young woman, she seemed now like a trusted aunt. Fighting beside each other to survive brings even strangers closer.

The Interpol agent asked, "So, how did your goodbye go with Bill Schmidt? I didn't want to eavesdrop on a private conversation, so I stood back."

Carrie shrugged. "I don't know. I'm so confused about our relationship. I do love him but . . ."

"And from what I've observed, he really cares for you." The agent contemplated for a moment. "I was once in a relationship with someone where we desperately loved each other. Unfortunately, that just isn't always enough to surmount the obstacles in your path. Sometimes it is. Every situation is different. You have to take a step back and logically examine what you want. I know it's hard to accept this now, but being apart will give you the breathing room to think and also free you to feel."

"It just seems that we keep getting flung back together like it was meant to be. But we never seem to get there at the same time."

"It's like that in life. One person may want something more than the other. A short time later, it may completely reverse." Surprising even herself, Katarina patted Carrie's hand. "Right now, you need to focus on just you. What do *you* want? What do you want your future to look like?"

Both rode in silence for a while. When they did talk, it was mostly about either Popov's childhood or Kate's seaside town art gallery. Long past thinking of her companion as an authority figure, Carrie suggested, "There's a stable close by where I used to ride. I think you'd like it; there's not a single western style saddle in the place. You should come visit and practice your jumping. You looked a little rusty in our upper pasture."

Katarina laughed. "I don't suppose you factored in the fact that we were under fire at that particular moment and the horse had never jumped before."

"I thought jumpers trained to perform under pressure." Carrie giggled. "How much difference can there be between hired assassins with guns and judges with clipboards?"

"Good point. Even though technically you and I haven't been officially associating since our interviews, I'd still like to come and check on you. Maybe even get a ride in."

"I'd like that."

Carrie knew someone would be waiting to give her a ride from the airport. Thinking Kate had just hired a driving service with a van to carry her pile of luggage, she was surprised at the familiar face holding up a sign with her name on it. As she headed toward the driver, Agent Popov stepped protectively between them.

"John!" Carrie grinned broadly. "What are *you* doing here?"

Popov glanced over her shoulder. "You know this person?"

"Yes, agent," Carrie laughed. "He and I were very close during my first summer in Long Island. My grandmother knows his family well."

Katarina studied the well-dressed young man for a bit, then asked over her shoulder, "Close, huh?"

"Yeah. In fact we dated until we both had to leave for separate universities. You can trust him. Really."

Popov stepped tentatively to the side, still with her hand pretending to be on a concealed weapon. Usually, that bluff was enough to deter minor threats. Carrie ran up to the young man.

"I can't believe you came!"

John hugged her. "You didn't think Kate would trust anyone else with her most valued cargo, did you?"

Carrie gave a formal introduction. "John, this is Interpol Agent Katarina Popov. Agent, this is an old, and yes trusted, boyfriend, John Spenser."

Still not completely satisfied, Popov checked his ID and phoned in a quick background check before allowing the young woman out of her sight. Before parting ways, Katarina warned one last time while being hugged, "Remember, no calling home. No running around making news. No online presence. I'll be in touch."

During the ride from the airport to Long Island, catching up on old times, Carrie asked, "So, what have you been doing? Out of school yet?"

"Yeah," he answered. "I'm working at my dad's firm in a new east coast satellite office." Pausing dramatically, he continued, "On Long Island. We'll see how long I can stand it before moving on."

She laughed. Relieved he didn't ask what she had been doing, she assumed Kate had filled him in on taboo conversation subjects. She asked, "So, where's Gramma now?"

"Oh, she's still in the long-term recovery center for a little bit yet. Her house is pretty messed up, and it'll be a while until the contractors can make it livable again." He looked at Carrie and smiled. "Don't worry. We've made arrangements for a place where you can live. She can stay there too until her house repairs are completed."

"Oh? Where?"

John's smile transformed into a huge grin. "The beach house. You have it as long as you need. It's a bit of a commute to her gallery but, hey, it's free."

"Thank you. That's so kind of you guys." Carrie turned and looked out the side window. Memories of the time she spent in the beach house were some of her happiest. She shook herself back to reality. That seemed like an eternity ago.

"You must be tired. Hungry."

She laughed. "You're forgetting my body is three hours behind yours. But yes, I'm starving."

"Which restaurant interests you?"

"Anything," she said. "Uh, on second thought, I've been traveling all day, and I'm kind of gross. Maybe I should clean up first."

John glanced at her and laughed. "You probably don't remember, but that was the excuse you used not to be alone with me when we first met. How about a compromise?" He pulled out his phone. "I'll call ahead and get some take-out. I can rewarm it while you shower."

"Sounds good."

Having trouble over the last few months making sense of her complicated relationship with Bill, Carrie needed time away to sort her feelings out. Kate's accident, while unfortunate, gave Carrie a good excuse to spend time away and think. With Agent Popov's help, her mind relaxed and cleared out some debris during the long cross-country flight.

During the drive to the beach house and being around the first completely sane non-related man or family friend she'd been near in years, her situation in the Palouse began to clarify.

Coming out of the shower, she headed toward the smell of food. Too drained to dig through her luggage for pajamas, she wore only the guest bathrobe which always lay in the linen closet. John sat on the living room floor with cardboard containers spread out on the coffee table.

He patted the floor beside him. "Dig in."

"So, you didn't say during the ride," she asked between bites. "Got a girlfriend? How's your love life?"

He shrugged. "I've had a couple. None that lasted very long. Nothing serious."

"That surprises me. You're a really good catch. Why?"

"I don't know." Glancing sideways at her, he murmured, "Nobody felt as right."

Carrie pretended not to see his look. "I've had a couple . . . none of them ended very well."

"I know." He put a comforting arm around her shoulder. "I don't know why, but Kate insisted on keeping me informed of your, umm, circumstances. She never got into specifics."

Somehow, their rapport from years ago instantly returned. It was as if they had just seen each other a few weeks before. Carrie opened up with John more than she had with anyone since he and her had parted for separate schools. She felt comfortable telling him things she couldn't tell anyone else and felt no judgment.

Then, it happened. Her relationship with Bill became crystal clear when John leaned over and kissed her on the lips. She pushed him away. "I can't."

CHAPTER FORTY-THREE
A YEAR OF CHANGE

Trying to make sense of his feelings toward Carrie, he didn't trust his burgeoning attraction to Sarah. The Hutterite girl was beautiful and had a wicked sense of humor, at least within the confines her religion allowed.

Then, there was the wide cultural gap between them. To him, the whole communal lifestyle and letting the community be involved in what he considered private matters was as foreign as walking on a distant planet. Now that she was twenty, colony leadership had been gently pushing her toward marriage.

During a candid moment, she confided, "I get free will to choose a spouse. Unfortunately, there is no one in any of the local colonies who interests me."

"That's tough," Bill answered. "You aren't allowed to just date anyone you choose?"

"Oh, no! That is strictly forbidden. If I did, I would probably be asked to leave the colony." Sarah sighed. "Although, we take finding a good mate seriously. That's why we have socials between colonies for young people to meet."

"You guys have your own singles club?" Bill laughed then realized that he may have gone too far. "Sorry. I didn't mean to be crude."

"That's all right. I've learned to make allowances for your

shortcomings." She smiled, then wistfully looked off in the distance. "It was at one of those meetings I met a young man from one of our Montana colonies. He's a few years older than I am but seems okay. I think he might propose."

"That's good, if you love him." He saw a lack of commitment in her eyes with that last comment. "Will he move over here?"

Sarah answered softly, "The woman virtually always goes to the man's colony."

Bill was aghast. "You mean you automatically have to leave your family and friends when you get married? What kind of deal is that? Who'll be your support group when you have a disagreement? What happens if he has quirks you can't stand?"

"That is our way." Sarah shrugged. "We are taught to forgive other people's shortcomings and make allowances for them. That is how we all can live so closely. Even if someone is obnoxious, we find a way to put them to use in a way that is beneficial to all."

"So, when are you and this guy going to start dating? Isn't it going to be tough with the distance thing and all?"

"I think he's coming over in a week or two for the Aufred Hulba."

Bill asked, "What's that?"

"He comes over for a few days, maybe a week. It's when he'll officially ask for my hand in marriage." She stared into the far, far distance. "At the end of the festivities, we'll travel to his colony and get married."

"What? How will your family attend the ceremony?"

"Only the ones who can be freed up from work long enough to make the journey will attend."

"How can you do that?" Bill was amazed at the faith it took to do what Sarah was talking about. "What if you don't fit together?"

She smiled weakly. "It's our way. We are taught to always put the other person's failings aside."

When she got up to leave, Bill didn't realize Sarah had been saying goodbye. It was their last shared breakfast.

Two weeks later, he had finished with the irrigation upgrades when Mr. Roberts walked into the shop. "You've done a good job for me. You deserve some R&R. Why don't you take some time off?"

"I'd like that," Bill answered. "I have to go home and take care of a few things. I'll be back as soon as I can."

Mr. Roberts smiled. "No, take longer. You deserve it. Here's a check for two weeks paid vacation."

"I know it's none of my business but, because you're back in the area, I take it you've solved that investor problem."

The older man laughed. "Yeah, *that* turned out to be a whole can of worms. Even Interpol was involved. Thank goodness it's all over now."

"How's Willa doing with all of this?" Bill asked tentatively, not wanting to overstep his bounds.

"That's another development I think I owe to you." Mr. Roberts put his hand on Bill's shoulder. "That girl has really turned her life around. She's doing great in school and still dating the same young man as last year. During summer break, they're heading off to the far east, as far away from southern Europe as possible." He laughed. "I wouldn't be surprised if she came back wearing a ring."

After work, Bill sat in a small diner. Glancing out the window, he saw two large passenger vans with Montana plates drive by, loaded with Hutterites. The vans pulled into one of the many upper scale Latina restaurants in town. He sighed as the term "Aufred Hulba" came to mind. The vans must be carrying the Montana delegation to pick up Sarah for her new life.

Pushing his meal around with his fork, he mulled over his own life for the last few years. It was his fault that this landslide had started. Jennie became tired of waiting and found a new love. Willa had gained her footing and now was moving on. Carrie had faltered but recovered. It was he who held on to the past and hadn't accepted the changes.

His talks with Sarah taught him something. He needed to

accept people for who they were now and not some past fantasy. He definitely wasn't perfect nor were those he loved. Bill stared at the Hutterite vans and contemplated.

A few days later, he sat on a rise and watched Sarah's wedding convoy leave her colony headed for Montana. She was riding in the second van passing his pickup. When they made eye contact, he saw a wistful smile on her face as she discreetly waved.

Now that his contract was up, he could get on with his life. Bill drove back to his small room to pack his gear. For some reason, he felt an urge to spend some time with his dad's cousin in North Idaho. It was as good a place as any to sort out his feelings for both Sarah and Carrie.

Driving up the long, two-rut road, Bill worried that he'd turned at the wrong mailbox until he broke out of the tree canopy into a meadow. On the far side stood a large, metal-sided pole-building shop with cars parked out front. Mara ran out of the walk-in door followed by four other girls.

She squealed, "Look! My cousin's here! Isn't he *hunky*? I told you so!"

Her father came out to rescue Bill. "Come on, I'll show you where you can stash your gear while you're here."

Inside the building, doors to smaller rooms lined the right side of the main bay. They walked past the motorhome to access a set of stairs to the second floor. On the second-floor exposed walkway, Paul leaned against the railing and explained his home's design.

"It's the North Idaho way. It can have bathrooms and bedrooms which we technically refer to as office spaces. As long as it doesn't have a kitchen, it's taxed as a shop, not a house. In the summer, I have the barbeque. In the winter, I use the motorhome's kitchen. If the urge strikes, I can pull out the RV and hit the road."

That night, at Mara's insistence, Bill sat beside the outdoor firepit and went into detail about how both he and his stepsiblings were related by blood. "I had to research my genealogy as a school project. Amazingly, somehow both my father and stepfather's bloodlines traced back to the same man in the sixteenth century—Pieter Smid. He had two children, one boy and a girl. My father is a descendant of the boy. My stepfather's lineage began with the only child of Pieter's daughter."

The excited girl wouldn't let him stop with just the men. "Tell them how your mother's lineage goes right back to the same town at the same time. They may have known each other!"

Bill glanced toward Paul, sitting silently on the fringe of the fire's glow. The older man's hand, instead of calming, seemed to shake even more as the night progressed. "You're right. Records indicate that the sole child of an English noblewoman was raised in Wales after the lady mysteriously disappeared in what is now modern-day Belgium. No one knows what happened to her mother. Charlie said he heard she was known in Antwerp as Mariken."

Paul leapt to his feet and stumbled away, mumbling to himself. With what little he heard, Bill wondered what his host meant when he said, "So, the slut really *did* sleep with him. Not only did she lie about that, but she bore him a child."

At dawn the next day, Bill heard rummaging on the shop's ground level. Curious, he went downstairs to see if he could be of any help. Wearing a fishing vest and waders, carrying a fly rod, Paul looked up.

"Good morning. I was heading out to catch breakfast. Wanna join me?"

"Sure. I don't have an Idaho fishing license, but I can at least watch and carry gear." It was obvious the older man wanted to talk, maybe get off his chest what upset him the night before. "With all that keeps happening whenever we're in the same vicinity, maybe we can take the time to get to know each other."

Bill raised an eyebrow when his host strapped on a shoulder harness holding a large caliber pistol. Paul shrugged and explained, "Bear country. Black bears may shy away with pepper spray, but a sow grizzly with a cub nearby will just laugh when you squirt jalapeno scented perfume at her."

"There are grizzlies around here?"

"Yeah, wolves too. They've both exceeded their proposed populations and are moving into populated areas."

"That kind of looks like my dad's old revolver. Mom still keeps it cleaned and oiled."

"Same brand. It was a .44 caliber, and this is a .50." Paul abruptly changed the subject. "We better get going before the fish quit biting.

Bill studied the expression on his host's face, curious why the man instantly became dour every time Karen was mentioned. As the morning wore on and they conversed, the young man wondered how Paul knew so much about his family. The older man even knew the caliber and type of pistol that was locked in the family gun safe. Bill only remembered meeting him the one time at his dad's funeral. At other times, Paul's demeanor seemed so familiar, it was almost as if it was his lap the younger man had sat in as a child.

"So, you gonna tell me the real reason you're here?" Paul glanced toward the shore while changing the fly on his line. "You didn't travel a hundred miles off the interstate just for the fun of it."

"It's that obvious, huh? I'm trying to make sense of a few things and need to be away from everybody to think. Familiar surroundings only confuse my thoughts."

After wading to shore, Paul sat beside Bill and put a hand on his knee. "Let me guess, that young lady who caused all the trouble during the party. Don't waste time denying it. The tension between the two of you was obvious."

"Yeah, I'm trying to figure out what I want."

"I can't tell you what to decide. All I can do is give an example of my own." Paul's left hand began to shake for the first time that day. "I once believed the sun rose and set around a woman. For a decade, I sacrificed everything to be with her, believing she felt the same about me. I missed all the signals until my whole world imploded. I guess I later found a faithful love, but because of my injury, I can't remember a thing about her."

Unable to stand the way his host's trembling hand made the pole violently oscillate, Bill carried the fly rod as they walked toward the shop. "Was it that obvious? We haven't been in contact since you gave her a ride to the airport. I was supposed to use our time apart to figure out what I wanted. I've just about made a decision."

Paul put his good arm around the young man's shoulder. "Just be sure that it's something you can live with and not just want. They say that time heals all wounds. That may be true, but it can't erase the deep scars those wounds left."

As Bill packed his truck for the trip back to civilization, he studied his new mentor. The man's past just didn't fit the timeline of his stories. To have put ten years into a relationship before he married and raised the family he had lost, he would have to be a decade older than he appeared. Paul seemed to understand him, almost like a father. Yet, there was something so sad about him. The only time he had ever seen joy on the older man's face was when Paul was basking in his adopted daughter's enthusiasm.

His mind made up, Bill headed south.

CHAPTER FORTY-FOUR
CELEBRATION OF LOVE

Driving from the gallery to the beach house after work, Carrie desperately wanted a trusted ear to confide in. Her time with the Appaloosa therapy horse had made a new person out of her. It helped ready her to step into new possibilities. Shortly after she arrived on Long Island, another troubled horse showed up in the stables owned by John's uncle.

Carrie had made progress with it, and even more on herself. She felt free, unbound by past mistakes and guilt. For the first time since leaving Greece, there was light ahead.

Her interlude with Nick, and how she handled it, reinforced her belief that she was capable of not falling into another trap. Carrie knew there was always going to be pitfalls in life. She knew now it was how she chose to navigate around them that mattered.

Something wonderful happened the night she arrived—unplanned, spontaneous, almost organic. The fog obscuring her feelings toward Bill blew away, and she could see clearly what their future was.

Now, things were changing, possibly moving too fast. Her grandmother was of no use at all. Kate's advice was so predictable, why even ask? Her parents had enough issues of their own, and she didn't want to bother them. Mandy was off on an internship in East Podunk and Carrie didn't have the phone number.

Since her own phone was shut off and hidden in her dresser back on the ranch, that left Bill, the only other number she knew by heart. Carrie reached for the beach house's landline receiver. With her hand gently caressing the earpiece, she fought her instincts to call. Even though it was her idea to have no contact for a year, he had agreed.

That left Katarina Popov. The Interpol agent hadn't been recalled to her home country but had been put on administrative leave after her superiors scrutinized every minute detail of the shooting. One thing in Katarina's favor was the cornucopia of new leads that the young woman who had been captive on the Greek island provided. Popov took advantage of her leave to spend time with Carrie, riding horses and mulling the possibility of retirement.

The two women acted as sounding boards for each other. She had never judged Carrie or pushed one way or the other. The girl from the Palouse had to smile while thinking, *Where was Katarina and her wisdom when my parents chose my shrink to help with my Victim's Dependency Disorder? I probably never would have become entangled with that ass Rod.*

Sitting at a table overlooking the beach had become Carrie's go-to place to quietly think. Why did she need to ask someone else's approval about something she wanted so very much? She hadn't second guessed this type of thing before going to Greece. Was she looking for someone to talk her out of it or chastise her?

Finally, she decided to trust her gut. She stood up from the table to do what her heart asked for and prepared to wholeheartedly take her decision one step further. There was no turning back now.

The situation in both Greece and Turkey had been handled, and authorities gave her the all clear. The only thing keeping her from leaving was a couple of loose ends that she not only needed, but wanted desperately, to tie up. Almost everyone would be happy for how she was doing—almost. Those that weren't were just going to have to deal with it. She couldn't please everyone.

Two weeks later, Carrie made sure the envelope with the plane tickets was in her purse for the twentieth time. The bags were packed. It was time to fly back to the Palouse.

Bill had made up his mind. Right or wrong, he knew what he had to do. He'd been sitting on the fence too long. While refueling the pickup at a truck stop, he pulled out his phone and called Mandy.

"Hey, my contract's up. I'm headed back home."

"That's great! Can't wait to see you."

"I have to run an errand in Spokane first." Bill absentmindedly replaced the nozzle before heading toward the convenience store for snacks. "So, I'll stop by your place before going the rest of the way."

"We aren't there," Mandy answered. "We're down at Mom and Dad's . . ."

Bill interrupted, "That's okay. It just means I'll get home quicker after my errand. Speaking of home, is Carrie back yet? She was supposed to be back from Kate's place about now."

"Yeah, she got back yesterday. Bill, there is something I have to tell you. Carrie . . ."

HONK!

"Crap!"

Jumping back startled, Bill dropped his phone. Not paying attention, he had walked out in front of a car going through the parking lot too fast. Bending over to retrieve his phone, he knew the conversation was over. The phone was crushed. *Oh well*, he thought. *They know I'm coming. Carrie's home at last.*

Late afternoon, when Bill pulled into his parents' yard, there wasn't a soul around. He shrugged. The person he really wanted to see was six miles farther down the road. Getting into the Bennett driveway was impossible. Cars lined the shoulder of the road in both directions. He smiled. Beth's latest art show must have been a real success and they were having a party.

Parking in the ditch five cars behind his parents', he walked toward the festivities. There was a banner hanging from the ranch's entrance log archway. *Congratulation Spensers?* Bill couldn't recall any of Beth's art friends with the name. Then, he admitted that he hadn't met that many.

Just as the rear porch came into view, Carrie and Beth walked out of the back door. Carrie, carrying a casserole dish, was absolutely radiant in the dress she was wearing. She and her mother saw Bill at the same time. Carrie handed Beth the dish.

"I'll go talk to him." She walked toward Bill, hands folded behind her back.

He gave her a huge grin. "Hey, stranger. It's been too long."

When he went to hug her, Carrie put her right hand on his chest. "Not here. Come on." She pushed Bill back down the driveway toward the road.

A male voice came from the direction of the stable, "Is everything all right?"

"Everything's fine," Carrie called back.

When she turned, the setting sun's reflection glinting off her left hand caught Bill's eye. The huge diamond on her ring finger had to be the largest he'd ever seen. His mouth moved, but nothing would come out. Carrie took his arm and led him down the driveway.

"You know that I love you, don't you?" Carrie said softly. "I always will. You've been my best friend for a decade. You've saved my life twice and have always stood by me. But you know as well as I do that there's just too much baggage between us."

"No, I've used our time apart to examine, *really examine*, my feelings and what I want."

"It's not just you, Bill. I have to make changes. I knew you could never be with me. I had to finally accept that and move on."

"So, you ran out and got engaged? How long have you even known each other?"

"We met during my first summer in Long Island." Carrie

didn't know how much she should tell her long-time friend. She owed him an explanation, but how much? "He was my first boyfriend after you. He put me back together then. We cared deeply for each other, but our schools were thousands of miles apart."

"So, you just picked up where you left off? How do you know you'll get along?"

"Bill," she put her hand on his arm, "we both felt our old connection immediately when we saw each other again in Long Island. We started dating and moved in together not long afterward. John knows everything. He understands and accepts me."

"Well, you have to break off the engagement. You . . ."

"Bill . . . Bill, stop. I can't break it off." Carrie's voice cracked. "This is . . . it . . . it's a wedding ring. We're married."

His future disappearing over the Palouse scablands, Bill couldn't think of a single thing to say. Instead, all that would come out was meaningless small talk. "So, is he moving out here?"

"No. His parents gave us their beach house as a wedding present. John has a good job at his dad's firm. His uncle owns a stable where I'm doing equine therapy part time when I return to school."

All he could choke out was, "Well, have a good life."

Pulling free from Carrie's hand, Bill turned and shuffled toward the road.

"I love you!" she called after him. "Will I ever see you again?"

He paused and looked back for a moment, then silently walked away. Reaching into his pocket, he dropped an object on the ground. Thinking it might be something he needed, she picked it up. Holding the tiny diamond engagement ring, crying, Carrie watched the destroyed remains of a ten-year relationship rip their tether from her heart.

Bill started his truck and blindly continued down the highway in the direction it was already pointed. After a half an hour, he realized he was going east, the opposite direction of his family's home. Stopping on the side of the road to wipe his eyes and compose himself, he considered turning around. No. He pulled back out into traffic and drove on.

He didn't know where he was headed. Maybe the Dakota oil-fields? Maybe the military. He didn't know. All Bill knew was he would never return to the Palouse. Nothing was there for him anymore.